Jesus at Walmart

...fire on the Earth

rickleland.com

Jesus at Walmart...fire on the Earth

Published by:
Freedom Shores Media
South Haven. MI

ISBN: 978-0-9833624-8-7

rickleland.com

Contents

Contents

Contents

Contents

Dedicated to:
Maria, Nohemi, Magaly, and Marco.

Love
Forever

Then I said, "O GOD! They are saying of
me: is he not a maker of stories?"

Ezekiel 20:49

1-1-2014

"Hello world," Malachi said to himself as he entered his personal sanctuary. "I think I'm awake."

He tipped the blue rimmed mug and sipped as he glanced at the clock—7:49. And then with his right elbow nearly touching the half-opened door, as he faced into the room, Malachi glanced at the calendar on the wall. It was a daily habit. There was no real point today. Simply his routine. He knew it was the first day of 2014.

He pressed the door closed with his elbow until he heard the clanky thud of the latch inserting into its resting place. He took three steps and sat down on a murky green recliner with mellow, oak-toned arms. He placed his cup to the left on a small coffee table constructed of raw framing lumber rescued from a jobsite bone pile.

Jesus at Walmart...fire on the Earth

To the right, in a black tubular stand, rested his mandolin.

He picked up the delicate looking instrument. The main body of the mandolin, the size of a dinner plate, was predominately the color of those oversized oak leaves that seem to cling onto the tree, even as autumn has bowed to winter.

Malachi strummed it with his thumb—his unorthodox playing method. The purist among mandolin players would assert: peculiar. Maybe even heretical.

Malachi slung the three-quarter inch chocolate-brown leather strap over his neck and cradled his musical instrument, almost like a mother would hold a newborn, and then strummed the G-chord. The two-finger version. Followed by a D. And next a C-chord sounded, as Malachi softly/tenderly began to sing:

Salvation and glory and power belong to our God

Hallelujah, hallelujah
Hallelujah, hallelujah

Salvation and glory and power belong to our God

Praise God, praise God
Praise God, praise God

Salvation and glory and power belong to our God

Hallelujah, hallelujah
Praise God, praise God
Salvation and glory and power belong to our God

To our God

He strummed a few more chords. No singing. And then

continued playing—no particular song. Noodling—as musicians call it.

He stopped, allowing the strap to carry the mandolin. Malachi turned to the left and reached under the coffee table. From a hidden place below, his hand withdrew a binder, a basic student-version in a passive green color.

Malachi smiled when he opened it, saying to himself, "God, You've given me so many new songs. Thank you, God. Thank You."

With his thumb, Malachi was fanning his way through the binder when he heard a slight rap on the door.

Followed by a voice not much louder than the knock,

2. Jump for Jesus

"**M**alachi," the voice said as it amplified a few decibels.

"Alex," Malachi said as he stood up and made his way to the door.

Without hesitation, Malachi opened the door and, in nearly the same motion, hugged Alex around the shoulder, "Happy New Year, son."

Alex's eyes opened wider as a small grin formed on his face, "Mom is still asleep, and I'm bored."

"You could clean your bedroom."

"You're funny," Alex said. "And besides, isn't it a national holiday?"

"I was just kidding, Alex," Malachi said. "Your room always looks decent anyway."

Alex glanced around Malachi's office and then said, "I think your room's the one that could use some attention."

Malachi laughed. "You're right. But ah...yeah, it's a national holiday. No office cleaning allowed."

Malachi touched Alex's shoulder. "Come in. Tell me what you've been doing all year."

"I guess, mainly sleeping," Alex said as he made his way to one of the other chairs in Malachi's office. A leather-like synthetic-covered chair. Tanish-brown—positioned three and a half feet away from the other chair. Placed in front of a computer.

Alex sunk into it and swiveled to face Malachi, who was back sitting in the recliner. Alex circled his eyes around the room, looking at the shelves and the stuff hanging on the walls. And then he shifted his attention to the computer monitor.

A Bible verse scrolled across the blackened screen. Two-inch tall letters in a whitish gray: Jesus said, "I came to send fire on the earth and how I wish it were already kindled."

Malachi merely watched Alex as he absorbed the surroundings with his eyes.

And then Alex said, "Is everything in here about Jesus?"

Malachi rubbed two of his fingers along his unshaven chin. "I ah...I never thought of it that way."

And then Malachi took his own look around the eleven-foot by ten-foot space, freshly appraising his haven from the world, when the door was closed.

Malachi let out a laugh, the kind when the mouth is closed and the sounding emanates from air pushing through the nose, a nasally chuckle: "I never thought of it that way."

Neither one said anything for a couple of moments. And then Malachi said, "Yeah, most things, well not everything in here, but yeah-a lot of things in here are about Jesus. I never saw it that way before."

Jump for Jesus

Malachi gazed directly at Alex. "Son, you're smart. That's very observant for a thirteen-year-old."

"Hey, on a different subject," Alex said, "can we talk about something I've been thinking about? Well…it's not a big deal. But can we talk?"

"You know we can. The first day of a new year—I can't think of a better time for a Father/Son talk."

"I was wondering if," Alex said, "I mean…can I paint my room a different color? And I want to paint it all by myself. Plus, I want to pick out the color."

Malachi grinned. "Oh, I thought maybe this was going to be a more serious matter."

"Well, maybe it's not serious," Alex said. "But it's kind of important to me."

"Well, yeah," Malachi said. "You're right."

"Can I?" Alex said. "And I know how to paint. I've helped you before."

"Here's the deal," Malachi said. "Your behavior has earned you the right—at school and at church and at home. Like the Bible says, 'You're reaping what you've sowed.'"

Malachi nodded his head up and down. "You sure can, Alex. I know you'll do a good job too."

Alex smiled. "Cool."

But then his body slumped further into the chair. As he sunk down, his disposition seemed to sag also.

"Malachi, there's something else I've been thinking about, mainly when my new friend Rollie started talking about it."

"Rollie Kirtner?"

"Yeah. You've never met him. But you know his Dad-Rollie Sr., don't you?"

"I sure do. I sure do. He pretty much runs downtown Manistee," Malachi said. "So, what were you and your friend talking about?"

"Malachi, do you ever start thinking about Jesus and God

and the Bible and start wondering if ah...kind of ah...I don't know...does it all seem logical? Does your brain get mixed up?"

"That's a big question," Malachi said. "So, where does Rollie come into all of this?"

"It started when I told him I couldn't hang out with him once because I was doing something at church. I mean, he had never put me down for it before...I don't know what happened. He said something like, 'Oh you just have to jump for Jesus. Whatever He says, you have to do. Can't you think for yourself?'"

And then Rollie stared at me. "Come on, Alex, don't you think some of that Jesus-stuff, this God-stuff, is just plain foolishness?"

"What did you say?"

"I said, 'No way.'"

"Well, good for you, Alex," Malachi said. "You know the Bible says, 'The message of the cross is foolish to those who are headed for destruction'. And it also says, 'This foolish plan of God is wiser than the wisest of human plans.'"

"Yeah, I guess I know that. But still. I started thinking over what he said. And that jump for Jesus stuff. I mean, Malachi... you ah...you definitely jump for Jesus. In a good way. And I think that's cool. But even you would have to wonder if..."

3. Wonder If?

Malachi heard Alex as he continued talking.

But the words *wonder if* stirred so many memories it was like a multi-burst of fireworks going off in his head, a grand finale of stimulation, with so much to take in.

His brain tried to anchor the rush of mental pictures. And Malachi riveted in on one especially pleasing memory, the kind that can salve over the wounds of lost life-battles, lost through human perspective that is.

Malachi was seeing Alex. He wasn't jumping for Jesus. But he was swaying and about as happy as an eleven-year old can get.

This deeply satisfying mental recall was the culmination of an eight-month life-season involving numerous *wonder if* episodes.

Jesus at Walmart...fire on the Earth

In the first episode, Malachi ended up wondering if God even existed. His cherished job as an associate pastor at St. Amos Community Church had ended, due to a no-win confrontation with a marijuana addicted Senior Pastor—Pastor Neil Renner, who had cloaked his activities by aligning his drug usage to medical marijuana, heavily emphasizing his compassion for suffering people.

And through missteps in trying to resolve the situation, Malachi encountered the fury of his wife, Annie. This was in essence a smoke screen of its own, as Annie was involved in an extramarital relationship at work.

Admittedly, a mistake in retrospect, Malachi jettisoned it all without telling anyone and moved to Manistee, Michigan.

Now, Malachi hadn't chosen Manistee on a whim. His Uncle Dale Marble, who was a very successful building contractor, lived there. They met the same day Malachi had left everything behind in St Amos at Uncle Dale's favorite downtown restaurant—*DT's Good Time Place.*

And Uncle Dale was actually in worse shape than Malachi. Uncle Dale was nearly bankrupt from an unexpected crash in the construction market plus an unhealthy propensity to visiting the casino north of town. With an added crush—he was battling cancer.

Somewhat by default, Malachi secured a job at Walmart. Manistee's economy was bleak—available jobs were scarce. And Malachi was desperate. But it was an odd incident that cemented Malachi's decision to seek employment at Walmart.

More like an odd person—Carl Lacombe, who intentionally encountered Malachi as he stood staring out over Lake Michigan, out to where the sky touches the water. From behind him, Carl had said to Malachi, "Are you finding what you are looking for?"

Wonder If?

Later, Malachi would find out from Carl that God would send him out on missions—essentially a job assignment. And this morning, Malachi's first in Manistee, he was Carl's mission from God.

Their first encounter, one Malachi deemed the strangest of his life, ended with Carl saying, "Maybe you should get a job at Walmart."

And then, not too many weeks later, Carl devised a way to get Malachi to give him a ride to church. As they sat in Malachi's Suburban in the church parking lot, Carl tugged on his emotions, convincing him to accompany him inside.

During the church service, unexpectedly, Malachi's heart was turned back to God.

And they returned the next Wednesday. That evening, the sermon was a call to get out into the world and make a difference for Jesus.

Malachi's soul was inspired. And before he left church, he was determined to start a Bible study at Walmart, or as he called it, "More than a Bible study."

From the start, the Bible study—later named Jesus at Walmart, constantly caused two wonder if's to plague Malachi's mind. I wonder if anyone will show up for Jesus at Walmart. And, I wonder if they will keep attending.

But now, Malachi smiled, his brain locked in on that precious memory of Alex. One from the first Jesus at Walmart meeting in 2011. This was seven months after Malachi had launched his middle-of-the-night ministry.

Both Malachi and Jesus at Walmart were coming off a low ebb. In the days preceding the meeting, Malachi had been fervently praying, "God please bring one new person to Jesus at Walmart. Please God!"

The clock had slipped a few minutes past the 3:00 a.m. starting time that night, with no answer to his prayer. And then, as a prayer was lifted up to initiate the proceedings, they heard someone at the door calling out, "Malachi."

It was Alex!

Thoughts raced through Malachi's head. "Why is Alex here! Is this an emergency like the first time? What's wrong?"

It wasn't a crisis, but when Alex explained why he was there, it was still difficult for Malachi to make the decision to allow him to stay.

Until, in an uncharacteristically stoic voice, Carl said. "You can stay, Alex."

Then Martin, one of the faithful-few, power punched the air, "Praise God. One more person—thank you, God."

For the meeting, Malachi had a new song to play, as he says, "A song God gave me," which he played on his new mandolin—a gift from Martin.

The song Awesome is the God stirred everyone:

Awesome is the God
Awesome is the God, Most High

Worthy
Worthy

Worthy is the Lord
Worthy is the Lord, who died upon a cross

Here's my life
Have your way

For You Lord
For You Lord
No cost is too great
Awesome is the God
Awesome is the God, Most High

Wonder If?

But no one was moved more than Alex was—that is, if the visual was the determining criteria. His body swayed-full of exuberance, as he enthusiastically sang out the chorus. His smile was radiant.

As Malachi sat in his chair, the first day of 2014, he locked his thoughts on this mental picture for more than a few moments. He drew in on this memory of Alex, like a desert wanderer ravishing the water at an oasis.

4. Flame of Fire

"Can I have some coffee?" Alex said.

"Oh ah...what did you say? Yeah. Ah yes," Malachi said.

"So, I can have some coffee?" Alex said.

"Coffee? No, I don't think so, Alex."

"You just said 'Yes'," Alex said. "I knew you weren't listening."

"I'm sorry. I really am," Malachi said. "What did you say?"

Alex smiled. "I said a lot of things."

"I'm sorry. I should have been listening."

Alex then glanced to his right and tilted his head upward. His eyes fixed on the t-shirt hanging on the wall that was adjacent to the chair he was sitting on. The t-shirt was black. In the chest area of the shirt, the size of a large hand, was a guitar pick. Bone colored. And in black block letters was the word *PICK*. Directly below, in larger lettering, slanted in an uphill direction, was the word *JESUS*—depicted in a cursive-like font. A small cross in a circle rested a quarter-inch from the uphill side of the inscription: *Jesus*.

Alex turned toward Malachi. "You're right," he said. "That's what I said. Well...I mean, that's where I ended up."

"Ended up?"

"When I was talking. And you were...you were some-place else."

"So, what am I right about?" Malachi said.

"Those Bible verses."

"Bible verses? 'The message of the cross is foolish to those who are headed for destruction,'" Malachi said. "And, 'This foolish plan of God is wiser than the wisest of human plans.'"

"Exactly," Alex said.

He then glanced back at the t-shirt and pointed. "I pick Jesus," Alex said as he turned back to face Malachi. "I have decided to follow Jesus." He shifted his eyes to the floor for a brief moment, "Not Rollie or his advice."

Neither one said anything. But inside, Malachi was like a kid who just did a triple flip on a trampoline.

And a brief snippet of Jesus' life sparked through his brain: "After this a lot of His disciples left. They no longer wanted to be associated with Him. But Peter replied, 'Master, to whom would we go? Only You have the words of real life, eternal life. We've already committed ourselves, confident that You are the Holy One of God.'"

"Alex, you've always been a flame of fire for Jesus. All the way back to that first Jesus at Walmart, the one you showed up at in the middle of the night."

Alex smiled. And then he rubbed his hands together, his lips pressed against each other as his concentration shifted to the wall above Malachi's head—slightly to the right.

"I just wish Rollie would see things the way we do," Alex said as his eyes fell downward until they met Malachi's. "Maybe you could talk to him sometime, because we're still really good friends."

5. Refined by Fire

"Maybe," Malachi said. "I mean sure...anytime. I would enjoy talking to Rollie, but only when he's ready."

"I've never thought of myself as a flame of fire," Alex said. "When you said fire, it made me think about that Bible verse that talks about gold being refined by fire. And we learned in science class—we saw a video of metal being heated until it melted down and all the junk came to the top, so they could get rid of the impurities."

Alex turned briefly and read the Bible verse scrolling past the screen. Jesus said, *"I came to send fire on the earth and how I wish it were already kindled."*

Alex quickly turned. It was more than a mere stare. It was as if his single-mindedness was a laser—reaching beyond the surface.

"What?" Malachi said.

"You're the gold refined by fire," Alex said in a slow, uncharacteristic cadence.

"What?"

"Yeah, I'm not a grown-up, but I see things," Alex said. "I see things, Malachi."

6. I See Things

"I've been watching," Alex said, "and listening. I see things."

"It says in Revelation 3:18," Malachi said, "'I advise you to buy from Me gold refined by fire so that you may become rich. And white garments so that you may clothe yourself.'" He paused, nodded his head up and down, and pointed at Alex. And then continued "'And eye salve to anoint your eyes so that you may see.'"

Alex grinned. "Eyes so that you may see." He then stood up. "No coffee?"

Malachi shook his head.

"I'm going to get some orange juice, maybe some breakfast. I'm getting hungry."

"Do you need some help?"

"No, I'm good."

Alex took four steps toward the door and turned around just before he made his exit.

"Malachi," he said. Alex pointed at Malachi in the same manner Malachi had pointed at him and said, "Gold refined by fire."

And he left the room, swinging the door halfway closed.

7. Into the Fire

When Alex said, "Gold refined by fire," and even before he walked out of the room, in that split second, Malachi's memory was triggered.

Like a long train passing by slowly enough to read every bit of the graffiti, images of the past started rolling by. These mental pictures set a course through Malachi's brain:

> Awesome is the God
> Awesome is the God
> Awesome is the God, Most High

Alex's exuberance far outpaced everyone else's. He sang out, "Awesome is the God," as his body swayed in his seat.

When Malachi finished, Alex said, "Let's sing some more."

"Maybe next week," Malachi said. "Remember I told you that this is a serious adult Bible study. You still want to stay?"

"Yeah."

"Since JC and Martin are going to be baptized in two weeks, I thought we should talk about what the Bible says about baptism," Malachi said. "And we know that baptism is a way for people to show others they are now followers of Jesus Christ."

Malachi began to explain the basics of baptism, but then he saw Alex waving his hand back and forth.

"Alex, do you have a question?"

"Does it cost anything?"

"Are you asking if JC and Martin have to pay to be baptized?"

"Yeah."

"No, there's no cost," Malachi said.

"But...I mean everything costs here at Walmart...even free food—somebody has to pay for it. For them to be baptized, it must have cost somebody something," Alex said. "Who paid the cost?"

"Let's see," Malachi said. "You're eleven and you've been to church some. Wow, that's a good question."

Malachi's eyes circled the room, actually looking over everyone's head—as if there was a blackboard with the answer on it. He then lowered his head slightly and looked at those gathered— Carl, Martin, JC, Elysia, and Alex. "Hey, let's shift gears tonight. Our friend here, Alex, has a great question. I'm going to see if I can answer it in a way he can understand."

"Absolutely," Carl said, once again, uncharacteristically stoic.

"Done deal," Malachi said.

"O.K. Alex, here's the deal," Malachi said.

Alex was nodding his head up and down, locking in on every word Malachi said, like a hunter peering through a scope.

"You asked about the cost of baptism. What we really need to do is to focus on the cost of what baptism represents. Baptism shows that a person is now a follower of Jesus Christ. Maybe like getting a tattoo that says: I follow Jesus."

"I have a question," Alex said. "Why don't they just get a tattoo?"

"O.K. maybe that was a bad example. Here's a better one. Baptism is like a high school graduation ceremony. It shows everyone that the student is now a high school graduate. Everybody knows. A public showing of what happened. So, the ceremony is minor in importance compared to what happened—thirteen years of study. Martin and JC are now followers of Jesus Christ. And the ceremony to show everyone is baptism."

"I have another question," Alex said. "What's Jesus' middle name?"

"Middle name?"

"Yeah. Jesus is His first name and Christ is His last name. What's His middle name?"

"Ah...O.K. ah. Let's keep our focus. I'll answer this one. But then you need to let me finish answering the first question. O.K."

"O.K."

"Jesus doesn't have a last name or a middle name. Back then, people called Him Jesus of Nazareth. That's how people knew Him from someone else named Jesus—because Jesus was a common name back then. Like this, you would be known as Alex of Manistee."

Malachi put his hand up—shoulder height, with the palm facing Alex. He could see another question on the verge of popping out of Alex.

"O.K. Christ is kind of a title, a job description...sort of. I'm Malachi Walmart Stocker. Christ means *Messiah, Savior*. Jesus came to save humans."

"From what?"

"Alex, slow down please," Malachi said. "Let me answer these one at a time. They're starting to stack up."

"I'm sorry, Malachi. I'll be quiet."

"O.K back to the cost," Malachi said. "Here's the…"

"Malachi," someone called from the doorway.

Everyone turned to look.

Alex stood up. "Timothy."

Malachi said, "Timothy, ah...come on in, Timothy."

He shook his head and motioned with his hand. "Can we talk?"

Malachi glanced back at the group. Martin had a big smirk on his face. He did a mini-power punch that went to shoulder height and barely louder than a whisper mouthed the words, "Yes. Yes. Another new person. Praise God."

Carl raised his chin and motioned with his head as he said, "Go. Go talk to Timothy." And almost simultaneously, he stood up and placed a gentle hand on Alex's right shoulder.

Elysia stood up also. "We'll answer Alex's questions."

When Malachi reached Timothy, he was slightly around the corner of the doorway—out of sight from those inside the meeting room. They shuffled a few steps to the airlock entry of the Walmart store.

The muted light cast down on them. And the moment they turned to face each other, Timothy pressed his head onto Malachi's chest and began to sob.

Not a few whimpering tears, but a torrent—enough to

moisten Malachi's shirt.

Malachi held Timothy. Actually, holding him, as he slumped as if he had no muscle control left. Possibly aided by the alcohol Malachi was smelling, which was beyond a scant whiff.

Malachi couldn't deny the awkwardness he felt. He exhaled some air out of his open mouth and hugged Timothy, almost like holding an eighty-pound bag of potatoes.

Psalm 37:5 surged into Malachi's head. "Commit everything you do to the Lord. Trust Him and He will help you."

Malachi knew, at this point, they both needed God's help.

So, he prayed, "God help us. God help us. I commit this to You. I trust You. God help us."

At first, it was a prayer in his head. And then he started to say it softly.

He continued for a few moments and then turned it into a hushed declaration: "God, I trust You. I know You will help us."

"I know You will."

Malachi rubbed Timothy's shoulder and kept repeating, barely audible, "God, I know You will help us."

In a few minutes, Timothy released himself from their embrace. He looked intently at Malachi. He shook his head back and forth. "I feel like I've been thrown into the fire."

They stood silently facing each other, until Timothy said, "Thanks, Malachi. You helped me a lot."

"I didn't really do anything."

Malachi noticed a hint of a smile. "You let me get your shirt all wet."

"The boss will think it's sweat," Malachi said. "I'll probably get a raise because of you."

Timothy smiled. "No, really, Malachi. Thank you. I know you're a man of God. I know I can trust you. And

I know you have to get back to work. So, can we talk real soon?"

"Of course. Absolutely. I'll call you down at DT's. I have the number," Malachi said. "Are you going to be alright tonight?"

"Yeah."

"You sure?"

"Something happened inside me," Timothy said. "I think God did something. I still need more help, but something happened."

Timothy hugged Malachi and when he stepped back, he said, "Maybe tomorrow?"

"Sure. Sounds great," Malachi said. "I look forward to meeting with you."

8. The Cost

Malachi walked back to the doorway and looked into the room where the Jesus at Walmart meeting had carried on without him. He stood back and slightly to the side, so he wouldn't disturb the group.

He had fourteen minutes before his overnight stocker's lunchtime ended. The room was adjacent to the store's entry vestibule, so it would take him two minutes to walk to the time clock and punch back in on time.

Malachi knew he could put the room back in order and pick up his mandolin and materials after the shift was over at 7:00.

He glanced at his watch again. He stood there reflecting on what had happened that night—the first Thursday of 2011.

Still, he couldn't help remembering a few months ago,

how a mini-revival had broken out and three to four times as many people started attending the Jesus at Walmart meetings. The catalyst for this spike in attendance was the death of a co-worker, whose funeral Malachi had officiated.

Malachi rubbed the side of his right cheek with his right hand and then let the hand cradle his chin. He watched the meeting as it continued.

He said, "Praise God," when his gaze settled on Martin and JC. They were the fruit of the post-funeral revival. The only ones who stayed around. Both Walmart employees. They were growing into strong, vibrant Christians. And as a bonus, which zoomed Malachi's emotions up another notch, they were courting with the hopes of getting married.

There was Carl. An ex-hippie, now in his seventies, he was a veteran of nearly forty years in the Jesus army. Would be worthy of a purple heart or two if there was a reward for those deeply wounded while serving the Lord. Malachi thought he was either a kook or a bum the first time they met. Probably both.

But now, Malachi was thinking, "Undoubtedly, Carl's Heavenly rewards will be significant."

And Elysia. Of everyone in the group, Malachi knew her the least, though he did invite her out for pizza a couple of days ago. He knew she is a true woman of God. She has served as a missionary for many years, her latest assignment being China. He and Alex met her when they were running and hanging out at the Manistee High School track. Elysia was a regular down at the track, also.

Malachi drew in air through his nostrils and then started rubbing above his right eye with his right hand. His face became warm on his right side. Between his ear and eye—above his cheekbone. He stood silently—not cognizant of his surroundings.

The Cost

"I'm at a fork in the road," he said. It was only a whisper. He nodded his head. "My life is at a fork in the road." And at that instant, his eyes were drawn to a spot on the floor seven feet away—near the wall. There he noticed a white plastic fork.

He took three steps, bent over, and picked it up. A fork—but not the brittle type. Malachi could tell because it had been flattened—maybe by the floor sweeper.

Malachi raised it to eye level. He smiled slightly. "A fork in the road." He let out a soft laugh.

And then he turned around when he heard sounds. The Jesus at Walmart group was heading toward him—led by Alex.

"So, Alex did they answer your question?" Malachi said as he glanced at the rest of the group and then looked directly at Alex.

"Yeah," Alex said. "Jesus paid the cost."

"What else did you learn?"

"A lot."

"Carl told me how to get saved," Alex said as he started talking faster. "Everyone has done something God doesn't like. A sin. This separates us from God, now and when we die. And if a person is separated from God when they die, that's bad news. Terrible. The worst thing that could ever happen. But God loves us; He loves everyone—no matter what they've done. So, God sent Jesus to Earth. Now, Jesus is God too. He's God with skin on. And Jesus never sinned. Isn't that cool? But they killed Him anyway on a cross. But He fooled the devil and came back to life. Now, Jesus didn't just die on the cross and come back to life just to freak everybody out. Well, here's the good news or like you say Malachi—here's the deal; He died and took the place of everyone. He paid the cost for what we owe because we have sinned. It's sort of like math. I owe God one life because of what I've done—I've sinned. But Jesus can take our place and become the life we owe. And He will give us His life as a gift, if you believe with faith and make Jesus the Lord of your life. *Lord* is kind of like *boss*—well more like *King*. You just do what He says. Like in the Bible and stuff. O.K. then here's the last thing. Well, there's probably more. You have to take the free gift of Jesus. No one forces you to take the gift. And if you refuse the gift—that's really bad news. Forever and ever."

Malachi got a big grin on his face. "So did you take the free gift, Alex?"

Alex smiled back. "No. No, I didn't."

Malachi looked at Alex. There was no smile, and his brow furrowed slightly.

"But I didn't refuse it either," Alex said.

"What do you mean?"

"It seems to me that this is the most important choice a person can make in their life. Nothing else is even a close second. Am I right?"

"Well sure. Exactly."

"If I was going to have your Uncle Dale build me a big house, I would need to take at least a little time to think it over to make sure I could pay the cost," Alex said.

And then Alex looked over at Elysia and back at Malachi. "Now, you wouldn't marry Elysia without thinking about your decision, probably a whole bunch, because you would want it to last."

Almost as an uncontrollable reaction, Malachi glanced at Elysia, as his face felt a little warmer.

But then Alex's next words drew everyone's attention, "So even a kid needs to weigh the cost of following Jesus."

"Wow," Malachi said in a hushed tone. And then he spoke up, "You are one amazing eleven-year old." He hugged Alex and said, "You're so right."

9. Good Time Place

"**M**alachi, thank you so much for coming down to the restaurant," Timothy said. "I hope you got some sleep."

"Enough."

Malachi didn't tell Timothy that his enough was two hours. Because when he got home, his mood was so elevated that he didn't feel like sleeping.

When Malachi arrived home after his third shift stint, he took a shower and then sat down in the living room with his mandolin.

The room was sparsely furnished. And nothing in the room was more precious to Malachi than his mandolin.

It was a gift from Martin a few days ago, while Malachi was visiting his home. An unplanned gift. When Malachi was admiring the mandolin, Martin had noticed. So, he let

Malachi hold the mandolin and then showed him how to play some simple chords. For some unexplainable reason, even considering the fact that Malachi played guitar, he caught on easily.

That night, Martin had stood motionless for several seconds. He stared unfocused—off to the right of Malachi. And then he looked directly at him. "I want you to have this mandolin. It's yours—on one condition—you always honor God with it—with the music."

As he sat there in his home in the town of Freesoil, Malachi was feeling what he calls the awe of God. And reflecting back on what had happened at last night's Jesus at Walmart meeting further roused his God-awareness.

And God had already given him another song to play on his mandolin. They were both simple songs; still, they would come to him quickly. It was as if they were already written—chords and all. When this happened, Malachi would remember the words from Psalm 45:1: "A Song of Love. My heart overflows with a good theme; I address my verses to the King; my tongue is the pen of a ready writer."

Malachi strummed his mandolin and began to sing:

> Jesus, Oh what You've done for me
> Jesus, Oh what You've done for me
>
> Loved me. Saved me. Set me free
> Loved me. Saved me. Set me free
>
> And who the Son sets free
> And who the Son sets free
> Is free. Free indeed
>
> Jesus, Oh what You've done for me
> Loved me. Saved me. Set me free
> Free indeed

Good Time Place

"Yeah, I got enough sleep," Malachi said. "Thanks for asking. How about you, Timothy?"

Malachi looked at Timothy. Before last night, he hadn't seen or talked to Timothy in a few months. He was the owner of DT's Good Time Place in downtown Manistee.

The street side was two stories of brick in the typical early 1900's traditional downtown look. The back of DT's overlooked the broad, murky Manistee River, which five blocks to the west fed into Lake Michigan.

On the backside, an ultra-modern deck was perched thirty-five feet from the meandering waterway. Quarry-tile red composite decking was underfoot, with an expanse nearly as large as the interior of the restaurant. A shiny, sleek tubular railing system with clear glass panels, in lieu of any spindles, protected the patrons from a tragic tumble to the ground two stories below, likely the savior of many a guest who had tipped too many Trinity Darks.

Timothy appeared as if he was at home on a stool next to a raised table.

The tables were a décor statement. Malachi had never seen anything like them. They could nearly pass for wood, except they were molded as one piece. Undoubtedly, some type of composite wood. The color and the shape were the tables' distinguishing features. The main color, the background color, was nearly fluorescent green. And was muted with a blood-red tone that highlighted the wood-like graining. This red tamed the green, while giving it a surreal, almost optical-illusion effect.

With its color and peculiar shape—a slightly elongated square with two diagonally clipped corners and two that were rounded, the table drew Malachi's curiosity. Almost begging those nearby to discover its mystique.

"Yeah, kind of," Timothy said. "Well, last night was my

best rest in a long time."

Before last night, Malachi had only one other noteworthy encounter with Timothy.

In contrast, the restaurant he owned became a venue of significance for Malachi, mainly because of his relationship with one of the waitresses, who had been employed by Timothy. Mandy Howard—Alex's mom. DT's Good Time Place is where they met; here their friendship grew and then blossomed into something endearing. And like a funeral, this is where the casket was closed on their relationship. Already dead, here is where Malachi saw Mandy for the last time.

He still mourned the downfall of their friendship.

"Do you ah...you want ah...do you want a beer or something?" Timothy said with a beer sitting on the table in front of him. Apparently, the house favorite—Trinity Dark.

"I'll pass."

"Do you mind if I have one?"

"Go ahead. It's your place, my friend."

It was easy for Malachi to recall the other time they had chatted at the restaurant. While their conversation had launched, as Malachi caringly inquired about Mandy, the corner quickly turned as Timothy transparently shared his own struggles. Not in a totally dropped-guard manner, yet truthfully soul revealing.

One thing Timothy had said in those regards had surfaced in Malachi's thoughts many times since: "Malachi, make sure you know the desire of your heart is the right desire. Because you know what? Now I'm trapped by what I thought was the desire of my heart."

What touched Malachi's heart the most, though, was when he said, "I never talk about it anymore, but I used to be really into God." But even before that, Malachi had felt a bond with Timothy—a feeling like—I think we could be good friends.

"Can I get you anything?" Timothy said as he held the Trinity Dark in his right hand.

"No. I'm fine," Malachi said. "Thanks."

Timothy fidgeted with the bottle of beer. For several seconds, he stared at it. And then fixed his gaze on Malachi.

"I'm so burned out," Timothy said. "I just want to put a closed sign up and walk away. I feel like I've been thrown into the fire. Everything," he shook his head and then continued, "everything that could go wrong is going wrong. I just want to leave. And not tomorrow. Today. Right now."

They sat diagonally to each other at a table snugged up against the exterior wall of the restaurant. A rust-red canopy with a matching fabric ceiling was suspended overhead. To Malachi, what appeared to be removable glass or Plexiglas panels, enclosed the area from the outside elements, like a three-season porch. Two overhead radiant heaters moderated the temperature nicely, though just a touch on the cool side.

"So, what are your options?" Malachi said. "I ah...how can I help you, Timothy?"

"Options?" Timothy said as his left hand brushed his neatly cropped black hair.

"Options?" He sat back, his shoulders resting against the chair back.

He had the restaurant entrepreneurial look. Black shirt with square tails, black corduroy tapered-leg slacks, and black shoes.

"Options?" he said as he peered at the Winter-scape through the glass.

"I remember a long time ago," Timothy said. "I think I told you I used to be into church and all that. I still remember that Bible verse I memorized back then, "The thief comes only to steal and kill and destroy.""

He half laughed, half snorted. "Options?"

"I could jump into the Manistee River," Timothy said.

He looked hard at Malachi for several seconds. "So, what do you think, man of God?" And then he tipped his Trinity Dark to his lips.

"Jesus said, 'I came that they may have life and have it more abundantly.' That's the conclusion of the Bible verse you just quoted," Malachi said. "What do you think of that option?"

"So bam. I do the Jesus thing and bam—I have abundant life."

"Yep. That's exactly how it works." Malachi shook his head up and down.

"What?"

"O.K. You're right. It might take forty-five minutes before all your troubles have vanished."

Timothy shook his head back and forth and almost grinned.

"Here's the deal," Malachi said. "If you wanted to start a successful restaurant, and you were new at it, you wouldn't expect success on the first day just because you opened the door and made a heartfelt commitment to be the best in town. Now would you? But even on that first day, you would expect to be a few steps down the road. Maybe garner a few lifetime customers. Maybe unveil a signature dish."

Timothy touched the three longest fingers of his left hand against his tightened lips as Malachi continued.

"Think about it, Timothy," Malachi said. "Even last night, down at Walmart, God touched you. Didn't your anxiety subside substantially—pretty much vanish? And then, as you said, 'Best rest in a long time.' That little package of abundance came...ah... express delivery."

And then Malachi slowly drew in air through his nostrils. He started rubbing above his right eye with his right hand. His face became warm on his right side. Between his ear and eye—above his cheekbone.

"What's wrong, Malachi?" Timothy said

"Fork."

"Fork? You need a fork?" Timothy said. "You want some food?"

"No. No," Malachi said. "You need to listen to me. This is really, really important."

Malachi stopped, like he had frozen. He looked behind Timothy, down at the floor. He stood up and went over to the spot where he was looking and bent over and picked something up in the corner—nearly obscured by a silk plant.

By then, Timothy had turned around and was watching him.

When their eyes met, he handed Timothy a flattened fork. "You're at a fork in the road of your life. Timothy, make sure you choose the correct direction. Make sure. Make sure, Timothy."

Timothy examined the fork. "Where did you get this? We don't have this style of fork here at DT's. What happened to it? You put it there. Didn't you?"

"When would I have done that, Timothy?" Malachi said. "We've been together the whole time."

"Fork in the road," Timothy said, drawing out each word to nearly two syllables.

He shifted his eyes from the fork to Malachi. Timothy's body tensed as he stood up. Both of his hands fingered through his hair—front to back, as he looked upward. And then he returned his gaze to Malachi. "I think the flames are surrounding me like a cage."

Malachi then stood up and put a hand on each of Timothy's shoulders. "So, if the Son makes you free, if Jesus makes you free, you will be free indeed."

10. God Please Change My Heart

Malachi arrived back at Freesoil in plenty of time for some sleep before his next overnight shift at Walmart.

Before he headed to his bedroom, Malachi went to the kitchen and broke loose a banana from the bunch lying to the left of the kitchen sink. He took two steps and was in the dining room. His laptop was set up on the table—an economy grade folding card table. He sat down on the only chair—a white plastic lawn chair, badly discolored because of its previous outdoor life.

A few clicks and he was scrolling through a thin selection of correspondences. Never much for personal communication via the media, though he did sense a spike of stimulation when the subject line of the third e-mail appeared—Baptism. This was enhanced when he saw who it was from—Stephen Johnson.

Malachi,

It's been too long since we've communicated. I hope God is blessing you.

Life flies by too quickly, and I apologize for not thinking of this sooner.

Actually, it's only because Sarah asked me about it (You know how amazing she is). She's being baptized this coming Sunday, and it would be so special if you could be there.

I know this is short notice.

Still, I hope you can make it. Also, I would enjoy getting together and catching up on life.

Please let me know.

God Bless,

Stephen

Malachi leaned back in his chair. "Wow. That's cool."

His right elbow rested on the arm of the chair as his hand brushed against his chin. "Hmm," he said. He sat motionless for forty-five seconds.

And said to himself, "I need to do this."

His fingers went to the keyboard:

Stephen,

Pray God will make a way. And on my end, I will do everything I can to make it to Sarah's baptism.

It would be so awesome to be there. And you and I need to catch up on everything—like you said.

Love,

Malachi

He leaned back in his chair again. And after less than two minutes, he said, "That's what I'm going to do."

He picked up his cell phone and scrolled through his contacts: *Sal.*

The overnight manager.

"Sal. This is Malachi. I hope I didn't wake you up."

"No, you didn't. I haven't gone to sleep yet. Is this an emergency?"

"No. But..."

"What is it?"

"I just found out about a baptism on Sunday where I used to live—in St. Amos. Someone very special to me. If I'm going to go, I would need a couple of days off work. I can come in tonight and then I would need two days off. I know this is short notice. But this would mean so much to me. But whatever you say, Sal."

"You can have the time off. You can have tonight off also. If you want it—so you can get ready."

"What?" Malachi said.

"The answer is *yes.*"

"Thank you so much, Sal."

"I think Walmart still owes you this one. The store won't be busy. It never is this time of year. And you know what, Malachi? So many of the associates just call in on a whim or they just lie so they can get out of work. You've never called in, have you? You've never missed a day, is that right?"

"Well no, I haven't," Malachi said. "Well...when I got arrested in the parking lot and all that."

Sal laughed. "I didn't mean that."

"Thank you, Sal. You're the best." Malachi said, "And if it's not too much, could you tell Martin that I'll be out of town for a few days?"

"Sure. No problem," Sal said. "Have a great time."

Malachi sent another e-mail to Stephen to tell him that he was coming and checked his cell phone to make sure he still had his phone number.

Then Malachi called Timothy.

"Hey Timothy, this is Malachi. Got a moment?"

"Sure, Malachi. What's up?"

"I told you I was going to come by tomorrow so we could talk some more. Something came up, so I'm going to head out of town for a few days."

"Some emergency?"

"No, a baptism of a very special, let me think...a very special twelve-year old back at the church in St. Amos, where I used to work."

"That's cool," Timothy said. "So what kind of work did you do at the church?"

"Well, I ah...I was the Associate Pastor."

"Are you still there, Timothy?"

"Yeah...I was just thinking. I mean...I'm curious...but you don't have to tell me. But I don't know...well, how does a person go from being a Pastor to a Walmart third shift stocker?"

"Malachi, are you still there?"

"I'm just thinking. Yeah...I'm just thinking."

"Well, you don't need to tell me."

"Yeah...I know what you're saying," Malachi said. "Timothy, do you know what a hypocrite is?"

"Sure. I mean I understand the concept."

"So, you and I are planning on meeting together some more. Probably quite a few times. And essentially, you'll be baring your soul to me as we attempt to rid your life of some junk—with God's help, that is. Right?"

"Yeah, that pretty much says it."

"But when it comes time for me to bare my soul a little bit...I'm like, no thank you," Malachi said. "I don't know for sure, but I think if I do, then I'm smelling like a hypocrite."

God Please Change My Heart

Neither one said anything for a couple of moments.

And then Malachi said, "This is how a Pastor becomes a Walmart stocker..." And then Malachi told Timothy the unsanctified version. The whole story.

"That's quite a story," Timothy said when Malachi finished. "Back in my church days, I think we called that a testimony. I mean it's only a testimony if you get to the good part. The part where God does something cool through all the mess. Is that right?"

"I never thought of it that way," Malachi said. "Yeah, you're right."

"Malachi, thank you for telling me your story. Your testimony really encouraged me. I feel like there's hope for me. And you know what, you're going to have another testimony when you come back. I don't know how you're going to face all those people. And what if you run into your ex-wife, Annie? Wow, you're a lot more of a man than I am. Imagine what people are going to be saying about you. I mean, leaving without telling anyone. Some people call that a coward. Wow...awful... it's going to be awful. People will be talking."

"O.K. O.K. Thanks, Timothy, I get the point."

"Well, I mean...you'd have to agree."

"I didn't really...I don't know," Malachi said. "I was just thinking about Sarah. And I got all excited. I know it's the Godly thing to do. But still..."

"Maybe you shouldn't go," Timothy said.

Malachi made sure Timothy would be O.K. while he was away and assured him that he was only a phone call away.

As soon as Malachi hung up, he wanted to yell, "Crap," as loud as he could. Instead, he held it in and let it rumble around. His insides were like a two-liter bottle of Coke after a vigorous shaking.

Jesus at Walmart...fire on the Earth

Finally, it shook loose, "Oh crap." But in a conversational tone—more like a declaration of surrender.

There was only one chair in the living room—overstuffed, covered in a black corduroy fabric. Malachi shuffled over to it and plopped down, more like a freefall into its plush interior.

His Bible rested on an empty plastic drywall-compound bucket turned upside down—to his left.

Malachi glanced at it. And then focused on nothing, except the pictures cascading through his head. A handful of minutes passed.

Then he shifted and fastened his eyes on the Bible. And picked it up and flipped through the pages. He stopped and then read—barely audible: "Why are you in despair, O my soul? And why have you become disturbed within me? Hope in God, for I shall again praise Him for the help of His presence."

Malachi leaned forward and picked up his mandolin, which was cradled in a stand next to the bucket.

He strummed four chords and then began to sing:
Oh God please change my heart
Oh God please change my heart

Holy Spirit let Your wind blow in this place
Holy Spirit let Your wind blow in this place

Jesus I will seek Your face
Jesus I will seek Your face

Oh God please change my heart
Holy Spirit let Your wind blow in this place
Jesus I will seek Your face
Oh God please change my...heart

God Please Change My Heart

When he finished, he placed the mandolin back in its stand.

And then bowed his head, "Father God, that's what I need. Please change my heart. Give me the power of the Holy Spirit to travel the road set ahead—so I may honor You. And Jesus, I will believe Your words. I receive them, 'Peace I leave with you; My peace I give to you; not as the world gives do I give to you. Do not let your heart be troubled, nor let it be fearful.' Thank you, Jesus. Amen."

II. Facing the Giants

Awful, *Awful* was in a shoving match with: *I can do all things through Christ who strengthens me,* as Malachi took the seven-hour trek south and east of Manistee.

It didn't seem like a standoff to Malachi. Still, seeing the St. Amos city limit sign ahead didn't feel like an invitation to ascend the victor's platform either. And he felt somewhat cowardly when he opted to use texting to confirm his plans and to attain the necessary details regarding the baptism.

And his decision to stay at the Motel 8 on the south perimeter of town made Malachi feel like he was hiding out. Because, he knew he was.

Though the last text he received from Stephen did boost his courage: "Please come early to church. Sarah is so excited you'll be there."

Malachi sat on the edge of the bed in Room 17. He was settled in.

He picked up his phone and re-read the last text from Stephen. His eyes rested on the words, "Sarah is so excited you'll be there."

It was like that bag of potato chips the hand can't resist. He had to have one more nibble of satisfaction.

Sarah Johnson was Malachi's favorite Sunday school student when he was the Associate Pastor at St. Amos Community Church. Now twelve, she was every Sunday school teacher's dream student.

And Malachi knew she was a reflection of her father, Stephen Johnson, and her mother, Gracie.

Stephen was the head elder at St. Amos when Malachi encountered his turmoil. Through it all, Stephen became Malachi's number one ally. Not a yes man, but a prober, with Godly wisdom to weigh matters carefully.

Even after Malachi bolted to Manistee, Stephen stood ready to help him. But after things turned around for Malachi, communication became sketchy between them. Until it ceased. Busy schedules, as with many, was the blamed culprit.

St. Amos Community Church, originally a denominational church going back over seventy-five years, re-invented itself a decade or so before Malachi's arrival. The metamorphosis entailed two main distinctives—contemporary worship music and pulling out of the denomination to become non-denominational. St. Amos employed most of the typical changes utilized when a church turns to the contemporary format.

Yet, St. Amos Community Church still held onto a shade of the traditional. They followed the church calendar, including the pulpit reading of set scriptures—the lectionary, with the sermon linked to these elements. Although Malachi initially had his uncertainties on this format, he soon grew to appreciate the approach.

The building was also the other traditional ingredient at St. Amos. The exterior was wrapped in buckskin colored brick. The roof pointed heavenward with its exaggerated steepness—every roofer's nightmare, and then cascaded to within five-feet of the ground—every roofer's dream.

The sanctuary's ceiling soared, planked with natural-tone pine boards and emphasized with massive, laminated arched-beams. The exterior's brick theme carried into the interior.

Malachi knew the churchgoers' favored method to remain inconspicuous, arriving late and sitting in the far reaches, was not available. He needed to honor Stephen's request to arrive early.

Actually, he felt fortified. He had been reading his Bible in the morning—like usual. And as he soaked in some scriptures, God started to change his heart. Though he read many passages, two familiar ones burrowed their way into Malachi's inner man.

"Therefore humble yourselves under the mighty hand of God, that He may exalt you at the proper time, casting all your anxiety on Him because He cares for you."

Humble became the word entitling his guidebook for the day's proceedings.

He thought to himself, "I'm Malachi, who totally screwed up. I'm the one who walked away from my marriage, my job, and God. I'm the Malachi who is now right with God. No pretending—I am who I am."

As Malachi approached St. Amos Community Church, he still wished he could blend in. Predominately, so the day could be about the baptisms and God. Not—look who showed up.

And Malachi couldn't deny that the inner punching match was now going another round. A feisty one.

If I can't arrive late, I'll arrive early; real early—Malachi decided. Beat the crowd. Sit on the back row and huddle up against the wall. There's something comforting about having a wall behind you. Plus, this sort of posturing, especially with well-planned body language and a determined focus on the weekly bulletin, seems to encourage—"Don't talk to me." Malachi had his plan.

Two cars in the parking lot. Now three.

Malachi's body wasn't fully through the church's front door, when he heard, "Pastor Malachi."

And before he could take two steps, Sarah Johnson had her head pressed against his chest in an embrace.

It was all he could do to fight back an all-out cascade of tears.

His eyes were glistening when he looked up and saw Stephen and Gracie. Both beaming.

Malachi swallowed hard. The inner *awful, awful* crashed to the ground with one pummeling blow. A single tear trickled down his cheek. His mind became engulfed with a singular thought, "This is the day the LORD has made. I will rejoice and be glad in it."

After two more hugs, the joyous, bouncy Sarah tugged Malachi up the aisle, nearly singing, "Sit up front with us."

While the Johnson's fulfilled their pre-baptism obligations, Malachi sat alone. Second row left. Two thirds of the way over—wall-side. He could hear people gathering as he looked toward the front.

Sitting there, he felt solitude, a privacy. He didn't look back. But he knew, because of church quirkiness, the three or four rows behind him would remain empty. Sort of a church no-fly zone. At least no regulars would occupy those rows. But if the church filled up because of the baptisms, the irregulars—visitors may have no other option.

Malachi looked at his watch. Twelve minutes before the service would begin. He looked up on the platform. It was three steps up. Two musicians were making some final preparations. A portable baptismal was up on the stage almost directly in front of him.

Malachi thought to himself, "I have the best seat in the house."

He shifted his eyes to the back wall of the platform. Hanging nine feet above was a four-foot by five-foot banner. The background was a vibrant new-leaf green. Dual striped edging each an inch wide, in pure brown, framed the perimeter. The featured Bible verse proclaimed: "I will praise the Lord all my life. I will sing praise to God as long as I live."

Suddenly, he felt a soft touch on his shoulder and someone spoke, "Malachi."

He turned around and froze for several seconds.

They looked at each other.

"How are you doing?"

"Really good, Malachi. Really good. And I mean it."

And then it happened as if without effort.

Malachi stood up.

And they embraced.

Just briefly.

And then Malachi said, "It's so good to see you, Annie."

"Can I sit down?" she said.

Malachi hesitated for the briefest of moments and then said, "Sure. This is the day the Lord has made. I will rejoice and be glad in it."

"What?" Annie said. She smiled, "You're still Malachi."

By then, Stephen, Sarah, and Gracie were sitting on his right.

When he looked over, Stephen gave him a curious grin. Sarah waved exuberantly. And Malachi was almost certain he saw tears in Gracie's eyes.

Stephen whispered as he pointed toward the stage, "Pastor Benjamin is doing an outstanding job. Did you know Pastor

Neil is in drug rehab in Florida? Pray for him. Marijuana was only one of his problems. He'll make it, though. I know he will. By God's grace."

Malachi felt a hand on his other arm. He looked over at Annie.

She said quietly, "I had an awesome God encounter two months ago. I've never been so close to God in my life. I don't really know how it happened."

And then Annie started to tremble slightly, "Were you praying for me?"

"Every day," Malachi said. "Every day, Annie."

Her face pressed hard against his shoulder. Her whole body quivered.

The worship leader strummed the G-chord and said, "Stand with me. Let's worship the Lord together."

And as the congregation rose to their feet, the worship leader began to sing: "This is the day the Lord has made. I will rejoice and be glad in it."

12. Birds of the Air

"**A**nother testimony," Timothy said. "You have another testimony?"

DT's was empty. Malachi and Timothy sat side by side on bar stools.

Even back in his partying days, Malachi wasn't much of a bar person. Marijuana was his vice, his sin of choice. If he did go to a bar back then, the music had to be loud enough so that you only heard two-thirds of the words of a conversation—even when practically yelling. So, you smiled a lot and nodded. And he still remembers, toward the end of that phase of his life, it seemed like all the bands sounded the same, all the beer tasted the same, and all the conversations were dumped out of the same can.

"Yeah. I sure do. God is good," Malachi said. "What

time do you close on Sundays?" He glanced at his watch—
10:16 p.m.

"I'm not open on Sundays," Timothy said.

Malachi had left St. Amos a little before 3:00 and had
called Timothy twenty minutes before arriving back in
Manistee.

"You used to be open on Sundays," Malachi said.
"Didn't you?"

"Yeah. But no more."

"Oh, I didn't know. When did you start being closed
on Sundays?"

Timothy smiled, "Today." He looked over at Malachi.
"I went to church."

"Wow. A testimony."

"Not really," Timothy said. "Church was awful."

"Awful?" Malachi said.

"Dreadful."

"Where did you go?"

"I'm not even going to tell you," Timothy said. "I know
I haven't been in church even once...I don't know...ten,
twenty years. Probably over thirty since I went faithfully."

"What was so bad about the church?"

"I don't know. Maybe it was just me," Timothy said. "It
just didn't do anything for me. It seemed more like a rock
concert with a comedian. The banter and video clips about
what was going on at church, they were longer than the sermon. I mean, one of the videos was so compelling, I almost
signed up to play on the church hockey team. And I don't
even play hockey. But I couldn't decide, because it might
interrupt pre-conditioning for softball season. Of course,
I'm actually best at volleyball—unfortunately, signups for
that have already ended. But maybe I could play volleyball
in Hawaii—if I can scrape together two thousand dollars—
I mean, if God provides."

Malachi scrunched his face. "Hawaii?"

"Yeah, Hawaii," Timothy said. "The men's group, the Men of Courage, are taking a mission trip to Hawaii in two weeks."

"Seriously, Malachi," Timothy said as he stood up, spreading his hands shoulder width—head high. "I mean, I was probably the worst sinner there. But even I know church is about God."

He started striding back and forth like a Pentecostal preacher revving up for the altar call. "It's not about us. Church is about God. Church is about God!"

"Church is about God," Timothy said—his volume subsided as he slumped into a booth behind where Malachi was sitting.

Malachi had spun his stool around as he followed Timothy's movement.

Timothy was staring ahead. So, Malachi was looking at the left side of his face.

"Wow," Malachi said. "Was there anything at the church...anything that you liked?"

Without hesitation, Timothy turned and looked at Malachi, "Yeah, but she's probably already married."

"What are you talking about?"

"The lead singer in the band. She was, well, as a pastor, I'm sure you don't know what this means—she was hot. Skinny jeans. Now I'm talking skinny jeans. Man, she had the whole package. And she could sing—just amazing."

Timothy turned his head. Once again, Malachi was looking at the side of his face. He kept talking, almost as if he was talking into the air.

"Her voice, she could really sing. Her voice was like an emotion-extracting instrument. I especially got into the one song. My eyes were closed. Her voice was an alluring, whispery tone. I was being drawn in. Her voice floated through the room: 'Jesus I love You. I love You. Jesus I love You.' And then, it was weird. I thought I smelled perfume— I mean the good stuff. I looked up. I started checking her out again. I couldn't help it. I thought to myself, 'I wish she would sing: Timothy, I love you.'"

He looked over at Malachi. He raised his hand like you do in fourth grade. "I know, I'm a total heathen. But I'm just telling you the truth."

"God can change you."

"Not at that church. Well, only if God pokes my eyes out. And that would just be a start."

Malachi smiled. "You probably don't like the Bible verse that says, 'If your eye causes you to stumble, pluck it out and throw it from you.'"

"Yeah," Timothy said. "Yeah. I'll do that next Sunday. I'll sit up closer to the stage. See if I can hit the pastor on the forehead with my eyeball when he pauses to let the first belly laugh of the day die down."

"Wow. You are a heathen," Malachi said. "You need to try another church."

"Well, that's sort of, kind of what I was thinking," Timothy said. "I want to show you something. But first, guess who I saw at church?"

"Ah...I don't know...Britney Spears?"

Timothy laughed. And then said, "Mandy Howard."

"Mandy?"

"Yep."

"Mandy? Wow," Malachi said. "How's she doing?"

"I didn't talk to her. I mean this church is like a mini-mall," Timothy said. "I saw her at a distance. I mean...I was trying to blend in. You know what I mean. I didn't really want to talk to anyone. But I'm positive it was her."

"Mandy at church. Hmm," Malachi said. "Mandy."

"Hey Malachi," Timothy said as he jumped to his feet.

"I want to show you something."

He motioned with his head toward the front door. "Let's go outside."

"Outside?"

"Don't worry. I'm a heathen, but I'm not going to roll you," Timothy said.

They both laughed.

"Put your coat on," Timothy said.

And then they stepped out the door. Timothy led Malachi a couple of strides to the west. Timothy turned around to face the building. And Malachi did the same thing.

"DT's is actually two storefronts," Timothy said.

Then he pointed slightly to the west. And I own the adjacent storefront. That one's not really in use. Well... kind of for storage. I own all three—free and clear. And the three stores are actually one building. I bought them back when they were super cheap. They still don't go for very much."

Malachi was following what he was saying. At the same time, he kept wondering, "Where's this going?"

The three storefronts rose up two and a half stories in front of them. Malachi could see the symmetry of the three/one building. All the storefronts were the same—essentially. Every one of the second story facades had three oversized double hung windows. Below, each one had a large plate glass window to the left and a door to the right. Except the middle storefront—where the restaurant's kitchen was located.

Here, the window and door had been walled off. Covered in vertical boards painted the color of the brick.

Timothy kept describing his building. "There's seventy-five feet of frontage and the building is like a hundred and twenty-five feet deep—something like that. And remember, it's basically just one building. One big building."

He then touched Malachi on the shoulder as his body shifted around. "Look back here."

They turned around. And Timothy pointed across the street, several degrees to the east. "See that spot where there are no stores. That's a walkway to the back parking lot. Plenty of parking. And most people don't think of it this way, but it's no further away than the far side of the Walmart parking lot. And then…"

"Hey…ah," Malachi said. "So, I'm…I'm thinking what your telling me is more than the verbal handbook for downtown Manistee merchants."

"I'm getting chilly," Timothy said. "Let's go back inside."

Malachi followed Timothy. They sat down at the same booth where Timothy had been sitting.

"You want something to drink?" Timothy said.

"I'm just not much of a drinker," Malachi said. "I don't drink."

"Forget the beer. I'm cutting back myself," Timothy said. "Water. I have the best bottled water on planet Earth. It's local—it's called Camp Eden Springs."

"Sounds good."

Malachi sat pondering as Timothy fetched the waters. "What's going on?"

"Here you go, Malachi."

"Hey, you're right, Timothy. This is good stuff."

Timothy took a swig of his Camp Eden.

Malachi noticed he had something concealed in his left hand. Timothy set his bottle down. He quickly brought his left hand from under the table. Raised it above the table, flipped it palm side down, and released its content.

Clang!

The fork fell on the table. The flattened fork from the other day.

Birds of the Air

"Fork," Timothy said in absolute monotone, "fork in the road."

He looked Malachi directly in the eyes, "DT's is no more."

"No more," Malachi said.

He shook his head back and forth. He stretched the words out as he pronounced them, "No more."

He shifted slightly in his seat. His gaze fell over Malachi's right shoulder. His elbow rested on the table. His left hand brushed against his chin.

They were both silent for several seconds.

"I'm...kind of...kind of shocked," Malachi said. "So fast?"

Timothy picked up the fork. "When you left the other day, I carried this fork back to my office. It was like—click, click— in my brain. I had this supernatural clarity about the whole restaurant situation. My entire thought pattern shifted in...in less than a minute. I went from thinking I can't close, to I can't stay open. Just like that."

"A sign from God," Malachi said.

"A sign I didn't need," Timothy said. "The sign from my accountant should have been enough. Or from any sane person. The fork just lifted a fog. An evil fog."

"Wow," Malachi said.

"And even you, like most people, could figure out all the insurmountable challenges to running a place like this. Of course, money, the money thing is a killer—but so much more than just that. A lot more. But I'm not going into all the messy details and all the *whys*."

Timothy fell silent. His chin sunk to his chest as his head slumped. And then he looked at Malachi. "Isn't there something in the Bible about God watching out for even the birds."

"Look at the birds of the air, they do not sow, nor

reap, nor gather into barns. And yet your heavenly Father feeds them," Malachi said. And then he reached across the table, gently touching Timothy's shoulder, "Are you not worth much more than they?"

13. Cows

"**D**oes that mean…" Timothy said. His facial expression shifted. Now, like that of a six-year old peeking over the edge of his grandma's casket. "Does that mean, I won't lose everything? That's what I really need to know. I wish I could have found out at church today."

He didn't say anything else, but his eyes were searching Malachi.

Malachi retracted his hand and leaned back against the seat's plush upholstery. He rubbed his hands together at lap level. Inside, he was pondering as fast as he could. At the same time, Timothy's near-glare was almost spooky. In the rush of all these thoughts, Malachi was praying silently, "God what do I say? What do I say?"

"You're a pastor too," Timothy said. "What do you say?"

Malachi's cadence was slower than usual. "I'm getting a clearer picture here."

Timothy's clenched lips relaxed. Both edges upturned almost less than slight.

"Timothy, I'm thinking what you're looking for, what you think would really help you is…is ah…," Malachi said. "I'm thinking two things. Plan A and Plan B. Plan A: tell you I heard from God, informing you that smooth sailing is just ahead. Inches away. And if that's not so—Plan B: the sailing is not smooth. It's rough, rough, rough. So, have faith, faith, faith. And if you have enough faith, not only will you get through it, but your life is destined to turn out more wonderful than it's ever been before."

Malachi halted for several seconds. "Am I right?"

Timothy's body relaxed a hint. "Yeah. Pretty much. I mean, not exactly…but ah…yeah. I mean, that would work."

"I do have a word from God for you."

A slight smile formed on Timothy's face. "You do? Really?"

"For what will it profit a man if he gains the whole world and forfeits his soul? Or what will a man give in exchange for his soul?" Malachi said.

"Thanks for the warm fuzzy," Timothy said.

And then his head wagged back and forth in slow motion, his gaze fixed over Malachi's left shoulder. "So true. So true."

After a few moments, he returned his attention to Malachi. "I do have an idea though."

"An idea?"

"Yeah," Timothy said. "This place is available. You should start a church here."

"A church?"

"Yeah, you know—God, Jesus, the Holy Spirit. Some people. Some Bibles."

"O.K. thank you for the theology lesson." Malachi said. "A church here? At DT's? In downtown Manistee?"

Cows

"Why not?" Timothy said. "And it's not DT's anymore. Why not a church?"

"Why?"

"Why?" Timothy said. "You need another theology lesson. O.K. here's one—to get souls of heathens like me saved. Keep us from forfeiting our souls. Is that a good enough reason?"

"That's not the point."

"That's not the point," Timothy said as he stood up and started pacing. His hands were talking as much as his mouth. "That's not the point. Not the point!"

He stopped right beside Malachi and looked down at him. "So what is the point? What's the point, Pastor? Pastor Malachi?"

"Wow Timothy," Malachi said. "I'm…I'm ah…you're blowing me away with your zeal, your concern for those who don't know Jesus."

Timothy's countenance sunk as his body slumped into the seat across from Malachi.

"No," he said.

His words rose slowly like a nearly extinguished campfire, sputtering, spark-less. "I need to generate some income. I need some cash. Get some money rolling in. The reality is, most businesses that open down here don't survive. I was thinking: church, bunch of people, God—that has to equal money—some for me, some for you—for the church. Even I could believe what I heard in the Bible. I mean, doesn't it say that God owns like all the cows on like a thousand hills? So, he has plenty. Sell some off. Raise some cash."

Timothy reached for his bottle of Camp Eden Springs in front of him. It was nearly full. He took a swig and then returned it to the table. His left hand kept its hold. "Malachi, I'm not going to pretend. I'm desperate."

He drew in a breath through his nose. "Desperate. A fork in the road. And you know…if God wants a church down here and I'm thinking, 'Why wouldn't He?' He could send some cows."

Malachi grinned—ever so slightly, "Cows?"

14. Grasshoppers

"**C**ows," Malachi said to himself as he hopped out of his Suburban and flipped the hood of his Carhartt coat over his head.

Malachi looked at his watch. It was 10:12 Monday morning.

Getting sufficient rest was an ongoing challenge for Malachi ever since he started working third shift. And the trip to St Amos and the other events of the weekend had radically a skewed his normal sleep pattern. So now, when he should be sleeping, Malachi was fully awake.

He parked on the southwest edge of the Days Inn parking lot adjacent to Walmart and headed several strides south and then west. He was on Merkey Rd. Lake Michigan was two miles ahead. A park perched on a bluff three stories above the shore was located at the end of the road. This he discovered on his first morning in Manistee—the day after his speedy exit from St. Amos.

As he walked west, he briefly thought about the park. In a way, a landmark in his life. His first date with Mandy took place there—her suggestion. A little over a year ago, on New Year's Day 2011, Malachi had stood on the edge of the bluff with the word Jump caroming through his brain. And that same day, his best friend, the ever-knowing Carl, showed up. And Malachi still remembers his words, "You know God talks to me. I heard that one of His sheep needed rescuing." The little park is also the place where he and Carl had met.

After walking a block on Merkey Rd., Malachi turned to the right. He was heading to Carl's place.

Malachi had so much on his mind. In these types of situations, Carl was always Malachi's first choice. Insightful, caring, a true lover of Jesus, biblically astute, and amazingly gifted in hearing the voice of God—enough to be spooky at times. But usually, more in the realm of being the fatherly-type, who always seemed ready to strengthen, encourage, and comfort.

Below his feet, Malachi knew it was a dirt and sand two-track but now, mostly covered by snow. Malachi made his way on the fluffed washboard track created by snowmobile traffic. And in some well-worn spots, the snow machines had cut down to the beach-like sand below.

Soon the trail dipped downward—the footing less sure. But still adequate. And then the snow track inclined upward to the right—climbing a story and a half. Malachi concentrated on planting his feet firmly with each step.

A scattered mix of hardwoods, devoid of any leaves, were a dark contrast to the dazzling sun. Aided in its illumination by the bed of pure white snow.

The trail then hedged down and slightly to the left. And

then back to the right, rising up to the trail's highest peak—a mound capped by medium sized pines. Whiffs of powdery snow decorated the bows.

The trail next descended into a valley. The trees became sparser as the vista opened up. At this point, Malachi was wishing he had sunglasses.

And he was cognizant that this spot was directly behind Walmart. Close enough so he could spy the highest reaches of the store's west façade.

The trail turned slightly left as Malachi made his final descent.

Then he stopped. Standing silently, taking in the beauty of the up north Winter displayed before him.

Snow and gleaming metal shone from the roof of Carl's simplistic cottage. The pond, two hundred feet to the southwest, was frozen around the perimeter. The water reflected the vivid blue sky.

The reeds around the pond were still, at attention—as if they were awaiting their next command.

Nearing the building, pondering the idyllic setting, Malachi thought to himself, "God, could anything be more peaceful?"

He shifted his head upward when that thought entered his mind. Looking skyward.

And then he looked thirty-five degrees to the right. He knew it was there. But today, his awareness was more astute. There, in the distance, on a high embankment, was the sprawling Mt. Carmel Cemetery, visible only because of the change of season. With this new perspective, it was as if the cemetery hung high above the northwest corner of Carl's cottage.

Malachi glanced uphill, once more, before stepping up to the door. And thought as he raised his hand to knock, "I hope Carl is here."

But in that instant, Carl pulled the door open. "Come in Malachi. I was expecting you."

Malachi stared at Carl for a second, before saying, "Wow Carl, you are so prophetic. You amaze me. You sure see things."

"Yeah, I am amazing."

"Carl...that's not like you."

"Yeah, but I see things," Carl said. "I'm amazing. I saw you through the window. Isn't that amazing?"

They both laughed.

"Now, I'm seeing something else. I think it's a vision," Carl said. "You're chilly. And you're ready to drink some coffee."

"As the prophet of Manistee has decreed," Malachi said.

They hugged.

"So, what brings one of the Lord's vessels to my citadel?" Carl said.

"Oh, wise sage, you know not?"

"Sit down, Malachi," Carl said. And as fast as a thumb can slide a flashlight to the *off* position, the glowy banter subsided.

"I ah...maybe I do know," Carl said.

Malachi's eyes circled over Carl's features. He thought he had noticed something several nights ago at the Jesus at Walmart meeting. But now, as they sat nearly face to face, it was obvious. Carl had lost a lot of weight in a short time. Always on the thin side, his face showed more of its age because of loosened skin. His eyes appeared deeper in their sockets. He looked older.

Carl smiled. "I'm so glad to see you, Malachi."

"I hope I'm not interrupting your day," Malachi said.

"This is my day."

Malachi loved visiting Carl's simple—peaceful—Godly abode. And he couldn't help recalling his thoughts from the lunch hour at Walmart, when he was thumbing through a magazine devoted to living simplistically. As he perused its pages, he had thought to himself, "They need to visit Carl. Their definition and Carl's definition of simple living are several planets apart. Maybe universes."

At the same time, Carl was well traveled, a seemingly endless inventory of knowledge, multi-talented, masterful in his conveyance of love, yet all his possessions would fit into Malachi's Suburban. Carl was the definition of the 2 Timothy 2 man: "No soldier in active service entangles himself in the affairs of everyday life, so that he may please the One who enlisted him as a soldier."

"Let me get some coffee," Carl said. "I just brewed a fresh pot."

Malachi could see Carl's back as he poured the coffee, placing it on an oval salmon toned platter, a small one, the size of a flattened football. Malachi smiled when he saw Carl reach to his left and retrieve a bag of Walmart donuts.

And then Malachi shifted his focus to the left while Carl finished up. There, above a window on the wall, hung a cross made of deftly woven pond reeds.

"Here you go," Carl said. As he handed Malachi the platter. On it was a cup of coffee, a coconut donut, three packets of sugar, three small pre-packaged containers of creamer, and a fork.

"You're not having a donut?" Malachi said.

"No. Not today."

"Coconut, that's your favorite," Malachi said. "You're not going to have one?"

"I'm fine."

Because of the platter's shape, it nestled neatly in Malachi's lap when he folded his leg. He sipped his coffee and placed it back down on the platter. And then he looked down. He thought to himself, "Carl knows I always drink my coffee black. We've had coffee together so many times. And a fork?"

He looked over at Carl. His eyes re-examined the change in his features and then he looked down at the platter. And then at Carl again.

"Is something wrong?" Carl said.

"Well, no ah...," Malachi said. "I mean...you know I always drink my coffee black."

"Of course," Carl said. "But life changes, especially when we come to a fork in the road." He nodded slightly, so slightly. "Wouldn't you agree, Malachi?"

Malachi leaned back, unfolded his legs, and placed the platter on the floor to his right in one fluid motion.

"So, what's God been telling you about me?" Malachi said.

"Not much," Carl said.

"Not much?" Malachi said.

"Not much," Carl said. "Usually, when I hear from God about a person's situation like this, they've already heard from God. So, I can encourage them by saying, 'Yeah I'm feeling the same thing.' Or when they know they've heard, and they're like the little kid intentionally talking real loud—trying to drown out their parent's instructions, then I become a prodder—more of a gentle, yet firm nudge. And then, for the person who refuses to obey, I become the pusher. I'm lousy at doing that. It seems either the person blows up or I blow up. Usually both of us."

He smiled at Malachi. "So, my friend, tell me about what's going on. Why are you here?"

Malachi grinned. "Can I talk to you about a couple of forks in the road of my life?"

He told Carl about finding the fork at Walmart and his own inner impressions.

And then he said, "I need to tell you what happened

down at DT's with Timothy."

Carl had met Timothy and had eaten at DT's a few times. However, he knew little about him besides the fact that he was Mandy's boss. And of course, Carl was there when Timothy showed up at the Jesus at Walmart meeting.

"Hey, this works good," Malachi said as he raised a chunk of donut he had pierced with the fork.

For the next eighteen minutes, Malachi recounted what had happened down at DT's during his last two visits.

Concluding with, "So this is all confidential. But Timothy was O.K. with me talking to you to get your input."

"Let's see. Timothy shuts down DT's Good Time Place. He's strapped for money, has some mixed reasons—kind of mixed-up reasons for a renewed interest in God, and thinks you should start a church in downtown Manistee—mostly for the wrong reason—to ease his financial pressures."

"Yeah," Malachi said. "I couldn't have said it better."

"Wow, that's a big one. Starting a new church," Carl said. He didn't say anything for nearly a minute.

Malachi glanced at him twice. But mainly he stared ahead.

"I think we can both agree that this coming season of your life is going to involve changes and decisions. Big decisions. Forks in the road—for your life. And I know you Malachi; you really want to stay on the path God has for your life. I'm sure of that."

He looked intently at Malachi. "So be ready for the ride of your life, my friend. Changes are ahead. But at this point…"

Carl then turned. He looked upward slightly. The fingers of his left hand drummed gently on his pant—near his knee.

"The church thing is just too much at this time in my life," Malachi said. "Plus, even Jesus at Walmart seems to struggle constantly. Where would we even get any money to launch a church? And then…"

"Grasshoppers," Carl said as he interrupted Malachi.

"Grasshoppers?"

"'We even saw giants there…we felt as small as grasshoppers and that is how we must have looked to them.' From the Book of Numbers," Carl said. "You know the story, Malachi. Two said, 'The Lord is with us. Do not fear.' But the ten said, 'No we are not strong enough,' And you know how it ends up; the two conquered with the power of God. The ten grasshoppers died before reaching the Promised Land."

"Yeah," Malachi said. "Of course, I know the story."

"Malachi, you already know this," Carl said. "A follower of Jesus should never back down from taking a fork in the road that seems impossible. On the other hand, don't be foolish and try to kill giants that aren't yours to kill."

Though Malachi was listening closely to Carl, fatigue started setting in. A tiredness from lack of sleep.

"I can't stay much longer, Carl. I do need to get some rest before I go to work tonight. And I have other matters I need to talk to you about. But another time. O.K.?" Malachi said. "So, could you give me a couple of bullet points of advice? Kind of your bottom line for today. Some Godly insight. I really need something to take with me."

Carl set his gaze on Malachi. "By the grace of God, I'll do my best. The church at DT's—your ministry down there, at this point, is to Timothy. A door has opened up for you. Walk through it—be Timothy's pastor. Kind of a church of one—well two—you know what Jesus said, 'Wherever two or three are gathered in My name, I'll be in the midst.' And if God wants you to take it further, you'll know. Jesus also said, 'My sheep know my voice.' But don't you dare be a grasshopper."

"Or you'll prod me?" Malachi said.

"No, I'll provoke you, Malachi," Carl said. "Hebrews 10:24 style—'Provoke one another to love and good works.'"

15. Please Don't

It was more taxing as Malachi trudged his way back to his Suburban. The rising temperature had softened the snow, creating greatly reduced traction.

And it was like he was hauling a thirty-pound sack slung over his shoulder.

Carl's words always carried weight.

Not like a burden. But a package that needed to be pondered properly. And transported with due respect.

Malachi encountered fatigue, even before he neared his Suburban. His need for sleep was an equal contributor with the questions crisscrossing inside his head.

He turned on the radio as soon as he started the vehicle and was thinking to himself, "I need to get my mind on something besides forks."

Jesus at Walmart...fire on the Earth

Moments after he shifted into gear, he heard the DJ say, "This is our song for New Music Monday. The brand-new release from Obedience to Him called Rise Up. Now if this song doesn't revive your heart and send some inspiration coursing through your veins, please seek medical attention immediately. Or talk to your pastor."

> Silver and gold have I none
> Silver and gold have I none
>
> In the Name of Jesus
> In the Name of Jesus
>
> Rise up. Rise up. Rise...Rise up
> Rise up. Rise up. Rise...Rise up
>
> In the Name of Jesus
> Rise up. Rise up. Rise...Rise up.
>
> In the Name of Jesus
> Walk and leap and praise the Lord
> Walk and leap and praise the Lord
>
> Silver and gold have I none
> In the Name of Jesus
> Rise up. Rise up. Rise...Rise up
> Walk and leap and praise the Lord

By the time the song had finished, Malachi was ready to phone in a request. But he was certain they wouldn't play the same song back to back. The song's danceable beat and celebrative cadence had Malachi bouncing in his seat. No forks were poking his brain.

And even after he awoke, following four dead-to-the-world

Please Don't

hours of sleep, the words were singing out in his head: "Rise up. Rise up. Rise…Rise up. Walk and leap and praise the Lord. Walk and leap and praise the Lord."

With a smile inside and out, Malachi picked up his cell phone, which was resting on the kitchen counter.

He was not surprised by whom the first two messages were from. But his mind did wonder about the timing—"So soon?" he thought.

Especially message one.

"Hey Stephen. This is Malachi. Just returning your call."

"Malachi. Thanks for calling," Stephen said. "And thank you so much for coming to Sarah's baptism. It meant so much to her and Gracie and me."

"Thanks for saying that," Malachi said. "But to tell you the truth, I think I received the biggest blessing. And thank you so much for having me over to your place—another huge blessing."

"Well, praise God," Stephen said. "Remember what we talked about back in my office?"

During the get-together, Stephen had asked Malachi back to his office for a private conversation and had informed him that his vacated associate pastor position had never been filled. Church turmoil had led to a significant decline in attendance. But now, with Pastor Neil gone for several months, many people had returned, and the church was growing.

Through it all, Stephen remained the church's head elder. So, he knew the elder board was now discussing the church's need for an associate pastor.

"Now, I told you on Sunday that this was just my idea," Stephen said. "I sure hope you seriously considered what we talked about."

"How could I get it off my mind?"

"Well good, Malachi."

"But I don't know, Stephen. It just seems too crazy."

"I know," Stephen said. "That's one of the things I love about it. It seems impossible. Yet so redemptive. Plus, you're qualified."

"I don't know. The idea seems...well...just so crazy. And I'm thinking I'm disqualified."

"O.K. This is what I did," Stephen said. "I called each of the elders on the Q.T. I floated the idea of considering you for your old position."

"Wow, you're brave."

"You know what, Malachi?" Stephen said. "Not one elder said, no. Everyone said they would consider you for the job."

"I can't believe it. How many arms did you break off?"

"Hey, they're all still attached to their bodies," Stephen laughed. "But really, isn't part of a leader's job sometimes to be persuasive?"

"Stephen, what you're trying to do is one of the kindest gestures anyone has offered me in my entire life."

"I think I'm hearing a *no*" Stephen said.

Even through the cell phone, Malachi could sense the warmth, the love of Stephen's words.

"Yeah, you're right," Malachi said. "A few hours ago, I was walking a snowy trail. At one point, my mind was fixed on your proposal. But as I tried to let the pros and cons debate inside my head, it was like a curtain came down with the verse, 'No one after putting his hand to the plow and looking back, is fit for the Kingdom of God.' I couldn't get around the curtain. I couldn't get under it. I couldn't get over it."

"Too bad you didn't have a knife with you," Stephen said. They both laughed.

"Hey, this thing was machete proof," Malachi said.

"Did you try fire?"

"No," Malachi said. "But I do know, I feel so certain, so much inner peace, God wants me to keep my hand on the plow up here. If I look back to St. Amos, I'll be enticed to go plow some easier ground."

They were both silent for several seconds. Malachi could almost feel Sarah hugging him. A vivid picture appeared in his mind. He held onto that mental image like a soldier going off to war.

"Are you still there?" Stephen said.

"Yeah, I am."

"Malachi, may God do an amazing work as you plow up in Manistee."

Malachi's left hand brushed against the bristles on his cheek. "You know what, Stephen, I think the most amazing work God's done up here is what He's done in my heart. And He's still plowing."

And next, Malachi figured message number two would be predictable, unsurprising, even before listening to it. But he was wrong.

The words, "I need your answer right away," sparked an inner restlessness, an uneasiness.

When Malachi heard those words, he thought, "Wow, I need to talk to Sal as soon as possible."

Malachi took a deep breath as he fingered the keyboard of his cell phone. It was as if his fingers wouldn't dial the number for the return call regarding message number three. And at the same time, Malachi was unable to predict the reason for the call.

The message simply said, "Hey Malachi, could you give me a call?"

He could sense the pronounced beating of his heart by the time he finally punched in the numbers.

And then, just past the cordial greetings, the words on the other end caused his heart to race. His face flashed with warmth.

"I'm just going to say it. I hope you don't think I'm crazy.

I just have to say it right now: will you marry me, Malachi?"

Malachi didn't say anything. The shockwave going through his head triggered confusion. Bewilderment. And churning emotions.

"Are you still there, Malachi?"

"Yeah..ah...yeah," Malachi said. "Yeah ah...did you say, I mean. Ah...'Will you marry us?' You want me to preside over the ceremony? Is that what you're asking? Is that right?"

There was a silence.

And then the voice on the other end spoke, but this time the words weren't as clear, "Will...will you...Malachi...will... you...will you marry me?"

No more words were spoken. But the sound on the other end was distinctive. It was the sound of fully unveiled emotions that could no longer be contained. Her tears poured out in waves, subsiding, only to crest again in uncontrollable sobs.

Malachi breathed in slowly through his nose. He swallowed. And tightened his lips as he shifted the cell phone to his left hand, using his right hand to sweep against his closed eyes.

And then, after several seconds, he spoke, "Don't cry, Annie. Please don't cry."

16. Warming Himself at the Fire

Malachi jogged the last block and a half—mainly downhill.

His feet crunched and slid on the frigid snow. His breaths puffed visibly from his mouth. And while his body temperature accelerated, he was still longing for some warmth.

He could see a column of white smoke drifting directly upward. Snow hung from the roof, curling toward the eaves like a hanging sculpture. Snowdrifts piled against the white cinder block structure made it appear squatter than it really was.

Malachi neared the door. The green door—the hue of

unseasoned walnut husks. He imagined Carl inside warming himself at the fire.

His body chill rushed back the moment he stopped. And he longed to feel the warmth inside.

Malachi glanced at the bag in his right hand. And quickly thought to himself, "I hope they're all right."

He rapped lightly with his left hand. The frost etching on the window obscured the view to the interior. Malachi glanced upward and to the left, briefly scanning the embankment high above, the one that had drawn his attention nine days ago.

And then Malachi felt sudden warmth as Carl opened the door.

His smile was beaming. "Come in. Come in, Malachi."

Malachi felt a queasiness ripple through his body as he thought, "What's wrong with Carl?"

His face was thinner than during his last visit. And he had only heard from Carl via brief messages left on his cell phone. One said that he wouldn't be riding to church on Sunday with Malachi. And in another one, Carl had apologized because he wouldn't be able to attend the Thursday night Jesus at Walmart meeting.

Still, both times, he ended with nearly identical wording. Cheery toned words: "Hey, everything's going great. No need to call."

And because Malachi had been so busy, this provided a no-guilt excuse for ignoring the note he had placed on his kitchen counter, "Call Carl. See Carl."

But now, face to face, Malachi was guilt-ridden. Remorseful because of his selfishness.

Malachi's body hadn't fully settled into the chair before he blurted out, "What's wrong, Carl?"

"God is good, Malachi. I'm doing great."

"No, you're not Carl. You've lost a lot of weight—it's

very noticeable. And in a short time," Malachi said. "You need to tell me what's going on."

And then Malachi opened the bag he had been carrying. "Here, have a donut. I have your favorite. Our favorite. Walmart's coconut donuts."

Carl raised his right hand to shoulder height. "No, I can't do that."

Malachi furrowed his brow. "It's not like you're on a diet or something."

"Everybody's on a diet," Carl said, "or something."

Malachi grinned slightly, "Or something."

Carl looked down at the floor for several seconds. And then fixed his gaze on Malachi. "You know, Jesus said, 'Whenever you fast, do not put on a gloomy face as the hypocrites do. For they neglect their appearance so that they will be noticed by men when they are fasting. Truly I say to you, they have their reward in full. But you, when you fast, anoint your head and wash your face so that your fasting will not be noticed by men, but by your Father who is in secret. And your Father who sees what is done in secret will reward you.'" Carl said.

He paused briefly and then continued, "Some people, when they receive a deep prayer burden from the Lord— one that won't go away, like something needs to be birthed through travail before God, they're almost driven to seeking the Lord through a time of fasting. You may know what I mean. Well, Malachi, I know a person this happens to. A thin person who seems to lose a lot of weight right in the face. The fast becomes so noticeable that they seek seclusion sometimes. Privacy in what God is taking them through. And I know this for a fact; they prefer not to talk about the circumstances. It would be sort of like chitchatting with a pregnant woman in the throes of final contractions."

Carl then looked straight ahead for several seconds. And then smiled at Malachi. "So, is there anything exciting happening in your life, my friend?"

Malachi smiled back. "Do you mean besides the fact that I turned down an opportunity to interview for an associate pastor's job, my ex-wife Annie proposed to me— wants to get re-married, and I quit my job at Walmart. No, not really. Why do you ask?"

They both laughed.

And then Carl said, "Do you need a fork? I mean...for your donut."

"Sure," Malachi said. "It seems to be the new house rule for donut eating around here."

Malachi glanced at Carl's micro-kitchen. "Mind if I grab a cup of coffee?"

"Help yourself."

As Malachi sat down, holding a cup of coffee in his right hand, Carl said, "I'm thinking you didn't come by so you'd have a place to eat your donut. Or just so you could warm yourself by my fire."

Malachi took another sip of his coffee. And then without any prodding, Malachi launched off.

When he finished detailing the decision-making process regarding Stephen's associate pastor proposal, Carl simply said, "I can see that. I see God's hand in that decision."

Malachi paid attention to Carl's words. And he could tell when his demeanor and body language indicated end-of-subject.

They were silent for several seconds. And then a few more. Malachi pushed off slower, even shaking his head back and forth, saying, "Now this situation with Annie. I'm really confused."

Malachi explained to Carl what had happened before

the church service at St. Amos and added, "But afterwards, it seemed a little awkward. Annie and I and Stephen, Sarah, and Gracie, we were all together. Sort of a group. Stephen had previously invited me over to their place for a celebration—food and all. Stephen kind of asked me a question with his eyes. He caught my attention, in a way Annie wouldn't see. He shifted his eyes toward her and mouthed, 'Annie?' I shook my head ever so slightly. Stephen then gathered his family and said so only I could hear it, 'See you in a little. Do what you think is right.' Then it was just Annie and me."

"Hmm," Carl said. "Things got a little unsettled."

"Kind of," Malachi said. "It was sort of this weird vortex between—casual chitchat, a whirling potpourri of caring, loving feelings, mixed in with a guarded don't-get-sucked in mind-set. I don't know; that sounds callous. Maybe *awareness* is better than saying *guarded*."

"Well yeah," Carl said. "You were just confused. Wondering what to do—on the fly."

"You got it," Malachi said. "I really love Annie. God gave me a love for her. I was praying for her every day. And when she said to me, 'I've never been so close to God in my life,' I mean...isn't that one of the best things a pastor can ever hear?"

"Absolutely," Carl said.

"My last words to Annie at St. Amos were, 'Let's stay in touch. O.K.,'" Malachi said. "I meant it. But I wasn't expecting this. But I did wonder...when we hugged to say goodbye, Annie seemed to hold on too long. Way too long. Sure I enjoyed the embrace. I won't lie. But in my mind, I thought, 'Wow. What's the deal?' But with all the excitement at Stephen's house, that thought dissipated."

"Until," Carl said.

"Yeah...until," Malachi said. He shook his head.

"Until—Will you marry me?"

They sat in silence. They both had the same expression. Lips pressed together. Focus—seemingly into the air. Body movement, nearly nonexistent.

Carl spoke first, "There are a lot of couples who get re-married. I have a pastor friend out in California who got re-married. God does hate divorce."

"That's what Annie said. But I just don't know," Malachi said.

"That doesn't sound like a *no*," Carl said. "So, what's the plan?"

"You know, I do love Annie. But one God experience doesn't make me want to re-marry her. And then there's..."

Carl interrupted, "What would make you want to marry Annie again? What would it be?"

"What I was saying; this is what we decided— well, Annie, kind of more than me. She's going to come visit in late March. But don't tell anybody. O.K."

"It's our secret," Carl said.

Malachi turned his head toward the door. He stared at the window as if he was trying to see to the outside— through the frost. And then, after several seconds, he measured out the words, "Pray for me, Carl. I need to be able to answer your question. I don't know what would make me want to marry Annie again."

"I'll pray for you right now," Carl said.

And they bowed their heads

17. That Fast

"God doesn't answer prayers that fast," Malachi thought to himself. He was less than two minutes from Carl's cottage—halfway up the first ascent.

"I know the answer," Malachi said to himself.

He stopped, turned around, and looked back down the hill. The frail looking Carl was standing outside, looking up at Malachi.

When he saw Malachi turn around, he pointed his index finger on his right hand skyward—his arm fully extended. A smile beamed from his gaunt face.

Malachi shook his head and laughed aloud. And then hollered at full volume, "I know the answer."

Immediately, Carl gave him two thumbs up.

Malachi turned to the trail ahead. Carl turned back toward his door.

18. Oh What You've Done for Me

The first words out of Malachi's mouth when he awoke were, "Thank you, Jesus, for saving my soul." More like a whispery prayer.

As he walked toward the bathroom, he softly said, "Wow. This is it."

January was a few days from being over. And today was Malachi's last day of employment at Walmart. Tonight, Thursday night, he would be leading the Jesus at Walmart meeting. Malachi thought to himself how amazing it was that Sal had agreed to let him carry on with Jesus at Walmart even after his departure.

"Praise God," he said as he made his way to the living room. Loud enough for the words to hang momentarily in the atmosphere. Like a spritz of air freshener.

Malachi walked over to his mandolin and grasped it with his right hand. He relaxed in his favorite chair as he readied his grip on the instrument. And then started strumming the strings as he began to sing the song he had prepared for tonight:

Jesus, Oh what You've done for me
Jesus, Oh what You've done for me

Loved me. Saved me. Set me free
Loved me. Saved me. Set me free

And who the Son sets free
And who the Son sets free
Is free. Free indeed.

Jesus, Oh what You've done for me
Loved me. Saved me. Set me free
Loved me. Saved me. Set me free
Free indeed

As Malachi sat there, he sensed God in a special way. And at the same time, he could still smell the freshly painted kitchen walls. The pungent odor, with a slight chemically tang, elbowed his mind to his to-do list.

"Hey, Uncle Dale," Malachi said as he pressed his cell phone against his right ear. "Just calling to let you know all the interior painting is finished except the living room. I saved the biggest and easiest room for last. And I'm coming down the homestretch on the punch out list as well—four or five hours at the most, and I'll be all done."

"Good man," Uncle Dale said. "You're going to be a valuable addition to the Dale Marble Construction crew."

Malachi smiled. And Uncle Dale's compliment was only a sliver of the reason for his sensation of joy.

In that moment, Malachi reflected back to the evening

when he and Uncle Dale reconnected—at DT's—his first night in Manistee. Malachi beamed, thinking to himself, "Wow. He was at the bottom. But now, look what the Lord has done."

Just like the song:
Jesus, Oh what You've done for me
Jesus, Oh what You've done for me

Loved me. Saved me. Set me free
Loved me. Saved me. Set me free

Forever one of the best memories of Malachi's life—the first night he visited Uncle Dale and Aunt Betty's home since his arrival in Manistee. Back all those months ago.

They ate steaks Malachi had purchased—at Walmart. And visited in the tiny dwelling—simply being family. Initially, Uncle Dale was embarrassed. It was obvious. The house they were living in was only slightly larger than the garage of their previous home. Their financial plunge had required radical lifestyle changes. There was nothing showy about the place they now lived, something Uncle Dale wasn't accustomed to.

Malachi focused on erasing the uneasiness by showing love to Uncle Dale and Aunt Betty. And appreciating them for being special people in his life.

Consequently, when Malachi asked Uncle Dale if he wanted to have *the talk,* the talk about his spiritual condition, there was not a *yes* or a *no.* There was only the love. And the conversation shifted from first gear to fifth gear without pushing in the clutch. Yet, there was not even a hint of jerkiness.

Just smoothed, refined motion to a conversation about Jesus Christ. The culmination of their exchange is eternally etched in Malachi's brain:

"You pray. Talk to God. Just talk to Him. Right now," Malachi had said.

"I can act like Jesus is here in the room? And start talking? As if He was with us in the room," Uncle Dale said.

"Uncle Dale, Jesus is here. Can't you almost sense His presence?" Malachi said softly, "God is with us. He's right here."

For several seconds, no one said anything.

And then Uncle Dale, with eyes wide open, said, "Jesus, this is Dale. I guess You already know who I am. And what I've done. I've messed up a lot in my life."

He looked over at Betty and took a deep breath. "I know that's sin. And I know, just like when I do wrong against Betty, it screws up our relationship. You know I've been in the doghouse plenty. With You, the doghouse lasts forever. And that's what Hell is all about. Except a lot worse. And I would deserve it. You created everything. God, You get to call the shots. Malachi has told me some good news. And that's what I want. I believe Jesus is Your Son. I know He's God too. I don't exactly know how that works. I know Jesus died on the cross to kill my sins. His death is the payment for my sins. It's a gift. But I've got to accept that gift, so You can take my sins away. And give me eternal life with You."

Uncle Dale held out his hand. "God, I'll take the gift of Jesus from You. Who wouldn't? I believe in Jesus. And I'm not going to be the same person. I'm sorry for all the stuff... the sin I've done. I'm going to quit. Please help me. Dear God, I think I'm through. Hope I didn't miss anything."

Uncle Dale stopped and glanced over at Malachi.

Malachi nodded.

Then Uncle Dale added, "Well God, that's it for now. I guess. Keep in touch. Thanks. You're the best. Amen."

Malachi's attention returned to Uncle Dale on the other end of the phone as he heard him speak, "So the plan is to meet at my place early Monday morning. Can you be here by 6:30?"

"You got it, Uncle Dale," Malachi said.

"Hey, Malachi, I think we need to drop the Uncle Dale out on the jobsite. I think it would be more professional if you called me Dale."

"Sure, I can do that," Malachi said. "Dale."

"So, we'll all go over to Cadillac together—at least for the first day," Dale said. "I'm running the Skytrack over to Menards tomorrow. So, we'll be ready to roll on Monday. I have two more guys—Raymond and William—we call him Wilks; besides you and Martin. We'll just take it one step at a time. Should be a great job. I still need to touch base with Martin and tell him what time on Monday."

"I can tell him," Malachi said. "I'll be seeing him tonight."

"Thanks. I would appreciate that," Dale said.

Malachi stood up and looked out the front window. He was so excited. He was prancing around the room, thinking to himself, "This is so cool. This is great. This is going to be an awesome job."

At Christmas time, when he was over at Uncle Dale's house celebrating, he had told Malachi about a sizable contract he was trying to secure at the new Menards store being constructed in Cadillac. The new store is part of a home improvement super store chain. Menards has a presence in fourteen states—mainly in the Midwest. But with locations as far west as Casper, Wyoming. Like most of the newer Menards, the one in Cadillac—a thirty-five-minute drive from Manistee, will also stock a wide array of other merchandise, somewhat like a Walmart. Except building materials are the overwhelming feature—the full spectrum. While everything else is available in a greatly limited variety.

Uncle Dale had asked Malachi if he would consider

working for him on the project if he secured the contract and added, "The building business is making a nice come-back from the bottom. I don't see any problem with having plenty of work for you." He also asked Malachi if he knew anyone to fill an entry-level construction position.

Immediately, he piped up, "My friend Martin. I could ask him."

And when Malachi told Martin about it, he got excited. He was ready to start—without delay.

Uncle Dale had said, "Keep this just between us—and your friend Martin. Until I know something definite."

Things moved quicker than expected.

And then, Uncle Dale called in early January and left a mes-sage on Malachi's cell phone, "Menards isn't messing around. I've got to get in there. They're pushing faster than I expected. So, either both you and Martin are in, or I'm going to have to pick up some other guys. I need your answer right away."

Malachi was tingling with jubilation. The new job, working with Dale, and the new opportunities this would bring—he was praising God for all that.

But there was more. So much more to praise God for. Dale knew Jesus. His cancer was no more. He was being blessed financially. And he and Aunt Betty faithfully attended Pleasantview Community Church—a small coun-try church about two miles from their home. It was obvious; Dale was growing in the ways of God.

Malachi couldn't contain himself. It was like the song gushed out from within:

> Jesus, Oh what You've done for me
> Jesus, Oh what You've done for me
>
> Loved me. Saved me. Set me free
> Loved me. Saved me. Set me free

19. Jesus at Walmart

"**C**rap. What the crap?" Malachi said.

He had been looking at the door leading into the room all set for the Jesus at Walmart meeting. And he was like a chain smoker. But instead of puffing, Malachi kept looking at the door. He looked and then looked again. Again. He tried to stop, but then looked again. A few seconds later, he looked.

And then the words boiled out. It was 3:09 in the morning. The meeting was scheduled to commence at 3:00.

He could smell the Swedish meatballs marinating in their sauce in the crockpot to his left. There, on a long table covered with a Walmart-blue tablecloth, the table was filled with food. The carrots and ranch dip in the vegetable section. Sunchips along with other crunchy items were placed adjacent to the crockpot. JC had brought her nearly-famous barbecued chicken wings. Malachi didn't even know what all was on the table. However, he had seen the sheet cake with medium blue frosting emblazoned with the white lettering: *GOD BLESS MALACHI AND MARTIN IN THEIR NEW JOBS*—a surprise from Elysia.

The words that had slipped out of Malachi's mouth were also a surprise. Malachi knew they were there, there inside, but he almost didn't realize they had spurted out audibly—loud enough for everyone to hear.

Everyone had been visiting—Carl, Martin, JC, and Alex. While Elysia was talking with Timothy, who had joined the regulars.

Facial expressions changed so suddenly that the final *p* barely puffed off Malachi's lips before he had everyone's abrupt attention. That pious look of disbelief ruled everyone's stares. Except Alex—a grin was trying to break loose to the next level. But almost as if it was a natural human instinct, he was able to crow bar his outer shell back to a semi-pious appearance. More likely due to the power of peer pressure.

This Jesus at Walmart meeting was supposed to be a celebration—to celebrate his and Martin's last night of work. One attended by a sizeable group of Walmart overnighters. Malachi had prepared a song to play on his mandolin, which he planned to follow with a short message featuring his personal testimony on the goodness of God.

In his estimation, it was going to be awesome. Sure to stir the souls of the lost and the found alike.

With all eyes on Malachi, he felt unable to speak. And he wasn't thinking about the goodness of God either. But in his mind, he did have one short sentence he yearned to blurt out—"I'm leaving."

But he didn't verbalize that thought.

And then Martin said, "Can I say something?"

"No, not really, Martin. The only Bible verse I want to hear right now is that one that talks about 'ashes to ashes and dust to dust.' And I want the person speaking it to be looking down at my body."

"I have a thought," Carl said.

He looked over at Carl. It was obvious that his weight was returning. Though he still looked thinner. But not scary.

"I don't know, Carl. I'm not in the mood for an elongated enlightenment on the Biblical merits of patience and suffering."

"That's not what…"

"Please Carl…thank you…but ah…" Malachi said. "I mean, seriously—could one Walmart worker stop by, besides the regulars. Just one. That could have happened by accident. Couldn't it? I don't know…"

"Here's a suggestion," Timothy said.

Malachi shook his head back and forth. "Put it in the suggestion box. And I'm sorry, but we've run out of our custom Jesus at Walmart coffee mugs that we give to our visitors. We can't keep them in stock; they're so popular. With all the visitors, you know."

Timothy grinned.

And then Malachi said, "I'm sorry Timothy; I'm just trying to figure out what I want to do. Trying to figure out what's going on. O.K.?"

Timothy nodded, "You got it."

Suddenly, Alex's hand popped into the air. He was waving it back and forth more than necessary.

"Hey everyone, our young friend Alex has some words of wisdom," Malachi said. "Let's listen up. This may be our answer."

Carl gave Malachi an affirming look.

Elysia and JC smiled.

Martin nodded.

"So, what is it Alex?" Malachi said. "What do you have to say to us?"

"I have to go to the bathroom."

The pop was almost audible. And the laughter spilled forth in one accord.

Even Alex started laughing. Even though his facial expression seemed to be saying, "What's so funny?"

"Sure Alex, you can go to the bathroom," Malachi said. "Hurry up. O.K."

Malachi sat facing everyone. He rubbed his hands together; his eyes were watching their back and forth motion. And after several seconds he looked up. "I'm sorry everyone. Forgive me. I'm having a hard time learning to expect the unexpected. My behavior was not worthy of the God we serve. The good, the awesome God we serve."

Malachi looked over when he heard Alex returning and said, "Welcome back. I was just apologizing to everyone. So, I want to tell you, Alex, I'm sorry for the way I acted. Forgive me. Sometimes, I get this attitude that nothing has happened as a result of these Jesus at Walmart meetings. I just want to see some results, to see something happen…"

"Something happened to me," Alex said before Malachi could continue.

"What do you mean?"

"Remember the first time I came to Jesus at Walmart, the only time besides tonight, and everyone was talking to me about, 'Who paid the cost?' Remember? When you were talking to Timothy?"

"Well sure. I remember," Malachi said.

"They told me about Jesus and why He died on the cross. And Carl told me how to get saved by the free gift of Jesus," Alex said.

Jesus at Walmart

"You said you wanted to consider your decision because you wanted it to last the rest of your life," Malachi said.

"Yeah, I couldn't sleep when I got home—I was laying there wide awake," Alex said. "And then I heard my mom when she got home. She always makes a lot of noise when she gets home that late. Sometimes, I hear her in the bathroom. She sounds sick—but I know what it is. Then I heard a voice in my head—something from one of the times my Aunt Nancy took me to church. 'Choose this day who you will serve.' The pastor said there were only two choices. I know I'm only a kid, but even I know my mom is serving the wrong side. And she's paying for it."

Alex stopped. He looked down at the floor. It was several seconds. JC pulled him into a gentle embrace.

And then he looked up. His face was scrunched. "I'm only a kid…and…ah…I crawled out of bed and got on my knees. I prayed, 'Please God, help Mom. Please help her.' And then I made my choice. I asked God to forgive my sins, and I told God that I have decided to follow Jesus as long as I live. I believe in Jesus. I believe His death on the cross can be the payment for what I've done—even at my age."

He looked directly at Malachi. "I took the gift of Jesus into my heart. I'm ready to pay the cost to serve Him. You know what? That happened because I came to Jesus at Walmart. Does that count—as you were saying—as a result? Is that a result, Malachi?"

Tears were already running down JC's face.

Malachi looked upward. He had to swallow hard to get any words to come out. But even that wasn't enough. He looked to his right and swallowed again.

He turned back, lowering his eyes to Alex. "Yeah…ah yeah," was all Malachi could manage to exhale.

"Good," Alex said. A big smile broke out on his face, followed by, "When do we get to eat?"

Jesus at Walmart...fire on the Earth

Malachi stood up and grabbed Alex in a hug, picking him up off the floor, spinning him around—his feet flying through the air. "We're going to eat right, right, right, right, right...now."

20. Unquenchable Fire

"**H**ow did your meeting go tonight?" Sal said as she invited Malachi into her office.

"It was great," Malachi said. "Thought you were going to stop by, Sal."

"Yeah…I…ah," Sal said. "I had some stuff I just had to take care of."

"So, you were too busy to stop by for like three minutes, say, 'Hey.' Grab a piece of cake and go?" Malachi said. "You know what? Besides Martin, not even one overnighter came by."

"Oh," Sal said as she looked away.

They stood there in Sal's office. Silent.

Actually, it was the office for all six of the store's associate managers. Small, not much larger than a generously sized walk-in closet. One computer was perched on an economy grade laminated countertop. Basic, boring beige. The office was stripped down to the essentials.

"So, Sal, what do you think is the reason for all the no-shows? You weren't the only one who assured me they would come by. There were several."

After a couple of seconds, Sal slowly turned to face Malachi. "You're just so intense, Malachi, like an unquenchable fire. It overwhelms people. Sure, you're so kind and considerate, but...ah...It's kind of like some of the Walmart regional manager's meetings I've attended. Certain managers are so intense, most of us avoid them. Sure, they're cordial and warm and all that—but overwhelming. It pushes people away."

"You know, Sal, I guess I prefer the word *passionate*."

"That describes it," Sal said. "But over-passionate."

"So, let me guess here," Malachi said. "So, these unquenchable-fire type managers, they're the ones who usually rise to the top. While the main group gathers together, pointing their fingers, complaining, and talking about their over-the-top zeal. The complainers—now those managers either quit or remain un-promoted—for the most part. Am I right?"

"Well, I never sized it up quite like that. Let me think," Sal said. "Yeah," she shook her head. "That's how it usually turns out. I never thought of it that way before."

"So how fiery, how passionate, do you think the CEO of Walmart is?" Malachi said.

"Mike Duke," Sal said.

"I don't know his name."

"You met him."

"Mike Duke? When?" Malachi said.

"At Stu's funeral. The tall man in the black suit. I saw you talking with him after the funeral. Didn't he introduce himself?"

"Well yeah," Malachi said. "But only as Mike. I had no idea who he was. But I liked him right away. I knew instantly he was a man of substance."

And then Malachi focused intensely on Sal. "And I'll guarantee you, he's an unquenchable fire for Walmart."

"No doubt," Sal said.

"So, if Mr. Duke showed up at the store tonight and offered free refreshments, how many of the overnighters do you think would be there?"

"Well, all of them." Sal said. "Of course."

"So, it's not the unquenchable fire, the intensity, the passion that keeps people away, is it, Sal?" Malachi said.

Sal shifted her body towards the countertop—away from Malachi. "Well, I never...ah..."

Malachi stepped away in the other direction.

He had never worked for anyone he respected more. No one could outwork Sal. She led by example. She was fair, but always pushed to draw the best out of those who worked under her. And Malachi had seen it many times. Sal the manager who knew how to punch up the volume to get the needed results, was soft as a marshmallow inside.

"Sal," Malachi said. "You're the best." And then he took several minutes to tell her how much he respected her, appreciated her, how much she inspired him. He wanted to tell her how much he loved her, as the love of God started to flood his heart. But he kept that part to himself.

"Sal," Malachi said. "The reason people didn't show up is because they believed the lie that came into their head. The lie convinced them that their lives are better off without the passion of Jesus Christ and the passion for Jesus Christ."

Sal shifted her head slightly to the left, staring past Malachi's right shoulder.

Malachi broke the silence after nearly three-quarters of a minute. "Can I give you a hug, Sal?"

They embraced lightly, as Malachi said, "Thank you for everything, Sal. Thank you for giving me a job when I was desperate."

He then stepped toward the door.

And then turned around in the doorway. "I'll be here next Thursday. I'll keep plowing. I'll keep fighting that lie."

Sal tried to smile as Malachi turned around to leave.

21. The Table

"Hey thanks for coming down, Malachi," Timothy said.

"We need to catch up on things, my friend," Malachi said. "Seems like we've been playing too much phone tag."

"Yeah, that's for sure," Timothy said. "Hey, that was some meeting last night."

Malachi smiled. "Once I let God take over."

"And Alex helped," Timothy said. "He seems to be rather amazing. How old is he?"

"Let's see. He's twelve now."

"He acts like he's eighteen in some ways," Timothy said. "I mean, a mature eighteen. A Godly eighteen."

"Especially considering that Mandy is not being much of a mother. He sort of fends for himself," Malachi said.

"Well, his grandma helps some—I think—when she and Mandy aren't on the outs."

"Alex sure looks up to you," Timothy said. "You're a great influence on him."

"I hope so," Malachi said. He rubbed his left hand along his stubbly cheek. "But too many times, last night as a prime example, Alex is the great influencer. And I'm the foul-mouthed preacher."

Timothy shook his head. And laughed just loud enough so Malachi could hear it. And then he said, "I was thinking, last night, when Alex was talking about getting down on his knees and praying for Mandy, when was that?"

"Well, it was after the first Jesus at Walmart meeting of the year. So, it was like around 5:00 Friday morning. Why do you ask?"

"So, two days later, that Sunday, that's when I saw Mandy at church."

"Hmmn," Malachi said. "Wow, I never thought of that. That's cool, isn't it?"

"I sure think so," Timothy said. "Can I get you a Camp Eden?"

"Sure. Sounds good."

Malachi rubbed his hand across the top of the table. He was fond of quarter-sawn oak. He looked around DT's— the former DT's. While it still projected much of its former ambiance, it was obvious Timothy had been doing some work.

All the Trinity Dark posters had been removed, as well as all the beer-posters featuring the gorgeous friends you attract by your beverage choice. And as Malachi inspected the room, he noticed that every wall hanging had been taken down. Except the six-foot banner hanging above the riverside wall—red and white, with black lettering. Featuring the winged wheel of the Detroit Red Wings and the

The Table

proclamation—*NHL PLAYOFFS: THE CUP CHANGES EVERYTHING.*

Gone were all the flat screen TV's. Malachi wondered how Timothy had managed to extract the largest one from the wall high above—since it was almost as big as a sheet of plywood.

Malachi looked over at the bar area. Everything was stripped clean. No bottles. No glasses. No tools of the trade. Stripped.

Malachi drew in through his nose. It even smelled different. Before, while it smelled pleasant enough, it always seemed that the undertone of stink was fighting for its rightful place at the surface. Malachi found the hint-of-lemon fragrance now whiffing over the table to be pleasing. Enlivening. Invigorating.

Timothy returned to the table and set down two Camp Edens—with the screw tops removed.

Malachi reached to take a drink. Timothy raised his bottle into the air. "Enjoy."

"I never connected it that way before. Mandy at church after Alex prayed. At the skinny-jeans church," Malachi said as a smirk emerged.

"Well, I was a heathen back then," Timothy said. "I see things differently now."

"Back then?" Malachi said. "What about now?"

"Things are different...now," Timothy said.

"What do you mean?" Malachi said.

"I had...ah..." Timothy said. "God ah..."

And then Timothy seemed mesmerized as he sighted slightly to the left of Malachi. With a swift shift in demeanor, like a flicking of a remote control—everything changed. Malachi could see Timothy trembling. His body then slackened. His head bowed as his hands covered his face.

Even the atmosphere felt altered. And Malachi sensed the words of Jesus: "For where two or three have gathered together in My name, I am there in their midst."

Words eluded Malachi. He searched his mind for just the right ones for Timothy. A scripture. Some words to strengthen, comfort, some encouragement. Maybe from his own life—an illustration. A testimony. Each idea he drew upon echoed back unsuitable—oddly forced.

Yet, one simple expression repeatedly pressed to the forefront of Malachi's mind.

One phrase.

"Jesus loves you, Timothy."

The torrent busted over the dam. More than a few of Timothy's tears moistened the table.

It was a hushed experience. For Malachi—like peering through a window, observing, but not fully grasping what was transpiring inside.

A face, lacking all composure, looked up after some time—even Malachi didn't know how long. The lingering of His Presence mystified the reckoning of time.

"Oh Malachi...I know Jesus loves me," Timothy said. Then his eyes sunk back toward the table.

This round only lasted a couple of handfuls of seconds. And when Timothy unbowed his head, a smile started forming on his moistened face. "I ah...I experienced that love a few days ago," Timothy said. "In a way...I ah, didn't even know..."

He drew in a couple of slow breaths. He motioned with his head. "It happened right over there."

Malachi turned. looking over toward the patio door leading to the riverside deck, and then turned back to face Timothy.

And then Timothy's words pushed off slowly. Like a child's finger setting a toy boat into motion on a still pond.

The Table

"I was in here all by myself. The words from that Bible verse you mentioned the last time you were here, they were alive in my head. 'For what will it profit a man if he gains the whole world and forfeits his own soul? Or what will a man give in exchange for his soul?' I was pacing around. Those words were cutting me up inside. I thought to myself, 'How could I be so stupid?' I used to be close to God. How stupid. I got down on my knees. I think church people call it, 'Crying out to God.' I raised my hands in the air—the universal sign of surrender. I said, 'God, I surrender. I give up. I'm Yours. This fifty-five-year-old heathen is now in Your service until the end of his days. I'm going to need a thorough cleaning. God, do whatever you have to. Make me fit to serve You. I'm ready for boot camp.'"

Timothy hesitated for a few moments. Malachi could see his eyes moistening again.

"I ah...," Timothy said. "I'm not even going to try to detail what happened. It would be like trying to watch a Star Wars movie on a screen the size of a fingernail. Human words can't properly convey what God did over there on the floor."

Timothy fixed his eyes on Malachi with an extra measure of intensity. "God did major surgery on me. It took some hours. And I went from my knees to my face on the floor."

By now, Timothy was smiling, "Malachi, by the time I got up off the floor, I physically felt lighter. I could feel it. I mean it. Wow...I started dancing around like a kid."

"Praise God. Praise God. Praise God," Malachi said, his volume climbing with each repetition.

"And praise God for you, Malachi, and your Jesus at Walmart meetings," Timothy said. "That's where all this started."

"I'm sure God was at work long before that," Malachi

said.

"I'm sure too," Timothy said. "But the results were a big zero before you and I connected."

"Thank you for your kind words," Malachi said. "I'm praising God."

"Hey, remember that idea I had to start a church here?" Timothy said.

"The I'm-Broke-Send-Cows Church of Manistee, that one?" Malachi said.

"Will yeah, I mean no," Timothy said. "That is, now that I'm different—why don't we start a real church down here? A Jesus Church. The real deal."

"Just like that," Malachi said.

"Just like what?"

"I mean...have you fully considered what it means to start a church? The process. What it all entails?" Malachi said.

"O.K. here's the process and the entails and the full consideration," Timothy said. "We move some chairs around. We hang a sign up outside. We invite people. And then, on Sunday, we sing about God. You preach out of the Bible. We pray. We all leave. Most of us are changed. Some aren't. And then the next Sunday— some people come back. And some don't. So, we invite some more people during the week. On Sunday, we sing about God. You preach out of the Bible. We pray. We all leave. Most of us are changed. Some miss out again. And we just keep doing that until Jesus returns."

"You're oversimplifying things."

"O.K. You're right," Timothy said. "We need to take an offering. Once a month, we do communion. And so, we can get to know each other, we'll have some meals together after church. I'll make the food. And when people get saved, we'll baptize them. And if they renew their life with

God, we give them a big hug."

"You're pretty set on this idea," Malachi said. "Aren't you?"

Timothy stood up and walked towards the back of the building. He stopped seven-feet before reaching the outside and four-feet out from the perpendicular wall. He turned, facing Malachi. He pointed down at the floor. "Right here, Malachi." He raised both hands above his head. "I surrender."

He then walked slowly back towards Malachi. "I'm going to call the church—The Table. From Matthew 9:12, 'Other outcasts came and joined Jesus and the disciples at the table.'"

Before he finished, Timothy was once again seated, facing Malachi. "I love you Malachi, but I'm telling you, I'm starting The Table, no matter what you decide." He then raised both hands again—above his head. "I surrender."

"Wow," Malachi said. "A fork in the road. The Table."

"Yeah, The Table," Timothy said. "And here's our slogan, 'The Church for You.' What do you think?"

"The Table—the church for you," Malachi said. "Sounds inviting."

For a few seconds, they were silent. And then it was a few more seconds before Malachi said, "I think I need to go over there and lay on the floor."

Timothy smiled, "So you might be in?"

Malachi rubbed his hands together and glanced upward for a few moments. And then his gaze again rested on Timothy. His words came out in a rhythmic cadence, "Other outcasts came and joined Jesus and the disciples at the table."

He smiled. "Might be."

"When will you know for sure?" Timothy said.

"How soon? How soon?" Malachi said. "Ah…let's see.

Ah...Godspeed?"

"Godspeed?" Timothy said. "What's that mean?"

"O.K, here's a better answer," Malachi said. "From Hebrews: 'Be imitators of those who through faith and patience inherit the promises.' Some patience, Timothy. It is one of the fruits of the Spirit."

"Yeah O.K." Timothy said. "Ah yeah...I can see my floor time didn't fix everything inside me."

"Timothy, as soon as I know, you'll know," Malachi said. "And just because God leads you a certain direction at a fork in the road doesn't mean that's the way I should go."

"O.K. I got it," Timothy said. "Godspeed."

Malachi stood up and reached toward Timothy as he stood up also. He hugged him and said, "I love you, Timothy. It's so awesome what God's doing in your life."

They walked toward the door. Outside, January-thaw was prompting a meltdown, with the temperatures nearing forty.

"It's really nice out here," Malachi said. "So, what are you doing to pay the bills?"

"Surgery," Timothy said.

Malachi's forehead wrinkled, "What?"

"Yeah, I'm cutting all the junk out of my life," Timothy said. "I can't believe all the stuff I own. At home and here. I'm just selling all sorts of things—on Craigslist, eBay, to friends, strangers, enemies. My house is on the block—it's priced to sell. And it's staged so perfectly that I've moved out. I'm living here. Sold my Escalade. Sell, sell, sell."

"You're going for it, aren't you?" Malachi said.

"You know what 2 Timothy 2:4 says," Timothy said.

"Yeah."

"No soldier in active service entangles himself in the affairs of everyday life, so that he may please the one who enlisted him as a soldier," Timothy said.

The Table

"So true," Malachi said. "Timothy, you sure have an exceptional recall of Scripture."

"I ah...I have kind of like a photographic memory," Timothy said. "I sort of messed it up with all the garbage—legal and illegal, I've ingested over the years. But ever since God took all that nasty out of my life, when I was on the floor, my brain is making a vigorous comeback. I'm just astounded."

"Wow. That's incredible. Amazing."

Malachi walked to the right a few steps—toward his Suburban.

"Check out my new ride," Timothy said. "I call it my Zipper. It's a 2002 Ford Escort ZX2."

"Zipper?"

"Yeah, it gets like thirty-four miles per gallon. It's great for zipping out of town on trips—my Zipper," Timothy said.

Parked two spaces behind the Suburban was the minuscule Escort. It seemed almost small enough to fit in the back of Malachi's vehicle. It was sporty and low slung. The black gleamed in the sun. But Malachi did notice scratches along the side of the car.

"It's nice," Malachi said. "I like the sunroof."

"See all those scratches?" Timothy said. "I got the seller to knock off four-hundred bucks because of those. God is good."

Malachi laughed. "So you said something about out of town trips. You've been traveling some?"

"Yeah ah..." Timothy said. "It's kind of a job. A job thing. Yeah, I'm just starting."

"A job," Malachi said. "So, what do you do?"

"I ah...," Timothy said. "Let's see. I ah...it involves a multi-faceted, transitional, funding enhancement process with government regulatory ties."

"Sounds complicated," Malachi said. "I bet your exceptional memory helps out."

"Yeah, it sure does," Timothy said. "It definitely does."

"God is good, Timothy."

22. Zeke's Table

"Your waitress will be right with you."

"Thanks."

Malachi had never dined at Zeke's, though he had noticed it before. And it had caught his attention when he drove past it after he had met with Timothy the day before.

The low-slung building looked out of place in downtown Manistee's cityscape. Located two blocks west of the former DT's—toward Lake Michigan and across the street.

Zeke's looked especially stubby compared to the now abandoned Vogue Theatre, downtown Manistee's tallest structure.

Located three doors down, Zeke's was in the shadow of The Vogue at 8:20 on Saturday morning.

Malachi had found himself repeating the restaurant's

catchphrase, displayed prominently above the entry door—*A more excellent place to dine,* as he walked into the dinner.

"No, I've never eaten here before," Malachi said. "How about you, Carl?"

"I've noticed it," Carl said. "But ah...nope, I've never been inside."

"I like the décor," Malachi said. "It seems larger in here than I expected."

"Good morning. I'm Carmel. I'll be your waitress this morning. Can I start you off with some coffee or something?"

"Coffee for me."

"I'll have coffee also," Malachi said. "And could I have a fork to stir it?"

"A fork?" Carmel said. "You want a fork?"

Malachi looked at Carl and tried not to smile. "I think this is a fork day. What do you think?"

And then he looked at the waitress. "Make that two forks."

She scrunched her face. "O.K. Two forks...with coffee."

"It's pleasant in here," Malachi said. "Kind of like a big cottage."

Divided into three dining spaces, separated by eight-foot doorways. The walls and ceilings were lined with narrow beaded tongue and groove boards. Reminiscent of a 1920's era cottage. Pure white paint covered the aged, noticeably flawed wood. The floor was a distressed wood of some sort. Malachi was thinking it was probably hickory. While not a dark brown, the color did lean heavily into that spectrum. It was obvious that the flooring was much newer, yet it fit perfectly with the cottage motif. The hint-darker-than-mustard color chosen for all the interior trim and doors added a spicy, funkiness to the space.

"Here's your coffee guys," Carmel said. "And ah...your forks."

They placed their orders. And then Malachi looked

directly ahead when he heard the entry door open again. "It's really busy in here."

Malachi picked up his cup of coffee with his left hand and the fork in the other. He tapped the fork's tines and held it near his ear. He looked at Carl, who was watching him. "Have you ever noticed that this fork represents a choice to take in our life's journey, yet at the same time, we must stay in tune with God as we seek which way to venture."

Carl scratched the top of his head. "Now you're making me wish I hadn't ordered the scrambled eggs."

"Why's that."

"I might scramble the message God is trying to get through," Carl said.

"You're funny, Carl," Malachi said. "O.K. I was probably trying to be too mystical."

"Amen."

"O.K. Here's the deal," Malachi said. "I mainly wanted to talk to you about one thing."

Malachi filled in the needed portion of details over the next eight minutes before ending with, "So that's what Timothy wants to do. Start a church—The Table. And he wants me to be a part of it, probably its pastor."

"Here's your food. Can I get you anything else?"

"Thanks. I think we're good."

Malachi pointed at Carl. "Could you offer the blessing?"

"Father, thank You that Your mercies are new every morning. Thank You that we are Your sheep. You told us in Your word that Your sheep hear Your voice. Thank You for this food, which You have provided. Help us to honor and glorify You with the strength we receive. In the name of Jesus, amen."

"Amen."

"So, I know we'll probably need to meet several times before we can make any kind of a reasonable decision on

Timothy's proposal. We'll need a lot of prayer. Maybe an extended season of fasting. We'll need to talk to all the Jesus at Walmart regulars. Some council from a couple of local pastors would be helpful," Malachi said. "And how would we even weigh out the budgetary issues? And what do you think Carl? Should we consider doing a demographics analysis?"

"Let's just start a church," Carl said. "I agree with Timothy."

"No, really Carl. This is serious. Let's stay on track."

Carl leaned backed as they fixed their eyes on each other. And were silent.

Malachi could tell Carl's face was even more filled out than just a couple of days before. He leaned back in the opposite direction. And rubbed his hands together. And then said, "You really mean it. Don't you, Carl?"

Carl slowly nodded his head.

"That fast. You just know. Just start The Table."

Carl was in no hurry to speak—that's how it seemed to Malachi.

"So, tell me again, what was that Bible verse Timothy gave you? The one he derived the name of the church from."

"Other outcasts came and joined Jesus and the disciples at the table."

"An outcast?" Carl said. "A person who doesn't know Jesus. A disciple—a person who knows Jesus. At a table—together. That could happen. Would that be a sign from God, Malachi?"

Malachi wrinkled his forehead.

Carl then peered over Malachi's left shoulder.

And then Malachi glanced to his left when he heard a voice, "Hey, Malachi."

And simultaneously, he heard the sound of a chair being scooted over from a nearby table. "Can I sit down? I only have a minute."

Malachi felt his heart inside his chest.

Thump, thump, thump.

"I ah…didn't know…ah…you worked…ah…" Malachi said.

And then Malachi heard, "I've never seen you here before either."

"No, this is my first time…ah," Malachi said. "My, our first time."

"It's O.K., Malachi," she said as she touched him lightly on his left shoulder with her long fingers.

"It's so good to see you, Mandy," Malachi said. "It really is."

"Thank you for joining us at the table," Carl said.

Malachi shifted his attention to Carl with a fleeting stare. And then he looked back at Mandy. "How are you doing?"

She stood up. "I just wanted to say *hi*. I have to get back to work."

Malachi rose to his feet also.

Mandy shifted closer. And said—so delicately—almost as if the words were fragile, "I went to church a few weeks ago." Then, it was somewhat of a hug from Mandy, as she spoke near his ear, "Thank you so much for everything you do for Alex."

Her body quivered. Malachi could see her facial muscles contorting. She pulled back. "I have to go."

And hurried off.

Then Malachi heard Carl say, "Other outcasts came and joined Jesus and the disciples at the table."

Malachi was still looking in the direction of Mandy's departure when Carl said, "What do you think, disciple?"

23. Ready to Roll

"**H**ere's the deal," Malachi said.

He looked over at Alex's beaming, attentive smile.

Malachi could see Mandy in his facial features as they stood facing each other. He was also noticing how much taller Alex was since they started meeting together over six months ago.

And Malachi still recalled what he had told Carl not long afterwards: "It's the strangest relationship I've ever been in. I typically do something with Alex once a week. We always have a great time. But I never see Mandy. I don't talk to her—ever. Just Alex. And Alex told me once, with sternness —an eleven-year old's sternness, 'Mom told me that you and I should never talk about her. O.K.?' But every time I'm with Alex, I want Mandy to be there too."

And besides Alex growing taller, other things had changed, situations had changed. They were meeting less frequently—with the time factor being the main reason. And the pull on Malachi's heart regarding Mandy had diminished considerably. His feelings for her just were not the same anymore. However, the incident at Zeke's earlier in the day had stirred up some unwelcomed confusion.

As usual, he and Alex had settled their plans over the phone. When Malachi arrived at their apartment, Alex would troop on out. And if the regular pattern prevailed— they would leave, have their outing, and then return as if Mandy Howard didn't even exist.

"You ready to roll, Alex?"

"Yeah," Alex said. "This looks like fun."

"You brought a change of clothes for when we go out for pizza?"

"In the bag I brought."

"And your mom...ah Mandy, she's O.K. if you get some paint on the clothes you're wearing?"

"Oh yeah. These are old clothes."

Malachi had already placed drop-cloths down around the perimeter of the room. And applied masking tape over the electrical outlets and switches.

"So Alex, you'll be working the roller. And I'll be using this trim brush to go around the edges."

Malachi picked up the roller, pressed it into the paint tray, and then began applying the paint to the wall in the classic W-pattern to assure a thorough coverage.

With the attentiveness of a puppy dog about to receive a treat, Alex watched Malachi.

"Now you try it, Alex," Malachi said. "Take your time. This isn't a race."

He watched Alex, adding a few pointers and then said, "O.K., you're on your own. Just take your time. Quality over quantity. Got it?"

Malachi then proceeded to paint the top of the wall and around the trim and other objects. *Cutting in*, as Uncle Dale called it.

Malachi glanced over at Alex. He smiled as he observed the care with which Alex rolled the walls. Malachi was thinking again how mature he was. And now it was showing in his workmanship.

After fifteen minutes, Malachi stopped what he was doing to inspect Alex's work.

Nearly half of the south living room wall had been transformed from dirty, splotchy off-white to clean, consistent off-white.

Except. "Alex, you're doing a great job," Malachi said. "Except, I'm seeing a few holidays."

"Holidays?"

"Yeah, holidays," Malachi said. "You have to look close. Real close. But there are a couple places that need a little more paint. We call them holidays—those missed spots."

He pointed out three places. Alex immediately complied by evenly applying more paint.

And then he looked over at Malachi. "Quality over quantity. Right?"

Malachi smiled. "You got it. The Bible says, 'Work as if on to the Lord.'"

"What does that mean, Malachi?"

"Work as if God is your boss."

"He is," Alex said.

Those words, *He is*, burrowed into Malachi's mind. It was as if they rode in the Suburban with them as they headed back to Manistee after the painting and clean-up had concluded.

"You know what, Alex?" Malachi said as they neared the southern edge of town. "That was the most fun I've ever had painting in my whole life."

"Me too," Alex said.

"Isn't this the only time you've ever painted in your life?"

"Yeah," Alex said. "I guess what I meant was, most of the best things I've done in my life have been with you, Malachi."

Malachi glanced over at Alex. He was smiling. And then he returned his focus straight ahead.

Neither one spoke for a bit

Until Malachi said, "Thanks, Alex."

"For what?"

"For being the most awesome twelve-year old on planet Earth." And then Malachi looked over quickly at Alex and smiled. "That's all."

24. I Surrender

"We're going to stop by and see Timothy for a couple of minutes before we head over to Mancino's for pizza," Malachi said. "There's something I want to tell him in person."

"Where does he live?" Alex said.

"Well, he lives downtown at DT's," Malachi said. "Well, it's not DT's anymore. Things have changed."

"What is it now?" Alex said.

"Let's see," Malachi said. "It's going to be called The Table."

"The Table?"

"Yeah," Malachi said. "The Table."

Alex smiled. "That's a really cool name for a restaurant."

"It's not going to be a restaurant anymore. Or a bar."

"Is he going to sell furniture?"

"Hey, I've got an idea," Malachi said. "You can ask Timothy

when we get there. What do you think?"

"O.K."

Malachi parked the Suburban and called Timothy on his cell phone. "Hey, I'm parked out front. There's no doorbell. Are you home?"

"Yeah, I just got back from Mt. Pleasant," Timothy said. "Yeah ah...I mean back from work."

"So how was your work trip?"

"Very profitable."

"Great. Praise God," Malachi said. "Hey, I've got someone with me who wants to ask you a question."

"A question?" Timothy said. "Well yeah. O.K. I'll be right out."

When Timothy opened the door and saw Alex standing in front of Malachi, he gave him a hug around the shoulder.

"Hey, come in," Timothy said.

"We only have a minute," Malachi said. "We're heading over to Mancino's for pizza."

Malachi glanced at his watch. "We're meeting someone special over there."

"We are?" Alex said. He looked back at Malachi.

"We sure are," Malachi said as he smiled at Alex.

"Otherwise, we would come in and then you could go have pizza with us," Malachi said. "We can do that another time."

Malachi then placed his right hand on Alex's left shoulder. "Go ahead, Alex. Ask Timothy your question."

"What is The Table going to be?"

Timothy placed both of his hands on Alex's shoulders. "The Table is going to be a church."

"Right here?" Alex said.

"Right here," Timothy said.

"I want to come," Alex said. He turned around and looked at Malachi. "Can we come? Please. Please, Malachi."

I Surrender

Timothy nearly shouted, "Yes! That's one."

Alex looked back at Timothy, who already had his hand in the air for a high-five.

And then Malachi extended his hand into the air. "Make that two."

Their hands slapped. And Timothy's "Yes!" reverberated down the block.

Malachi glanced at his watch. "We have to get going, Timothy. We're almost late. We'll talk. O.K.?"

They took two steps in the direction of the Suburban and then Malachi turned around, looking back at Timothy, who was watching them depart.

"Godspeed," Malachi said.

Timothy raised both hands skyward. "I surrender." As he bowed his head.

25. We're a Family

"**S**o, who are we meeting here?" Alex said as they pulled into the Mancino's parking lot.

"You'll see."

As they walked in the door, Malachi was looking around. Alex was by his side.

Italian-eatery smell hung pleasantly in the air. So pungent it seemed to raise the humidity level, stirring Malachi's appetite several notches.

"I sure am hungry," Alex said.

Malachi glanced around the restaurant again and, at the same time, he thought to himself, "Is this a date?"

He quickly weighed all the circumstances and concluded after a single round of bouncing thoughts, "No way. This is not a date."

And then he heard someone off to his left, "Hey Malachi."

Alex responded first. He spun around and said, "Elysia!" And instantly hugged her.

Malachi smiled to the point of softly chuckling.

But even as he smiled, he was sensing an inner churning. And it was almost impossible for him to avoid an Annie filmstrip, followed by a Mandy filmstrip, flickering through his head. It was a rerun. And more than once today.

He had wrestled with the thought of canceling. The day's circumstances—especially with seeing Mandy, could be excuse enough.

Though he would have had to tell Elysia something different.

In addition, when Malachi had asked Elysia out on New Year's Day, it was more or less whimsical relief from overwhelming stress. And not a well thought out request. So he saw a way to use that circumstance to rationalize opting out.

Still, at the time, he really meant it. And then cemented the deal on Thursday night at the Jesus at Walmart meeting, essentially because of an obligation that needed to be fulfilled.

He was able to wrangle all his thoughts and emotions down to: "I need to do the Godly thing. This is simply some good Christian fellowship."

Plus he had concluded— rightfully so, "It's not a date at all."

Moments after they sat down, well before the sixteen-inch family-style pizza was brought to the table, topped with Genoa salami, onions, mushrooms, banana peppers, and a few jalapenos—just a smidge. Before the arrival of the oven-baked bread sticks, sprinkled delicately with Mancino's signature parmesan cheese and all that sat

on the table were two Cokes and some eight-flavor con-
coction Alex had brewed from the self-dispensing pop
machine, Malachi felt the lightest possible touch on his
left hand as it rested on the table.

And Elysia said, "Thank you so much for inviting me,
Malachi. It's been quite a while since I've been out on a
date."

Malachi fixed his eyes on Elysia. It had happened
before when he was around her. The warmth of the Presence of God rested in the atmosphere.

"Woman of God," he said in his mind. "Awesome
woman of God."

"Have you ever had these stupid concerns come into
your head, Elysia?" Malachi said. "And then while that
thought is still rumbling around inside, you sense the
Presence of God so distinctly that clarity returns to your
thinking. And not only does the dim-witted thought
leave, you're left with an extra measure of Godly wisdom,
Godly insight. And it totally defuses your apprehension—
making it seem silly."

"When the enemy comes in like a flood, the Spirit of
the Lord lifts up a standard against him," Elysia said. "I
know exactly what you mean, Malachi. Yes…I ah…"

And then Elysia said, "Can I bless you, Malachi?"

Malachi bowed his head.

Elysia reached across the table, placing her hand on
the top of his head. "Arise, shine. For your light has come.
For behold, the darkness shall cover the Earth. And deep
darkness the people. But the Lord will arise over you and
His glory will be seen upon you. The outcasts shall come
to the light of Jesus because of you. And leaders, to the
brightness of your rising."

Malachi kept his eyes closed. He was glad he was sitting. He had no desire to move. And he wasn't even sure

if he could stand.

Though he did open his eyes when he heard Alex exclaim loudly, "That was cool." Enough so that the people at the next table turned to look.

Next, Elysia focused her attention on Alex, who was seated next to Malachi— "And for you, young man of God."

Alex jumped to his feet and reached his hands toward Elysia. She held his hands.

Alex bowed his head and Elysia spoke, "Do not say that you are too young. But go to the people I send you to, says the Lord. And tell them everything I command you to say. Do not be afraid of them, for I will protect you. May the blessings of the Lord rest upon you all of your days."

The pizza was the best Manistee had to offer, according to Alex, who proclaimed the fact at least three times as Malachi drove him home.

Malachi was hoping Elysia's blessing was the main reason for Alex's exuberance.

Malachi knew his own elevated mood certainly was launched by his blessing experience. And was fully nourished by the God-centered conversation that flowed the entire evening.

But Malachi did suspect Alex's consumption of two tall glasses of Alex-brew was a contributor to his liveliness.

Malachi parked the Suburban in front of Alex's apartment. Always well mannered, Alex expressed his appreciation. And then he said, "We're a family. I mean...it was like you, Elysia, and me were a family tonight."

At that point, Malachi had no desire to speak. Alex's words radiated so much tenderness; they were too precious to unwrap in a hurry. Malachi's thoughts hung in the warmth of the moment.

And before he was ready to speak, Alex said, "Only God could do that."

26. Like Uranium

"**H**ey, thanks for coming down on such short notice," Timothy said. "Good, you brought your mandolin."

It took Malachi's eyes several seconds to adjust to the muted lighting inside. Outside, it was a brilliant Sunday morning, enhanced by a fresh four-inch blanket of snow.

Timothy's smile was every bit as radiant as the day. And with a sweeping hand motion, he said, "Malachi, Carl, welcome to The Table."

Now everyone was smiling.

By now, Malachi's eyes had adjusted to the interior lighting as he looked around. "It's different in here. The booths are gone. What happened?"

"Craigslist," Timothy said. "Just like that. Someone contacted me. I've been getting rid of so much loot. Not money to live on, but praise God my tiptoes aren't hanging over the edge of financial disaster anymore. I just may be out of debt before the sell-off ends."

"And you have a new job," Malachi said.

"Thank God for that," Carl said. "So what's your new job, Timothy?"

Malachi looked off to his right at Carl. "It's pretty complicated."

"Yeah ah," Timothy said. "It's investing that entails a high-level of numerical analytics. The speculation spectrum is a multi-faceted endeavor that falls under the umbrella of an array of governmental regulations."

"He travels a lot," Malachi said.

"'Not really a lot," Timothy said. "This week, for example, I'm thinking, like two days."

"So where does work take you this week?" Carl said.

"Well ah," Timothy said. "Just around ah...the state. You know."

Carl's eyes fixed on Timothy for a few moments. And then said, "No. I don't know where you're going. I was just curious."

"Of yeah," Timothy said. "Tuesday and Wednesday, I plan on making stops in Wayland, Battle Creek, New Buffalo, and Michigan City if I have time. Hey, enough of all that work stuff. Let's sit down."

Seven round oak tables had been pushed against the wall immediately to the left of the entry door. Not only touching the wall, but each table snugged against the adjoining table. Stringing out along the wall, nearly one-third of the length of the long wall. Opposite, was the bar itself. Resting on it, near the riverside end, was a black and yellow toolbox. It was open. A cordless screw gun, slightly askew, was housed in the container.

Timothy tapped his hand on the bar's horizontal surface as they walked toward the back of the building. "This goes next. I'm trying to figure out how to take it apart. And then put it on Craigslist or something. Or maybe we can rework it and make it into something useful for the church."

"God's good at that," Malachi said. "Re-working. Look what He did to you."

Timothy laughed. "Yeah, this bar should be nothing compared to this old heathen."

"So, what do we have here?" Carl said. As he eyed the rearranging that had taken place in front of the patio doors leading to the deck.

Though the patio door was not visible, a pleated curtain draped to the floor blocked the view to the outside. The fabric, with three-inch stripes—in muted fall colors—green, brown, dirty yellow, and an understated shade of orange, covered the twelve-foot by eight-foot area on the riverside wall.

Three rows of seven chairs each, chairs that formerly gathered around the restaurant's tables, formed a gentle arc. The first row being twelve or so feet back from the curtained wall they faced. And in front of the seating arrangement, facing the chairs, was a metal music stand in a flat black with a slightly hammered texture. The carrier portion of the stand was adjusted to the proper height and angle to accommodate someone using it as a podium.

"I was just messing around," Timothy said.

He looked over at Malachi and then Carl and then back at the seating array and then back at Malachi. "Do you see chairs there?"

"Well yeah, I see the chairs there," Malachi said.

"Me too," Timothy said. "But I see them all filled up."

"Amen," Carl said.

"So, Pastor Timothy, what's on the agenda today?" Malachi said. "Here at The Table. It does seem a bit hectic. Do we need to get some more chairs? It sure is crowded today."

"Oh, look at that," Timothy said. "I didn't see those up front. But there are three seats left. We better grab them right away."

He was grinning.

Carl and Malachi sat in the front. Before finding his place, Malachi placed his mandolin case down to the left of the music stand. Timothy repositioned his chair, so they were all facing each other.

"The Table," Timothy said slowly. "Let's do church. What do you think?"

"I was glad when they said to me, 'Let us go to the house of the Lord.'" Malachi said.

"Psalm 122:1," Timothy said.

"Impressive Timothy," Carl said. "You must have a good memory."

"When I was younger, it was kind of like photographic. Not quite. But close. I messed it up—if you know what I mean. But praise God, I'm clean. And it's coming back. It's great because learning Scriptures comes easily."

"And it helps him in his new job," Malachi said.

"Yeah, it does," Timothy said. "But hey, what do you think about this? Malachi, you do the music. Carl, I'm thinking you're a 2 Timothy 4:2 man: 'Preach the word; be ready in season and out of season.' So can you give us some Word today?"

"Sure," Carl said, "Absolutely."

"And my part is over there at that table," Timothy said.

Carl and Malachi had noticed it resting against the west wall, almost at the point of being an extension of the front row of chairs, with a five-foot walkway between. A table with a rust-red tablecloth held two white-cloth covered objects. One was as tall as a beer pitcher. The other was nearly flat—only a hump was visible.

Malachi proceeded to unlatch his mandolin case. And then he opened his green ring-binder.

When he finished. He stood at the podium facing Carl and Timothy. "I would like to welcome everyone to The Table this Lord's Day morning. The Table—the church for you."

Malachi then picked up his mandolin, placing the strap over his shoulder. He strummed a few chords softly. "Father God help us to realize, help us always to acknowledge that this church is for You—may the words of our mouth and the meditations…"

And then everyone's attention was drawn to the noise reverberating from the door. It was a firm rapping sound, almost a pounding. Someone was saying something outside, but the words were too muddled to understand.

"Well, praise God," Timothy said. "People are trying to knock down the door to get into church."

He made his way swiftly to the door and opened it, as Malachi and Carl remained at the other end of the building.

But they could hear Timothy. "Well, come on in, Rollie."

"So what's going on down here?" Rollie said as he moved his sunglasses from his eyes to his head—just above the forehead.

"Come on in," Timothy said. "I want you to meet some friends of mine."

Rollie was looking all around as he walked toward Malachi and Carl. And said before he reached them, "Been hearing things around town, mainly down at Zeke's—so you shut down DT's. Well, I guess they were saying the state came in and shut you down. Of course, when you hire illegal aliens—that'll catch up to you too. What was the name of that cook you had, that Mexican guy—that got deported?"

"Bill," Timothy said. "That's the only Hispanic-looking

worker I've ever had."

"Yeah him."

"He was born in Ludington," Timothy said. "So he deported himself back to Ludington. He's a high school science teacher there. This was his summer job."

"Oh," Rollie said.

"So what did the state shut me down for, Rollie?" Timothy said. "What did *they* say it was?"

"I don't know for sure," Rollie said.

"Can you do me a favor?" Timothy said.

"What's that?" Rollie said.

"Can you go down to Zeke's and find out why the state shut me down? And then tell me, so then I'll know."

Rollie shook his head. "O.K. Just give me the straight scoop. What's going on, Timothy?"

"Thanks for stopping by, Rollie," Timothy said. "I want to introduce you to two very good friends of mine."

Handshakes and cordial greetings followed. Rollie— Rollie Kirtner seemed pleased when Timothy called him, "A mover and shaker in downtown Manistee." He was the owner of three downtown properties, chairman of the Manistee Downtown Authority, and presently was heading up a 2.4 million-dollar fund raising effort to benefit the restoration of The Vogue Theater. He also owned other rental property around the Manistee area.

As Timothy talked on about Rollie's credentials, Malachi watched Rollie, who kept peering around the room.

In addition, Malachi was noticing his t-shirt. Much of it exposed under his winter coat. Spruce green—its design made it look like an Army jacket with flapped chest and waist pockets. And a vertical button cuff. None of it was real. Just printing. The imaginary upper pocket flaps were oversized. On one flap, the printed words said, *War is over. If you want it.* And on the other pocket flap, while the image was small, Malachi knew it had to be John Lennon.

Rollie's eyes were gazing at Malachi's mandolin when Timothy had completed his tribute.

"Are you having a concert down here or something?" Rollie said.

"Something," Timothy said.

And then over the next seven minutes, Timothy told Rollie all that had happened to him. How his life had changed. It was a testimony of God's goodness.

Twice, when Timothy was especially revved up, Malachi saw Rollie eyeing the door. Also he stepped away from Timothy, increasing the space between the two of them. But like a good mystery book, Timothy's story drew Rollie in, holding his interest—even though the plot didn't appear to be his genre.

Timothy nearly sung the last two lines of his monologue, "We're going to start a church here. We're calling it—The Table."

With not even a speck of hesitation, Rollie said, "You can't do that."

Timothy instantly volleyed back—with zero uncertainty, "Yes we can."

"You're full of it, Timothy," Rollie said.

"You're right, Rollie," Timothy said. "Well almost."

"What?" Rollie said.

"I'm full of Him. The Holy Spirit," Timothy said.

"Another bunch tried to start a church downtown," Rollie said. "We had to run them off. If you let one church move in downtown, it's like uranium; they'll pretty much never go away."

"I see that as a good thing. A group committed for the long haul. Never going away—like uranium. Except, we'll be committed to bettering the world around us."

"I don't see it that way," Rollie said. "And the other

merchants and investors won't see it your way either. I'm sure of that."

And then Rollie repositioned his sunglasses—covering his eyes. And said, "You better change your plans." With that, he abruptly turned around, marching to the door as Timothy, Malachi, and Carl silently looked on.

They stared at the door for a few moments after it thudded closed louder than necessary. No one said anything for several seconds.

And then Malachi said, "I think Rollie left without his new visitor's welcoming gift."

"That's funny, Malachi," Timothy said. "But not funny enough to make me laugh."

And then Carl said, "In the words of Pastor Timothy, 'Let's do church.' Now we need it more than ever."

Malachi walked back up front. The other two sat down.

He strummed his mandolin. "I can't exactly remember what I was saying...let's see."

And then he heard Timothy saying quietly, "Father God help us to realize, always help us to acknowledge that this church is for You—may the..."

"Words of our mouth and the meditations of our hearts be pleasing to You," Malachi said.

Malachi looked at Timothy, smiled and nodded his head. And then said, "Early this morning, God gave me this song. Well, part of it is from a hymn—probably written a hundred years ago. I never even gave this song a title."

He strummed a G-Chord, a D, and then a C. And then he said, "Maybe I could entitle it, *Like Uranium*. Because this song is about a rock. But that title wouldn't really work. Because this Rock lasts forever and is solid. Eternally unmovable."

> Solid is the Rock upon which I stand
> Solid is the Rock upon which I stand

Like Uranium

Savior, Lord, You're my King

Solid is the Rock upon which I stand
Standing, standing, I'm standing on the promises
of Christ my Savior
Standing, standing, I'm standing on the promises
of Christ my Savior

Savior, Lord, You're my King

Solid is the Rock upon which I stand
Standing, standing, I'm standing on the promises
of Christ my Savior

Savior, Lord, You're my King

Malachi looked directly at Timothy. Their eyes met.
Malachi played three chords. Closed his eyes and sang:
I surrender all
I surrender all
I surrender all

Savior, Lord, You're my King
Savior, Lord, You're my King

Malachi removed his hands from his mandolin and
raised both of them overhead. His eyes remained closed.
And he kept singing the words:
I surrender all
I surrender all
I surrender all

Savior, Lord, You're my King

Jesus at Walmart...fire on the Earth

Savior, Lord, You're my King

Malachi could distinctly hear Timothy's and Carl's voices. His voice connected with theirs. He returned his hands to his instrument:

The singing continued. Those five lines. Those eight words.

Malachi was caught up into a dimension, a realm he had been before. But not to this degree. Almost as if he was encountering what the Scripture says: "Whether in the body or apart from the body I do not know, God knows."

I surrender all
I surrender all
I surrender all

A solemn hush permeated Malachi's inner man. Only one stream of thought saturated his mind. Immersing his spirit:

Savior, Lord, You're my King
Savior, Lord, You're my King

I surrender all
I surrender all
I surrender all

And then, after some passing of time, like a person deciding to place their feet on a descending escalator—one foot, then the next, Malachi took the step. The descent began.

Near the reentry point—back to where his body stood, Malachi strummed the final three chords—G-chord, D-chord, C-chord. Singing the final three words:

I surrender all
D-chord, C-chord. Singing the final three words:
I surrender all

29. Fire on the Earth

It was a foggy transition—in the holy foggy sense.

Normal human reactions were lacking. Perspectives askew. Comparatives seemed sorry. Like looking up into a nighttime sky with the uncountable stars slicing through the blackened backdrop with all their majesty and then turning to a companion, commenting, "Have you seen the LED flashlight display at Walmart? It's awesome too."

Malachi spoke first, after several moments of looking at each other. And then, it was as high as he could reach, "Wow. That was amazing."

Timothy shot a little higher. Still the trajectory was anemic. "Awesome. God is awesome. Wow, God is good. Praise God for His goodness."

They all fell silent for a few seconds. Or more.

Until Malachi said, "Yeah. Ah yeah...let's see? Carl, you have some Word for us today?"

Carl and Malachi exchanged places. Carl stood at the pulpit as Timothy and Malachi sat facing him—six-feet away.

"O.K. then...ah..." Carl said, as he leafed through his Bible, spread out before him. And then he looked up and smiled. "I usually like just a little more time to prepare. Give me just a minute here."

He took less than his allotted sixty seconds. He prayed and then read:

"I have come to cast fire on the earth and how I wish it were already kindled!

But I have a baptism to undergo, and how distressed I am until it is accomplished!

Do you suppose that I came to grant peace on earth? I tell you, no, but rather division. For from now on five members in one household will be divided, three against two and two against three. They will be divided, father against son and son against father, mother against daughter and daughter against mother, mother-in-law against daughter-in-law and daughter-in-law against mother-in-law."

Carl looked up:

"Those are the words of Jesus. He's talking about fire on the Earth. And the example He gives is one of division. Division to the highest level of pain and sorrow. Remember, back in Jesus' time, family meant everything. Extended families lived together. Worked together. Cried and laughed together. Birth and death was experienced—together. So this division Jesus talks about cuts or, I should say, tore apart the fabric of life. Painfully so. Fire on the Earth.

Now two-thousand years later, we can expect to experience this at even a more challenging and elevated degree and in so many forms.

And today, we experienced that—right here. I'm not sure, but I bet Timothy and Rollie were on good terms before today."

Carl motioned his head. "Maybe they drank some beers sitting over there at the bar. Had some laughs. Talked about business. They were at peace."

Timothy nodded his head.

"And then one thing changed all of that. We could name some peripheral circumstances, concerns etc. as the reasons. But they are not the reason for the departure of peace, for this fire on the Earth."

"Remember Jesus' words in our text."

Carl looked down at his Bible. "'But I have a baptism to undergo and how distressed I am until it is accomplished!' And then not too long afterwards, Jesus cried out from the Cross, 'It is finished.' And now, Timothy has embraced Jesus Christ, who died on a cross for the sins of mankind. Now, Rollie is likely O.K. with the: Away in a manger no crib for a bed; the little Lord Jesus lay down His sweet head—Rollie is O.K. with that Jesus. The Christmas Jesus is good for business. It's the Jesus who laid down His life on the cross—that's the reason today, right here, before our eyes, we saw peace turn into division. Fire on the Earth."

Carl stepped away from the podium—holding his Bible. "But there's also another fire on the Earth."

With his thumb, he flipped the pages from right to left as he looked down. And then he said, "Here's what it says in Acts 2:1-3."

Carl glanced up, and then he returned his eyes to the Bible he was holding.

And began reading, "When the day of Pentecost had come, they were all together in one place. And suddenly there came from heaven a noise like a violent rushing wind and it filled the whole house where they were sitting. And there appeared to them divided tongues as of fire and they rested on each one of them."

Carl moved back to the podium and set down his Bible.

"More fire. Divided—divisions. Now, while this fire was divided, it brought peace and unity. Each person received fire—they received the fire of the Holy Spirit. While everyone received their divided piece, it was all the same Holy Spirit. Something only God could achieve. And less than two months prior, Jesus had told them this would happen, the last words He spoke before ascending heavenward."

Carl paused. He shifted his eyes downward. A page rustled.

And then Carl said, "The words of Jesus, 'You will receive power when the Holy Spirit has come upon you and you shall be My witnesses both in Jerusalem and in all Judea and Samaria and even to the remotest part of the earth.'"

He looked up, "Fire on the Earth. For power. Power to proclaim the only true peace. The inner peace of knowing Jesus Christ. And power to unite believers—in one accord—to go out and make known this message of eternal peace."

Carl moved away from the podium. He held out his left hand.

"Fire on the Earth—strife, division at its worst. Some form of peace—but only on the surface, superficial, never the real thing."

And then he held out his right hand. "Fire on the Earth. Holy Spirit power for every believer—though for many, it remains smothered. But the fire is there. It is real. It brings true inner peace—as turmoil swirls all around. Powerful for uniting believers in the cause of proclaiming true, soul satisfying, eternal peace through Jesus Christ."

28. A Good Monday at Menards

It was dark. It was early. It was cold.

And inside, Malachi was going through a clash. Sort of a skirmish. A mental vortex.

New job anxiety—with it's unknown—like the vista into a black gorge whirled inside, counter-directional to the light of hope, Holy Spirit-style, encountered one morning earlier. Though tainted slightly with the splotch of black Rollie splashed onto the new white canvas.

Malachi glanced at the clock in his Suburban—5:33 a.m. He thought to himself, "I'm usually finishing up my last break, before making the final push of the night. I'm just not use to this."

Dale had called him last night with a change of plans. He told him to be at the Cadillac Menards at 6:45. The Dale

Marble Construction tool trailer would be out back in the lumberyard area on the north side of the main building.

Malachi was sure he could make it in less than an hour, but he had to find the job-site, and he didn't want to take any chances of being even a minute late. And even though his body felt tired, the excitement had spiked his adrenalin—he was ready to roll.

Malachi had talked to Martin after Dale called. They discussed the possibility of carpooling. After talking, they concluded that the logistics, for now, were too complicated—without further map scrutiny.

While Malachi lived in Freesoil, Martin's residence was in Brethren. One of the most uninhabited areas of the vast Manistee National Forest was located squarely between them. All the convenient connecting roads seemed to be dirt. Many unplowed this time of year—the first Monday in February.

Malachi and Martin had talked for twenty-five minutes. Much of the conversation was regarding The Table.

Malachi had called Martin on Sunday morning to invite him to yesterday's meeting, but he and JC had commitments at their church.

Martin had said, "I wish I would have known sooner. I definitely would have stopped over."

Malachi laughed. "Timothy only called me like thirty minutes ago. So I understand."

As Malachi described the day, the service, the run in with Rollie, all that happened, he could tell that Martin's interest in The Table was stimulated.

Still, Malachi ended their conversation on the matter with, "Now Martin, just because Carl and I've decided that this is God's direction for our lives, I don't automatically assume the same for you. I know that you, you and JC, are making connections at Living Water Bible Church. So you need to decide for yourself."

A Good Monday at Menards

After Malachi had said that, there was a silence on the other end.

Enough so that, after several seconds, Malachi said, "Are you still there, Martin?"

The words on the other end came forth slowly—the volume ascended only a few decibels above faint. Yet they were certain. More like a proclamation revealing an inward musing: "Another Holy Convocation. That's what we need."

Malachi had responded, "Hmmn. Maybe?"

To anyone listening in on the conversation, Martin's next question would have seemed like an abrupt gear shift—without pushing in the clutch. "What about Jesus at Walmart?"

'It's over," Malachi said. "I'm moving on. Jesus at Walmart is no more."

"Just like that."

"Yep. Just like that."

"How do you know?" Martin said. "Is it God? How do you know?"

"I know it is," Malachi said. "I didn't jump into this decision—like it might seem. Yes, it happened in a compact time frame. But I actually made my decision before I committed to The Table."

"You did?"

"Yeah. I never told anybody this. I was waiting for the right timing," Malachi said. "But when I said goodbye to Sal that last night at work, I told her just before I left, 'I'll be here next Thursday. I'll keep plowing. I'll keep fighting that lie.' And then the instant I turned around, I knew, I was positive; Jesus at Walmart was over. The inner knowing is the way I describe it—it entered into me. I sensed it. The thought was new to me; it surprised me. But just like that, I was positive it was from God. In faith, I accepted it. I said semi-out loud as I walked through the store—heading to the exit, 'O.K. Whatever You desire, Lord.' Immediately, I was at full peace. Three minutes earlier, I was gung ho to press on, no matter what the cost. But then—bam—peace. It was a done deal."

"Still it seems so fast." Martin said. "I mean—like bam?"

"Here's the deal," Malachi said. "At least for me, it's usually like God moves too slowly, and then when something happens so fast, it's like, 'Slow down, God. Let me catch-up.'"

"But what if you...ah?" Martin said. "What if that really wasn't God? And you missed it? And totally messed up?"

"This is how I gauge it. A two-perspective mind-set," Malachi said. "One, if I start developing a track record for missing it—determined in retrospect; I need to put the brakes on my existing method of determining God's will. Then two, say the opposite is true, but on some rare occasion, I go into a sideways skid and hit the wall—certainly some introspective evaluation is called for. However, I believe what Romans 8:28 says, 'And we know that God causes all things to work together for good to those who love God, to those who are the called according to His purpose.' So what I take away from this verse is: if your heart is right, say if you crash point-blank into the wall, God's going to make something good happen out of it. No matter how screwed up it may seem. And tell you what, Martin—I've experienced this—for real. It's like what those verses in Lamentations say, 'Through the Lord's mercies, we are not consumed. For God's compassions never fail. They are new every morning. Great is His faithfulness.'"

"That's good, Malachi," Martin said. "That would preach."

When Malachi arrived at Freesoil Road, the main street of the rural burg where he resided, he turned left. He was only two blocks from home. Instinctively, he wanted to go right and head into Manistee. His habit.

Nine miles out, Freesoil Rd. turned into Eight Mile Rd. Four and a half miles further west, it ended. With one option—Johnson Rd. North.

A Good Monday at Menards

Malachi was driving in the heart of the Manistee National Forest. Darkness pervaded. More like, dominated the immense publicly-owned tract of land. Lighting from the scant scattering of homes or other sources was negligible.

Malachi was making his way north to Highway 55—a primary road leading directly into Cadillac.

During the first few miles of his journey, Malachi reflected on yesterday at Church. The Rollie run-in had raised concerns; yet his mind was glued to the opposite spectrum of the day's events. As the joy of the Lord was still welling up from within.

However, a few miles back, it became necessary for Malachi to shift his attention to finding his way in the black-cast of murkiness.

Next Johnson Rd. veered into Seamen Rd., which then dead-ended into Hoxyville Rd.; a left for less than a quarter of a mile, and then Seamen Rd. re-appeared to the left. A crucial turn north that Malachi almost missed. He hit the brakes and made a hard, but rather smooth transition onto the final leg before arriving at Highway 55.

The road hooked left, and within three-quarters of a mile, it curved back to the east. And at that point, Malachi saw a glow ahead, slightly to the left. He figured it was the blink-and-you'll- miss-it town of Wellston, which was just south of the eastbound main route into Cadillac.

He slowed down as he came around the bend, the Suburban maneuvering back to the right. And then he slowed down even more, cutting his speed to a slow roll.

There on an embankment rising four-feet from the road-bed was one of the few, very few, remaining outdoor Christmas lighting displays.

Life-size figures of Joseph and Mary—in glowing white, were kneeling in the snow. The Baby Jesus was nestled in the snow in front of them. Heaping snow had nearly obscured the manger, and it appeared as if Jesus was laying in the snow—peeking over his blanket at Malachi.

Jesus, His manger, and the nearby snow emitted a goldish glow. A seven-foot tall wooden cross, wrapped with white lights, radiated onto Jesus and His adjacent surroundings.

"Wow," Malachi said to himself as he crept by.

The illuminated display was like an illustration to the contrast Carl had talked about yesterday: "Now, Rollie is likely O.K. with the: Away in a manger no crib for a bed; the little Lord Jesus lay down His sweet head—Rollie is O.K. with that Jesus. The Christmas Jesus is good for business. It's the Jesus who laid down His life on the cross—that's the reason today, right here, before our eyes, we saw peace turn to division. Fire on the Earth."

And soon, Malachi was singing. And within four minutes, he was on the main road, heading directly into Cadillac. His mind—driving-wise, went to autopilot as Malachi's thoughts returned to The Table.

Highway 55 ran into US 131. North six miles to Boone Rd. Left 1.5 miles just past the Walmart store. And then on the same side of the road—go past the main entrance and take the second one. Go straight back to the lumberyard—the future lumberyard.

Malachi easily spotted Dale's Hawaiian blue trailer. The v-nosed trailer with dual axels was already backed in. The rear tip-down door had been lowered to form a ramp into the trailer's interior.

Twice the length of the Suburban, Malachi could make out the words Dale Marble Construction. *The Job's Not Complete Until You're Completely Satisfied* in a yellowish hue of tan.

Malachi smiled when he walked up to the trailer and saw the kissing arcs of a Jesus-fish displayed right below the word *Satisfied*. White and large enough to avoid the impression that the displayer was squeamish about what it meant.

A Good Monday at Menards

And while Malachi knew the Jesus-fish had been abused as a marketing ploy over the years, he knew positively, for Dale, it was motivated by the purest of intentions.

Malachi smiled and said, "That's so cool. I love it."

He raised his hands toward the sky and said, "Praise God."

He took another glimpse at Dale's job-trailer. He inhaled the cold morning air. And then he said to himself as he exhaled, "Yeah. It's a good Monday at Menards."

29. Does that Cross Mean Anything Special?

It was the cold side of chilly as they stood in an exterior alcove large enough to park two eighteen-wheelers side by side. A future material's storage area in the lumberyard.

Malachi could tell Dale was nervous, noticeably edgy.

But when he spoke to the crew, he became more confident as he outlined the game plan—like a veteran commander ready to charge into battle.

Dale made the introductions. Besides Martin and himself, there were two other men. Both small-scale independent contractors—Wilks and Raymond. They both had worked on numerous projects with Dale.

Malachi was surprised when Dale said, "Most of what we'll be doing here at Menards will be new to me. And I think to Wilks and Raymond also."

Wilks nodded. And Raymond said, "I'm sure. That's construction."

"That's O.K. though," Dale said. "Pay attention. It's not rocket science."

He then issued hardhats—a shade darker than lime green, with the explanation, "I want my men to look professional."

Everyone took a couple of minutes to adjust their helmet. And soon, the Dale Marble Construction crew was sporting a new look.

He then outlined his expectations for the crew. He emphasized seven key characteristics. "Professional, quality workmanship, cooperative, courteous, hardworking, flexible, and safety conscious—these are the hallmarks I require for those who work for Dale Marble Construction."

When Dale quit talking for a moment, Martin said, "Just like Walmart third shifters."

Wilks looked over at Martin. "You were a Walmart overnighter?"

"Yeah."

"Me too. Back in 2003 and part of 2004—in Ludington," he smiled. And then gave Martin a knuckle bump. "Cool."

"So was Malachi."

"Cool."

Dale smiled. He looked at Raymond. "So what about you?"

"Oh man," Raymond said. "I've never worked there, but I spend enough money at Walmart to have my own personal stocker."

It was a good laugh for everyone. Dale's tension balloon deflated drastically.

As the laughing subsided, Malachi saw Dale removing his hardhat. He said, "Is anyone here uncomfortable if we say a quick prayer before we launch the work day? As we start this new job?"

Does that Cross Mean Anything Special?

Facial expressions all appeared to be thumbs-up. Dale looked at Malachi for an elongated moment.

Malachi shook his head up and down and pointed his right index finger at Dale, mouthing the words, "You can do it."

With everyone holding their hat in their hands, standing somewhat in a circle, Dale began to pray: "Dear God, thank you so much for giving us this really good job. Times have been lean."

Malachi heard Wilks say softly, "Amen."

Dale continued, "We thank you for this job. Help us to represent Your ideals well. Stir something inside us when we veer from that. Keep us safe by Your protection. Help each of us to be a blessing to the Menards Corporation, the general contractor of this project, and anyone whom we come in contact with. May Your kingdom come. Your will be done on earth as it is in Heaven. For Yours is the kingdom and the power and the glory, forever and ever. Amen."

And then, the crew followed Dale inside to attend the mandatory Monday morning meeting led by the project's General Contractor.

While Malachi didn't try to count, he figured nearly a hundred workers were gathered around a make-shift office area. Three laptops were set up on three church potluck size walnut-brown folding tables arranged in a *U*. There was also a printer. Several blue prints—mostly rolled up. While one was spread out, covering nearly half of one of the tables.

"Quiet everyone. Listen up," the general contractor hollered. "Let's get started."

Dale maneuvered his way near the front of the crowd. He was holding a tablet and an ink pen.

Malachi and the rest of the crew remained on the outer edge of those gathered around.

Then the contractor said, "My name is Evonda Presley."

Malachi could barely hear what she was saying. Her voice was not very loud, even at first. And after the introduction, it dropped back several decibels, going from nearly a shout to a slightly elevated conversational level.

Yet, as she spoke, she did up the volume to stress certain points. The three most distinctive being, "Don't throw your cigarette butts on the ground, we need to be a lot less gross in the porta-potties, and hangovers will not be tolerated as an excuse for missing work."

Much of the rest sounded like a drone—nearly impossible to understand.

Evonda did raise her voice near the conclusion. "Does anyone have any questions?"

Malachi did.

But he didn't ask it, even though he thought of it the moment Evonda stood up and introduced herself.

From back in the crowd, Malachi had noticed a small cross with a thin chain dangling from Evonda's neck. He was too far away to see much detail, except to notice its color—gold.

Malachi wanted to know.

He didn't raise his hand, but he did hope he would be able to ask Evonda a question before the completion of the project: "Does that cross mean anything special to you?"

30. I Surrender-Not

They reached the door at the same time.

"Martin, you look as tired as I feel," Malachi said.

"Oh man, I'll tell you, Malachi; this level of exhaustion is something I've never experienced in all my days," Martin said. "I thought I was going to die the first week. But now I'm thanking God; I'm getting used to it—somewhat."

Then he smiled, "Or maybe my body's just numb to the pain."

They both laughed.

The Dale Marble Construction crew had turned into The Beam Team. For the past two weeks, they had concentrated their efforts on one aspect of the Menards project.

Building the beams. In commercial construction jargon, this meant they were assembling massive commercial grade shelving. And more specifically, they were working outside in the future storage alcoves. Still essentially outside.

The word *beam* is used because all these massive shelving units, some over twenty feet tall, are constructed of I-beams. Five, six, and eight-inch beams in a dizzying variety of configurations were assembled with chunky bolts and nuts using electric impact drivers.

Much of the first day was spent gathering parts for the first configuration they were preparing to erect. Pieces were scattered all over the expansive lumberyard area. And then a deciphering of the blueprint was required to determine sometimes only a nuance of differences between the beam configurations.

Dale seemed undaunted by the slow start. The blueprint was his constant companion, either tucked under his arm or rolled out on any flat surface that could serve as a desk-on-the-fly. Malachi also noticed, even when things were chaotic in the first day or so, Dale, like the sea captain steering directly into rough seas, never flinched. He always had the next answer.

By noon the second day, the Dale Marble Construction team had hit their stride. Dale manned the Skytrack—his telescoping lift truck. And by now, it seemed as if he had absorbed most of the blueprint. Beams that appeared to be the same to Malachi, only required a glance from Dale, and then he'd say, "That one goes right there."

Malachi became the parts chaser. Since he had long ago been a factory forklift driver, he darted around on one Evonda had provided. Though Malachi drove the forklift, much of his efforts involved manual labor to restack, sort, and drag the bulky beams. All of this was accomplished at full velocity. Malachi had discovered early on—don't keep Dale waiting; he's all about efficiency.

Martin, Wilks, and Raymond were the assemblers. With Martin mainly focusing on pre-assembly—assembling a manageable array of parts to be lifted or manhandled into place when they were next in the queue.

Wilks became Dale's go-to man. If Dale had to leave to consult with Evonda, he simply said, "Wilks, you're in charge."

While Wilks was half a notch down in drive and efficiency from Dale, he was a seasoned veteran, who knew how to move the project along proficiently.

So much so that Dale put him in charge after he left for the day—usually after nine hours, but sometimes less. The rest of the crew usually pressed on for three more hours or until they heard Wilks say, "We're at a good stopping place. Let's roll 'em up."

And on those first two Saturdays, Dale put Wilks in charge for the entire day. They were shorter days. Both ended after eight hours—no matter what.

"You know what, Malachi," Martin said. "I'm really thanking God. I've never made this much money in my life."

He looked over at JC and said, "This is really going to help with our future plans."

JC was already smiling—like always. But a special brightness illuminated her countenance.

Martin had announced their *future* plans at a get together at his home in Brethren very early in January. Martin had called for a Holy Convocation, and as part of the afterglow of that Holy gathering, Martin made an announcement.

And at that moment, in his mind, Malachi was hearing those words again:

"Hey everyone, we…ah have something we want you to know. God has done an amazing work in my heart and in JC's heart. And by what seems like God's hand, JC and I have traveled the spiritual road together. The road to knowing Jesus as our Savior and beyond. We are now launching into a God-honoring dating relationship—we're courting. We're hoping this journey takes us to marriage."

Malachi reached around and pulled them both into an embrace. "You two are so awesome."

And then Malachi said as he released his hold, "What do you think of the banner?"

Jesus at Walmart...fire on the Earth

All three of them stepped back and looked overhead. Suspended two feet above, from the rust-red canopy, was a large vinyl fabric banner. Quite a bit longer than the arm span of even a tall man. Medium green and yellow were the background colors. Designed like a striped flag. Green, yellow, green. Except that the yellow portion, on the upper border, the middle one-third, arched upward six inches or so.

In the upper green section, the words: The Table, were printed, nearly filling the space vertically—using a mildly playful font. Printed below, nestled slightly into the arch, was the word: *Coming*. The word: *Soon* was printed below it. These words were somewhat smaller than those above, and the font was less adventurous. To the left, cutting through all three color swatches was a cross. Black, like all the lettering, it leaned back slightly with a hint of curvature. And was accented with a drop-shadow effect.

JC spoke first, "Makes me want to go inside."

"Well, now everybody knows it's not DT's anymore," Martin said.

"Well yeah," Malachi said. "Hey, let's head on in. Timothy told me the door would be unlocked."

The interior was set up exactly as before, except the largest of the tables had been pulled away from the wall, separated from the rest. Seven chairs were set up around the table.

And then Malachi noticed something else new.

Timothy was sitting in the front row of the seating array—still set up from the other Sunday. The last seat on the left, up near the table, which still had white cloths draped over two humps.

He sat motionless. His head lowered. His chin nearly resting on his chest. The chair he was sitting on had been slightly repositioned in a counterclockwise direction, facing an object that had been added to the décor.

Standing in the corner, the bottom out slightly, so the top could lean back and touch the point where the two walls intersected— was a cross. Five-foot tall. The color of an old copper penny. Rough sawn, as if it was hewn from a small log. While the roughness was tempered by a semi-glossy glaze.

Stillness prevailed. And by now, Malachi and company were standing in back of the last row. All their eyes were surveying the cross as Timothy slowly stood up.

He turned around, smiling, "Welcome to The Table."

"The cross is beautiful," JC said.

"It sure is," Timothy said. "Saved my soul." He smiled slightly as he glanced back. "This one's really nice too."

And then he looked back at the group. "A buddy of mine, well ah…a regular at DT's made it for me. Had a tab to pay off. A desperate soul. But he's talented, more so when he's sober. He made it from an old cedar telephone pole. I was just praying for Wierick. If the cross can change me, it can change him."

"Amen. I agree," Malachi said.

"Thank you everyone for coming to The Table today," Timothy said. "Is Carl coming?"

"Yeah," Malachi said. "He told me he would. Said he didn't need a ride. Unusual, but I've learned not to question Carl. He sort of falls outside of the boundaries of usual. And I think we all praise God for that."

"Elysia has a commitment today," Martin said. "She said she would swing by, but may miss us, depending on what time we leave."

Timothy directed everyone over to the table he had arranged and then went to fetch some Eden Springs.

When Timothy returned, he sat down, and said, "I know you all have been praying about The Table. And I think everyone is aware that today is not going to be like a Sunday church service. The plan is to have some prayer, some discussion, some trying to figure out the heart of God for The Table."

Everyone affirmed the agenda for the day.

And then Timothy said, "I do have something I had planned for two weeks ago when Malachi, Carl, and I met. But God had another idea."

He looked at Malachi and smiled, "And we thank Him for His interruption of our agenda."

"Yes, we do," Malachi said.

"And now I think I see why," Timothy said.

And then Timothy unscrewed the top of his water, took a sip, and said, "Did anyone see anything different outside today?"

"Outside?" Martin said.

JC laughed. "Like anybody in Manistee could miss your giant banner."

"Well, it's not a banner," Timothy said. "Sure, when I went to the Vistaprint website, they tagged it as a banner on their drop down menu. But it's not a banner."

"So O.K.," Malachi said. "What is it?"

"It's a flag," Timothy said. "During our last meeting, we had one of those mighty times in the Lord. And we surrendered to Him. We kept singing, 'I surrender all.'"

He then looked directly at Martin and JC. "And I'm sure you know we had a visitor last time, and he decided he didn't like what we're doing here."

'Yeah."

"Sure did."

"He wanted us to surrender to his wishes. And maybe a lot of people's wishes. I don't know. I'm sure we'll find out," Timothy said. "So that's a flag out there, boldly declaring: I surrender—not. I will not surrender to the desires of man over the desires of God."

And then Timothy stood up, closed his eyes, and started quoting Scriptures: "Yea though I walk through the valley of the shadow of death, I fear no evil, for You are with me."

Within moments, everyone in the group followed suit. Their voices swelled into a declaring proclamation. Their eyes were closed:

"Your rod and Your staff, they comfort me. You prepare a table before me in the presence of my enemies. You have anointed my head with oil. My cup overflows."

And then Malachi heard a voice from behind. Moving closer. Reaching a crescendo with theirs: "Surely goodness and mercy will follow me all the days of my life. And I will dwell in the house of the Lord forever. Amen."

Malachi stood up and turned around. There was Carl directly behind him—with a grin beaming from his face.

But Malachi barely noticed.

Mental pictures rifled through his brain.

His emotions spiraled, ebbed, and swirled faster than a strobe light.

His words came out like a man determining if the ghost in front of him was real, "Mandy? Mandy!"

They embraced. Mandy began to sob.

Malachi's heart was thumping. He sensed the pounding even in his ears.

JC joined the embrace. Mandy looked up at her. JC's hand caressed the tear away on the left side of Mandy's face. She kissed Mandy on the forehead. "We love you so much."

Malachi stepped back. JC pulled Mandy in closer.

And then there was quiet. The kind that's so precious, you don't want to make a sound. Something this treasured seems so delicate—it must be fragile.

And then the silence broke. But the precious remained.

Mandy looked up at Malachi. "I found Jesus."

Church got noisy.

Malachi discovered Timothy was a good praise dancer—even though it was probably his first try at it. And nobody could out jump Martin.

But Malachi couldn't even move. And he tried hard not to cry. But that didn't work either.

And then over the next several minutes, everyone found a seat at the table. No one took charge. There was no plan set in motion.

Until Malachi said, "Mandy, can you tell us what happened?"

Mandy smiled.

And smiled even more when Timothy said, "Testimony."

"I don't really know what happened," Mandy said. "Well, I know what happened. But I don't know why…exactly. Something happened…inside me. I had this strange desire to go to church. So I went on the first Sunday of the year. I've never done that—in my whole life. Gone to church by myself."

She looked over at Timothy. "I saw you there. But I didn't feel like talking to anyone. I was hoping I could sort of be anonymous."

She looked down at the table for a few moments, staring at its surface before raising her head back up.

"What really touched my heart was the singing. The lead singer—I could sense her inner beauty. Her voice. She sang so amazingly. Her voice was like a heart surgery instrument. I really got into the one song, all of them—but this one, by far the most. My eyes were closed. Her voice was, I guess holy and alluring. I was being drawn in. Her voice almost floated through the room: 'Jesus I love You. I love You. Jesus I love You.' And then, it was weird. I thought I smelled incense—the most fragrant kind you could buy. I looked up. I couldn't help it. I thought to myself, 'I wish I could love Jesus like she does.'"

Everyone drew in on each word Mandy spoke, except for the brief moment when Malachi's and Timothy's eyes met. Timothy's shoulders shrugged just a hint before they both returned their gaze to Mandy.

"I almost left the church, even though I wanted to talk to the lady singer. So I went back in. She was sitting on the side steps that went up to the stage, talking to two teenage girls. So I went up there. And when the girls left, she looked over at me and said, 'Hey, how you doing, girlfriend?'"

Mandy stopped for a couple of seconds and looked directly at Malachi. "It was so cool, Malachi. It was like something you would do."

She returned her attention to the whole group. "I told Clarinda,

I Surrender—Not

that's her name, 'I think I'm going under. I'm not going to make it.' She put her hand on my shoulder, 'You're not going under, Mandy.'"

She looked over again at Malachi. "She told me that God had given her a song. Like you."

Mandy faced the group again. "Clarinda went up on stage and brought a guitar back and said, 'God just gave me this song. It must be for you, girlfriend.' The picture of her singing that song to me is beyond precious. That moment will never leave my mind. The words of that song are forever etched on my heart:

> Jesus in the waves
> And I'm in the boat
>
> The boat's going down
> But I won't step out
>
> Come to Jesus
> He'll hold Your hand
>
> Come to Jesus
> He'll hold Your hand
>
> Jesus in the waves
> And I'm in the boat
>
> The boat's going down
> But I won't step out
>
> Come to Jesus
> He'll hold Your hand
>
> Come to Jesus
> He'll hold Your hand

31. I Fell in Love

The "Praise God's", four acapella rounds of *Awesome God*, and most of the joyous giddiness was over before a knock sounded at the door.

It was Elysia.

"Everyone sure is in a good mood…I mean even more than normal," Elysia said as she approached the table.

"You've never met Mandy. Have you?" Malachi said.

"You're Alex's mom. Aren't you?"

And before Mandy had a chance to respond, Malachi said, "Yeah she is. And she just gave her testimony of how she got saved."

"God is good," Elysia said. "'Thank you, Jesus."

Mandy shared a few highlights with Elysia.

And then, as if he couldn't contain himself, Timothy said,

"Anymore testimonies?"

Martin looked over at JC, who was sitting beside him. Their eyes, a few subtle head motions, and some lip movements were communicating something between them.

And then Martin turned to the group seated at the table. "We do," Martin said. "Kind of that and an announcement."

He looked over at JC. Her smile brightened. "I fell in love with JC pretty much at the same time I fell in love with Jesus. And likewise, JC fell in love with Jesus and me at the same time. We told everyone who came over to our house earlier this year that we were courting. Well now, by the grace of God and all the glory to God, we have decided to get married this April."

Accolades resounded for several minutes.

Timothy was still laughing and talking at the same time when the words spilled out, "Anymore testimonies?"

"Yeah," Elysia said. "I have one."

"All right," Timothy said. "Let's do it."

"When I heard Martin say, 'I fell in love', I knew this was the time to share my testimony," Elysia said. "A short time ago, a man of God took me out—kind of like a date. And I fell in love."

Malachi rubbed the side of his face with his right hand.

"It was one of those special times that changes your life," Elysia said.

She looked around the circle of people seated at the table.

Malachi felt a warmth on his face and the back of his neck, as her eyes moved past him.

"We need a lot more true men of God," Elysia said. "And I need to honor one today."

She looked directly at Malachi. "I bless you, Malachi, for helping me to fall so much deeper in love with Jesus Christ. Your words to me, the way you received my words, and your demonstration of love in action reached into my heart that special evening. Through you, I felt God's love. Thank you for stirring my love for Jesus to a new level."

Malachi peered at her for a couple of moments before he spoke, "I ah…Elysia…thank you for your kind words…again…"

She smiled and then focused on the group gathered. "And I'm going to need the ever-abiding love of our Savior. I'm returning to China. So, I'll be leaving Manistee this Thursday."

"Praise God," Martin said. "The church has its first missionary to support. Let's take up an offering for Elysia. Timothy, can you get something to pass around?"

Timothy went and looked under the bar. "Will this do? This is all I have." He held up a plastic beer pitcher.

"Perfect," Martin said. "Just like all of us. From a vessel of destruction to a vessel for the glory of God."

The pitcher ended up in Malachi's hands. He held it with both hands, looking at Elysia for several seconds. But no words would come out.

And then Carl stood up and began to sing the old hymn:

> Blest be the tie that binds
> Our hearts in Christian love
> The fellowship of kindred minds
> Is like to that above
>
> Before our Father's throne
> We pour our ardent prayers
> Our fears, our hopes, our aims are one
> Our comforts and our cares
>
> Blest be the tie that binds
> Our hearts in Christian love
> The fellowship of kindred minds
> Is like to that above

Jesus at Walmart...fire on the Earth

When we asunder part
It gives us inward pain
But we shall still be joined in heart
And hope to meet again

32. Holy Hands

"Isn't that why we scheduled this Wednesday night meeting? So we can put together a church mission statement, get a steering committee, a leadership team, plan a budget," Malachi said. "Something—before we just start."

"I was simply suggesting we gathered together, the core group and start doing church," Timothy said. "And I know the plan on Sunday was to talk more nuts and bolts. But I'm thinking, Mandy showing up was a little more cool than figuring out what color to paint the walls. Can I get a witness?"

The *Amens* and robust approvals were unanimous.

Martin power punched the air, but apparently, long hours at Menards impeded his jumping ability. But still, it was a noteworthy attempt.

"So, we start doing church," Malachi said. "Just like that? Without going through some level of formality?"

"I'm sure that's what they did back in the first days of the church," Carl said. "People started meeting together. And then it became a church."

"Come on, Carl; this is 2011," Malachi said. "Things are a lot more sophisticated. There's no comparisons."

Carl focused his attention on Malachi. "So, if we're so sophisticated, why is the church in America such a mess? Here's a comparison for you—who's had better results? Unsophisticated, total reliance on the Holy Spirit or reliance on the endless assortment of manmade...I don't know...stuff; which has worked better?"

"God can use both," Malachi said.

"Absolutely," Carl said. "But using and reliance—that's a big spread. They don't mean the same thing at all. Malachi, I've been to the churches with the megatrons and the lattes. I like lattes. A lot. I bless the churches that have all that...all that stuff."

Carl didn't say anything for a few moments. No one did.

And then he started talking again. "It's been a few years ago. It was a sizable church. Lots of nice stuff. Big screens. A good-sized platform with all the goodies. Balcony. Perfect lighting. It wasn't a mega-church, but just a step down. It was at a Wednesday night gathering; in a side room—the pastor was leading a Bible study. Less than a hundred people were there. And I have no idea exactly what triggered it, but the Holy Spirit came down."

Carl looked straight ahead. And drew in a couple of slow breaths. "Things changed. The Holy Spirit came down. There was no Bible study; however, the Bible was happening right before our eyes. Everyone was touched. I can only describe it as a Holy hush, even though there were sounds of tears, people crying out to God. I guess some people call it—the Glory. Two people got saved. People were on their knees. On their faces before God. Words of exhortation went forth. Yet divine order prevailed."

And then Carl looked directly at Malachi again. "After the meeting ended, no one seemed to be in a hurry. The pastor was talking to people. And so was I. And we ended up right beside each other. We stood back to back—but not fully. I heard him talking to someone. And it wasn't like it was a private conversation; actually he was talking to two or three people—that's what it seemed like. He was excited as he declared the awesomeness of what God had done that night. And then I heard him say, and these words will always stick with me; his tone totally shifted, 'After what happened tonight, I wish I could start this church all over again.'"

Carl's eyes corralled the group of men sitting at the table and then he said, "I basically agree with Timothy."

"I feel the same way," Martin said. "And it seems to me that we ah…pretty much by the hand of God have a leadership team—Malachi, Carl, Timothy, JC, and I'm thinking Mandy—I guess. Well maybe."

"JC and Mandy?" Malachi said.

"Well, I'm not sure about Mandy," Martin said. "But why not JC?"

"Because the Bible says so," Malachi said. "And none of the churches I've attended allowed women in leadership."

"It's in the Bible?" Martin said. "Show me. You got a Bible, Timothy? I want to see it for myself."

Timothy walked back into the kitchen, past the bar to the right. He returned quickly with his Bible.

"Here you go, Malachi."

Malachi thumbed the pages back and forth as he looked down at the Bible. And then said, "O.K. here it is. 1 Timothy 3:2-4: 'An overseer, then, must be above reproach, the *husband* of one wife, temperate, prudent, respectable, hospitable, able to teach, not addicted to wine, not violent, not greedy for money, but gentle, peaceable, free from the love of money. He must be one who manages his own household well, keeping his children under control with all dignity.'"

Malachi looked up, directly at Martin. "The husband of one wife—a man. That's a qualification for an overseer, a leader of a church. That's what I've always been taught."

Martin stared at Malachi for several seconds. He furrowed his brow before he spoke, "So that's what you've been taught?"

"Yeah," Malachi said. "It's pretty clear."

"It is?" Martin said.

"Yeah," Malachi said.

"O.K. then," Martin said. He stood up. "Hey, let's go down to Zeke's and get something to eat. I'm buying."

"What are you talking about? We're in the middle of a discussion about this church—about The Table," Malachi said.

"Can I see the Bible?"

Malachi handed it to Martin who then read, "Husband of one wife. Overseer."

And then he placed the Bible on the table. "Malachi, no one here qualifies. Carl doesn't, Timothy doesn't. I don't. You don't."

"Seriously. Seriously, Malachi," Martin pointed directly at Carl with his right index finger, still looking at Malachi. "This man of God, this man of God. God's saying he can't be a church leader. The Bible says, 'husband of one wife.'"

Martin looked at Carl. "Carl, are you the husband of one wife?"

"Calm down a bit, Martin," Carl said. "You know I'm not."

"And I also know that you chose to remain single, so you could serve God more fully," Martin said.

"What do you think, Carl?" Timothy said.

"Do I have to answer?" Carl said. "This question is one of

those classic church-splitters."

He looked around the room and then focused on the group. "I'm sorry to say this, Malachi, but I totally, well, more like fervently disagree with you. So many reasons; there are so many. That Bible verse is mainly addressing the character of the person. We all know it's easier to determine if a person is a husband of one wife. But when you start prying into a person's character qualities—well, much of the present church culture today calls that off-limits. So it's avoided. They circumvent the character issue and go for the easy."

Carl turned toward Malachi. "You know, Malachi, if I suggested to you that every time the Bible referred to the male gender it strictly meant men, you would disagree with me."

"Martin, can you hand me the Bible?" Carl said.

In just a few moments, Carl found his place and began to read, "I desire therefore that the men everywhere pray, lifting up holy hands, without wrath and dissension. Likewise, I want women to adorn themselves with proper clothing, modestly and discreetly, not with braided hair and gold or pearls or costly garments."

He set the Bible on the table. "So if I was going to make a doctrine based on gender reference: Men pray with holy hands lifted. Says only men. No women allowed. Now the women dress modestly and discreetly. And since it only says women, men can dress any way they want."

Carl beaded in on Malachi. "So what do you think?"

"Ouch," Malachi said. "You're bending me. But don't break me."

Malachi stood up. He extended his hand to Martin. "I misspoke. I should have said, 'Your beautiful fiancé—inside and out, is needed to help guide this church. I look forward to being blessed by her wisdom.'"

They shook hands. And then Martin scooted around the table and hugged Malachi.

"So what about Mandy?" Timothy said.

"Let's just go for it," Malachi said. "I'm thinking she'll have some insights none of us have. And we're still so informal, if something doesn't work, and we know that's going to happen—we'll fix it. By the grace of God."

Timothy laughed. "Malachi, you've been converted in only an hour."

"What do you mean?"

"When we started, you were all about structure," Timothy said. "Now, you're—Hey, let's do church."

"You're right," Malachi said. He lowered his head for a couple of seconds. And then it was as if he was speaking to himself—that intermingling point between barely audible and being just a thought. "How did that happen?"

33. Fire Drill

Timothy returned from the kitchen hugging eight bottles of Camp Eden Spring water and carefully lowered them onto the table.

"What are you doing?" Martin said. "There are only four of us here."

"Rollie paid me another visit," Timothy said. "He was so hot when he saw the banner; I mean, the I-surrender-not flag. Really hot. I was afraid if he touched anything combustible, he might set the city on fire."

Timothy passed out two bottles of water to each of the men at the table.

And then he said, "I know our last conversation raised the temperature in here. And I'm thinking this round might jack it up even a few more notches. So we each have one bottle to drink and one to pour on any hot spots that might flare up."

"And if that doesn't work, you need to remember," Martin said, "stop, drop, and roll."

Everyone laughed.

Except Carl.

"Carl, it's a fire prevention thing you learn in elementary school," Malachi said. "A fire drill."

"Oh. Before my time," Carl said.

"Well, back to business," Timothy said.

Malachi started rubbing above his right eye with his right hand. His face became warm on his right side. Between his ear and eye—above his cheekbone.

"He was yelling. Full volume," Timothy said. "He told me to take the banner down. Plus, he added a few non-family-friendly descriptives. For the banner and for me."

Malachi continued to rub above his eye.

"Only by the power of the Holy Spirit was I able to stay unruffled," Timothy said. "My adrenalin was kicking in, but I softly said to him, 'We're not ready to make that decision. Thanks for the suggestion, Rollie.'"

Malachi was still rubbing his eye when he said to himself, "Like Sal."

He thought he had said it to himself. But then Timothy said, "Did you say something, Malachi?"

'What ah…yeah," Malachi said.

"Have you been listening?" Timothy said.

"Ah yeah…I mean no," Malachi said. "No I haven't. I mean some."

"What do you mean?"

Malachi looked down at the table for a couple of seconds. He was rubbing his hands together as he looked up. "I know what to do."

"You haven't been paying attention and now you say you know what to do?" Timothy said.

"Are you alright?" Martin said. "I know work's been brutal.

Fire Drill

Maybe we should have waited for the weekend to meet."

"I know what to do," Malachi said.

"How could you?" Timothy said. "I haven't even finished yet."

"He threatened to start circulating a petition to get us to leave," Malachi said.

"Yeah," Timothy said. He stared at Malachi for a few moments. "Well, anybody could guess that. Isn't that what always happens in situations like this?"

"I know what to do," Malachi said.

"So just tell us," Martin said.

"I can't," Malachi said.

"You know what to do, but you won't tell us," Timothy said. "I'm going to dump this water on you."

"He knows what to do," Carl said.

Martin and Timothy looked at Carl.

Malachi didn't say anything and then he spoke. "Martin, have you ever written a song, it was pretty much finished, could sing it to yourself, but just weren't quite ready to bring it out for everyone to hear? You needed a little tweaking, so you weren't ready for its public debut."

"Well yeah. Of course."

"Timothy, do you know what to do?" Malachi said.

"Besides calling my attorney," Timothy said.

"Probably not a good idea," Carl said. "So if Malachi says he knows what to do, let's get behind his idea. No one else has one. If he needs to tweak something before he's ready to share it, let's trust him. And if his plan, or anything we try here at The Table, doesn't work out, let's do what it says in Hebrews 10:24: 'Let's see how inventive we can be in encouraging love and helping out.' What do you think, men?"

"I'm in," Martin said.

"I've got your back, Malachi," Timothy said.

"Now there is one detail to work out," Malachi said. "I'm not ah...I'm not sure..."

"I know what to do," Carl said. "The Table fire drill."

"Fire Drill?"

"Stop, drop—to your knees, pray. Fire drill," Carl said.

He went to his knees right beside his chair. He bowed his head, nearly touching the table. Within moments, everyone was kneeling.

Then Carl began, "Dear Father, we believe what Your Word says, 'Commit to the Lord whatever you do and your plans will succeed,' We commit all our plans for The Table to You Lord—is that right, men?"

"Amen."

"Yes, Lord."

"We surrender—to You."

34. Out on The Table

"I don't like missing work," Malachi said. "But Dale had told me before I started that he would be flexible—to a degree if, on occasion, I needed time off for ministry. Still when I called him, after the meeting last night, his, 'Well sure,' didn't sound like *well* or *sure*. But it was late. And I know he's under the gun. So, I need to get over to Cadillac as soon as I can."

"Have a seat," Timothy said. "Coffee? Water?"

"Yeah. Coffee. We do need to discuss a few things before we launch," Malachi said. "You said you talked to Rollie. And he's expecting us. What time?"

'I'm not sure if it fully qualifies as talking,' Timothy said. "But we did communicate and settled on 10:15."

As Timothy walked toward the kitchen, Malachi glanced

at his watch—8:41.

"Hey, Malachi," Timothy called from the doorway of the kitchen. "Come back here. I want to show you something."

Malachi followed Timothy back to his office. A walled-off corner of the kitchen—small, the size of a large walk-in closet. Crammed toward the back corner was a miniature dark-oak desk—imitation oak—a poor imitation.

The flat screen of his computer cast a glow in that quadrant of the room.

"Look at this, Malachi. What do you think?" Timothy said. "I placed another order with Vistaprint."

"So is this one a flag or a banner?" Malachi said.

"This one's a banner," Timothy said. "This one's a declaration."

Laid out vertically on a yellow background—the same yellow as Timothy's other Vistaprint creation. Set in from the edges was a frame—formed by sizeable green dots. The wording inside the frame was in a chunky, stately font, a font that would be perfect for a modern rendition of the Ten Commandments. The letters were big enough, bold enough so that about half the lines contained only one word. The message was unmistakable: "Commit to the Lord whatever you do and your plans will succeed."

Malachi smiled. "It sure is. That's definitely a declaration."

"You like it?"

"You have a gift, my friend," Malachi said. "So, does that one go inside or outside?"

"I ordered two."

They walked back into the *main sanctuary* and sat at the table.

"O.K. defog me, brother," Timothy said and then took a sip of his Camp Eden Spring.

Malachi looked at his watch again.

"We've got time," Timothy said. "I told Rollie it might be

as late as 10:30 or so."

Malachi pursed his lips. His eyes were on Timothy. He rubbed his hands together under the table.

"O.K. Let's see," Malachi said.

He shifted his eyes a little to the left and upward. Timothy was sitting to his right with his back to the bar.

Malachi then looked directly at Timothy. "Here's the deal," Malachi said. "I rarely talk to anybody about what I'm going to share with you. O.K."

"Yeah. O.K."

"God shows me things. I see things. I've never been able to figure it out. And it may seem really cool to some people. It's not. Not at all. But I'm not going into all of that. I guess I'll just say it—I have visions."

"Visions," Timothy said. "You mean like I read about in Acts: 'And it shall be in the last days, says God, I will pour out My Spirit upon all flesh. And your sons and your daughters shall prophesy, and your young men shall see visions, and your old men shall dream dreams.'"

"Yeah," Malachi said. "I guess."

"So what are these visions like?"

"Remember this doesn't happen very often. Close to zero sometimes. But it's happened a few times recently. And I never know when," Malachi said. "They're kind of like a movie in my head. Like I'm watching it. And God gives me a message."

"O.K."

"But here's the hard part—well two things," Malachi said. "I only see enough to know what I think God wants me to do. The step of faith set before me. I don't see the results ahead of time. I can't control what a person will do, and God won't control what a person does; He gives everyone their own free choice. And the vision I had last night, while you were talking, has a piece missing. I guess that's how I would describe it. That's why I was hesitant to tell everyone. I was thinking I would get the rest, the last piece from God, before now. But I didn't. And I did meet with Carl over at Walmart for a few minutes before I came by here. That wasn't the answer either. At least I don't think so. Still I feel certain, something inside, a peace, is telling me to move forward."

"Wow," Timothy said. "Ah O.K....ah...I'm still not seeing the light."

"Here's the deal. Here's what I saw. And what I know because of what I saw," Malachi said. "Rollie is desperately hurting for money. I'm talking serious stuff. He's ah...ah...it's awful what I saw."

He hesitated for a few moments before proceeding.

"This is another reason these visions aren't that pleasant," Malachi said. "Rollie's on a razor thin edge, emotionally. His financial destruction is to the point of utter desperation. My heart is heavy. His burden has become my burden. A part of me has entered into his misery. I..."

Malachi stood up. And turned away from Timothy. Tilting his head upward, he breathed in deeply—twice, before he shifted his focus back to Timothy

"It's so weird; it's like a pastor being happy because he gets paid to do a funeral for someone he loves. I'm happy, I'm joyous because I see God has made a way for The Table to stay downtown, but I feel this burden for Rollie. We're going to help him, but he still might not survive."

"So how are we going to help him?" Timothy said. "How's this all going to work?"

"He's so desperate; we're going to go down there and buy him off. I know you said he pretty much runs downtown. Like—what Rollie says goes."

"He's the king. All the merchants bow to him," Timothy said. "But you're saying he's that desperate?"

Malachi nodded his head up and down slowly. "Pushing bullets into empty chambers desperate."

"Oh," Timothy said. He turned, staring out toward the street for several seconds.

And then slowly back toward Malachi. "O.K. I see," Timothy said. "And I think I see something else. You're missing piece to this puzzle—it's the cash. Isn't it?"

"Yep. It sure is—seer of the puzzle."

"That one was as difficult as fitting in a corner piece. Probably easier than that," Timothy said.

They sat there in silence.

Then Timothy said, "How much, my friend?"

"This is going to sound stupid. Rollie's at rock bottom low—ten thousand dollars will buy off his hopeless soul. Here's the..."

Malachi looked down for a couple of seconds and then raised his head back to eye level. "The burden inside is too unbearable to merely buy him off, though."

Malachi leaned back in his chair. His body trembled. Not enough for Timothy to notice.

Malachi had to swallow before he spoke, "I've been to the edge."

Their eyes fixed on each other for several seconds.

"Yeah...I've been there too," Timothy said. He gazed upward as he said, "Only by the grace of God."

The next moments passed in silence.

And then his eyes returned to Malachi. His first word came out like an exhaling of air, "Yeah."

"Yeah," Timothy said. "Only by the grace of God."

Timothy smiled a little. "What are you thinking? Twenty thousand?"

"That would be nice," Malachi said.

"We would spend more than that for an attorney," Timothy said.

"We don't have money for that either," Malachi said.

"I'll get the money," Timothy said.

Jesus at Walmart...fire on the Earth

"This is serious stuff, Timothy," Malachi said. "No joking around."

"Malachi, I'll get the twenty thousand dollars," Timothy said. "I mean it. I'm serious."

"O.K. help me out here," Malachi said. "Not too many weeks ago, you told me you were selling off everything you own. And you told me that was so you could hopefully break-even—get out of debt. It was like you were throwing all the cargo over the edge of the boat just to stay afloat. You're driving a two thousand dollar beater and living here...Oh. O.K., I know. Your house sold. Right?"

"No," Timothy said. "And when it does, I won't even break even on that deal."

"But you've got twenty thousand dollars tucked away."

"No, not now."

"You're going to borrow it."

Timothy laughed. Kind of like a grunt, "No. My credit is so screwed up with the banks and everyone I know."

"You seemed pretty boxed in here, my friend," Malachi said. "An impending inheritance? That's it."

"No."

Malachi leaned back in his chair, folded his arms, and stared at Timothy. He didn't say anything for a few moments. And then shook his head back and forth.

"What?" Timothy said.

"Man, you've got to be careful what you watch on T.V.," Malachi said. "A lot of those preachers are scammers. So how much seed money did you send in for your expected harvest?"

"Seriously," Timothy said. "It takes a...come on. That's just sad. That stuff's garbage."

Timothy took a long drink from his bottled water. Set it on the table and cradled it with both hands and then said, "I think I have about two thousand dollars in the back. More or less. I'll go on a work trip blitz. I'll bear down hard for a week or two. Maybe three. I should be able to have it by then. If I really bust it."

Now Malachi was really staring at Timothy. Intensely. "So you can make eighteen thousand in like two, three weeks. That's thousands a week. So if you made that much every week for a year, let's see—that's like almost half a million dollars. Right?"

"I never thought of it that way," Timothy said. "But it doesn't really work that way anyways."

"Let's just lay all the cards on the table, Timothy," Malachi said. "You need to tell me how you're going to get this money. No mumble jumbo. Put the cards on the table. Right now—on the table."

"God told you," Timothy said. "Was it one of those visions?"

"Visions?"

"Is that how you knew?" Timothy said. "And you're acting the way Nathan the prophet did to David. Aren't you?"

"That's how I knew...what...?" Malachi said.

"You knew that I was earning money playing Black Jack," Timothy said.

"What!" Malachi said.

He stared at Timothy for several seconds. Before speaking. And then he said, "Now I get it. Mt. Pleasant, Wayland, Battle Creek, New Buffalo, Michigan City—casino towns."

"So God didn't show you?" Timothy said.

"Well no," Malachi said. "But maybe in a different way."

Timothy shifted his focus to the riverside wall. And then after several moments, he looked back at Malachi and said, "You know what; it's just good to get it out on the table."

"I'm ah..." Malachi said. "O.K. my friend, do you have a confession or do you have a testimony?"

"Well, that's actually how it started," Timothy said. "I was talking to a buddy, Wierick—the guy that made the cross, a week or so after everything happened. Telling him how my life has changed—my testimony. As part of my sharing with him, because I knew he could relate to it, I told him how my brain was getting healed and my nearly-photographic memory was returning."

Timothy stopped and took a sip of his Camp Eden Spring. "Wierick really started listening intently. His facial expression changed. I was thinking, 'God's touching him.' His head started nodding up and down. And when I stopped talking, Wierick blurted out, 'You'd be killer at Black Jack.'"

"So the prophet Wierick spoke, and now you're a gambler," Malachi said.

"I'm not a gambler. Not at all. I'm a businessman. I have a mandate: From Proverbs 13:22, 'The wealth of the sinner is stored up for the righteous.' I'm just going and getting it. I'm taking back what the devil has stolen. I'm extracting the precious from the vile—that's from Jeremiah 15:19."

"So how's this ah...this business work?" Malachi said.

"I've always had kind of a knack for Black Jack. But back then, like most gamblers who have winnings, you keep playing until you lose it all back. But now I'm using the brain God gave me and with self-control—a fruit of the Spirit and Kingdom of God motivated business practices. It's all changed. So this is what I do..."

For the actual card playing, Timothy based everything on statistics—the odds. He had memorized charts to the degree that he could be watching the cards played and exact numbers, reflecting the play, would display in his brain.

For example—he would analyze the array of cards at the table and those already played. And then as he looked down at his own cards, he would instantly recall the odds chart in his brain—bam, forty-three percent chance if I take the next card I'll go bust. Chart two pops up in his head. Personal statistic—subject to change over time, updated daily. This reflects his track record in this type of a situation. Like a flash card in his brain: sixty-four percent of the time, for him, considering the cards played, he did better when he took the next one. Flash card three in his brain—the co-efficient. Forty-three is index with the sixty-four. Pop—into his brain a number between one and fifteen appears. High is *yes*. Low is *no*. In between is gut.

"It's simple, at least for me," Timothy said. "It's like five quick snaps of the finger in my brain: cards, odds chart, personal history chart, co-efficient, decision."

Timothy snapped his finger. One, two, three, four, five. "Cards, odds chart, personal history chart, co-efficient, decision."

"Just like that," Malachi said.

"It's a business. One that God gave me the brain for. And there are peripherals to the main focus. I'm new at it. But this is what I've done so far…"

Timothy was developing a circuit of casinos where he would do his work. He knew that casinos were continually on the lookout for people like him. What he was doing fell under the general umbrella of what is called card counting. Timothy didn't see it that way—"I'm just using the brain God gave me."

While card counting is not illegal, a casino has the right to ask any player to leave. They do it all the time. So Timothy was keeping a book on the different casinos he was visiting—mainly trying to figure out how much money he could extract without being suspect.

And to thwart any detection, he always used cash. Additionally, he had four different looks, essentially disguises—the gray-pony-tailed, old-hippy look— wearing a baseball cap; the all black look—squared shirt tails, thick rimmed glasses in black; the cowboy look—boots, hat, fake mustache; and the casual look—Hawaiian shirt, sunglasses, Dockers.

He was also focusing on keeping his overhead low. His

thirty-four mile per gallon Zipper served well as economical transportation. And often he slept in it—calling it, "Camping." The rear seat folded nearly flat, so sleeping overnight was comfortable. And in the passenger-side front seat, Timothy had set up an on-the-road office."

"It's a business, Malachi," Timothy said. "Plain and simple. A business."

"So if it's just a business, why were you being so secretive?" Malachi said.

"You know why."

Neither one spoke. They were both focusing differently. Malachi off to his left. His right hand rubbing his cheek. Timothy was looking down at his Camp Eden Spring on the table in front of him.

Malachi turned facing Timothy, "You hiring?"

He laughed.

Malachi tilted his head back and stared at the ceiling. Shaking his head back and forth. And then he peered at Timothy. "This is so beyond insane. So beyond idiotic. God could take our enemy out with his own bullet. No. Instead He pokes the heart of two guys the enemy hates the most. And the one guy's hobby is to antagonize the enemy as much as he can with oversized, flapping in the wind banners. And then, because of a usually-drunk prophet named Wierick, he decides Black Jack is the best way to help God get some of His cows on a thousand hills to downtown Manistee. Because he needs an impossible amount of cash to save the enemy's life—even though things would seem to work out better if he was gone. So the seems-like-gambling money, but it's not really gambling, would be used to rescue the enemy. Now it gets even crazier. Because guy number two, who thinks he's a pastor, is almost convinced this is a good idea. Even though he should know better."

And then he looked directly a Timothy. "Is this beyond

insane? Totally nuts? So far beyond any rational thinking?"

Timothy cocked his head a bit, and his right hand brushed his hair on the side of his head. From front to back. "Do you know what I'm thinking?"

Malachi shook his head. "I do."

They looked at each other. Like looking in a mirror.

Malachi stood up. So did Timothy. They embraced.

They stepped away. Facing each other.

It was only a few decibels above a whisper, "Yeah...Jesus on The Cross...that was insane."

"So beyond any kind of rational thinking."

"Yeah."

"O.K. then, let's go see Rollie."

"Let's go."

35. War is Over. If You Want It

"**I** have the money," Timothy said. "Cash. Two thousand dollars. You know what a friend once told me?"

"What's that?"

"Cash has no enemies."

"I'll receive that," Malachi said.

Their eyes needed a few moments to adjust to the brightness when they stepped outside. The sky was a brilliant blue. The blue that always seems a hue darker near Lake Michigan, as if it had been tweaked by photo editing software.

Cold. Yet the stillness of the day seemed to hold back the icy chill that often penetrates downtown Manistee this time of year. With the big lake being only four blocks away, it was like the mouth of River Street inhaled the west winds off the lake. While the opposing flanks of the downtown buildings created a near-flawless wind tunnel.

"It's not too bad out here," Timothy said. "You don't mind walking, do you?"

"No. Not at all," Malachi said. "You know, I never come downtown. Except for DT's. Well now, The Table."

"That's the problem with downtown," Timothy said. "With all the shopping and restaurants out on the highway, people avoid downtown. It's a fight to get people down here."

They crossed the street. Making their way on the south sidewalk, they passed Larry's Books and Vintage Mart. The next three buildings were vacant.

And then Timothy said, "Right here—before this business was A Place in Thyme—this is where some people tried to start a church. The one Rollie said he ran off."

Walking by the eclectic blend of stores captivated Malachi's attention. He sensed a creative vibe that he realized could only be experienced at street level. One store past The Purple Polka Dot Petunia, Malachi slowed down and then stopped.

"Thou Art," Malachi said. "What's this place, Timothy?"

"That one?" Timothy said. "I'm trying to remember. This one was open so briefly, it was like they took down the *Opening Soon* sign and turned it around to read, *Going Out of Business Sale*. Let's see? They sold Christian artwork stuff. Leaning toward, well the only thing I remember was one of those fuzzy-textured pictures—the Elvis- type. They had a Jesus one in the window. And maybe one depicting the Last Supper or something. Not actually art. That's probably why—thou art gone."

Malachi laughed.

"That's another problem in downtown Manistee. So many businesses come and go—all the time," Timothy said. "In a way though, it's kind of cool, because not all of them fail. But many of the ones that succeed move out to the highway. So the cheaper downtown rents are utilized as a springboard for savvy entrepreneurs to get their start. But then they're gone. Another empty building."

Then Timothy stopped so suddenly that Malachi practically went into a faltering skid.

"Beth's Bakery," Timothy said. "I'm going in here, but you can't. You're not allowed."

"It's a bakery. I love bakeries," Malachi said. "I bet they have coffee too. So why can't I go in?"

"Amazing coffee. The best," Timothy said. "But the Bible tells us not to be a stumbling block to our brothers. This place is addictive. I'll probably need to start a Beth's Bakery Anonymous group down at The Table to help get the captives free."

Malachi darted for the door.

Timothy hollered, "Am I my brother's keeper?"

"I'm just looking," Malachi said as Timothy stepped next to him.

And then Malachi said, "Hey let's get Rollie one of those Dutch apple pies."

"Yeah. That's a great idea," Timothy said. "You know what they say?"

"What's that?"

"Dutch apple pies have no enemies," Timothy said. "Especially the ones from Beth's."

After they went back outside, the banter subsided. More so when Timothy pointed with his left index finger, "It's that reddish-pink one with the blue awning."

It was a much larger building than Timothy's. A two story also. But to Malachi, it appeared to be taller. It was two storefronts combined into one building. Each storefront was nearly as large as Timothy's three combined. While the buildings face was not the original brick, it still projected a historic ambience. Even though the paint and all the exterior accoutrements were fresh looking.

"This is where we enter; Rollie's office is upstairs," Timothy said.

Between the two storefronts, flanked by sizeable win-dowscapes, was a standard smooth-faced door—painted in a blue tone to match the awning.

"Rollie owns this building?" Malachi said.

"Yep, this is one of his."

"They're both empty?"

"Yeah," Timothy said. "So do you know what you're going to say?"

"*Yes* and *no*," Malachi said. "Probably more no. I have this tendency to script everything out in my mind ahead of time. And then the script never runs out as planned. So then I weird out."

They stood there. Some silence passed. Looking at the door more than each other.

"Save a life. Save a church. Cash has no enemies," Malachi said. "And beyond that, I keep wrenching my mind back to the words of Jesus, 'When they bring you before authorities, do not worry about how or what you are to speak in your defense, or what you are to say. For the Holy Spirit will teach you in that very hour what you ought to say.'"

"Well, let's go then," Timothy said.

"First," Malachi said. "Fire drill."

"Right here?"

"Yep. Right here," Malachi said. "Stop. Drop. Pray."

Malachi pondered a few moments as he prepared to pray.

And then he heard Timothy, "Malachi, have you ever read any from the Message Bible?"

"Yeah ah…" Malachi said. "I'm…ah getting ready to pray. We can discuss versions of the Bible at another time. O.K. So let's see ah…"

"No, that's not what I'm talking about," Timothy said.

"Timothy, let me pray," Malachi said. "O.K."

"Can I pray. I read something this morning. It seems

fitting," Timothy said. "I think it's all still in my brain."

"Well yeah, go for it."

"1 Corinthians 13," Timothy said:

> "If I speak with human eloquence and angelic ecstasy but don't love, I'm nothing but the creaking of a rusty gate.
>
> If I speak God's Word with power, revealing all his mysteries and making everything plain as day and if I have faith that says to a mountain, Jump, and it jumps, but I don't love, I'm nothing.
>
> If I give everything I own to the poor and even go to the stake to be burned as a martyr, but I don't love, I've gotten nowhere.
>
> So, no matter what I say, what I believe and what I do, I'm bankrupt without love.
>
> Love never gives up.
>
> Love cares more for others than for self.
>
> Love doesn't want what it doesn't have.
>
> Love doesn't strut.
>
> Doesn't have a swelled head. Doesn't force itself on others. Isn't always, me first. Doesn't fly off the handle. Doesn't keep score of the sins of others. Doesn't revel when others grovel.
>
> Takes pleasure in the flowering of truth. Puts up with anything. Trusts God always. Always looks for the best. Never looks back. But keeps going to the end.
>
> Love never dies. Inspired speech will be over some day; praying in tongues will end; understanding will reach its limit.
>
> We know only a portion of the truth… we don't yet see things clearly. We're squinting in a fog, peering through a mist.
>
> But it won't be long before the weather clears and the sun shines bright! We'll see it all then, see it all as

clearly as God sees us, knowing Him directly just as He knows us!

But for right now, until that completeness, we have three things to do to lead us toward that consummation: Trust steadily in God, hope unswervingly, love extravagantly.

And the best of the three is love."

"And so God, we pray, only by Your strength, help us to have that kind of love for Rollie. Amen."

And then Malachi prayed, "God, only you can change a heart. We ask that You change three hearts today. Father God, start with ours."

"Amen."

They were up off their knees. Up the stairs. And Timothy knocked on the door.

When it opened, Timothy said, "Good morning, Rollie. We brought you a pie."

"Some leftover rejects from your church potluck?" Rollie said. "It must be awful. I thought church folks would scarf down anything sweet. Must have maggots on it or something."

"No, it's fresh from Beth's Bakery," Timothy said.

"From that overpriced, Health Department nightmare," Rollie said. "I'm not eating any of her tainted garbage."

Malachi and Timothy glanced at each other as they stood in the doorway leading to Rollie's office. Timothy was holding the pie. But he had lowered the carrying bag to thigh level.

Malachi could see into Rollie's office. Mainly appointed in darker-toned woods. Appearing to be an upper grade of quality—as did the desk and shelving.

Heaps and piles of paperwork, books, and booklets, as well as periodicals and the normal outfittings of an office, covered all horizontal surfaces, including the windowsills. While the amount of stuff was immense, it appeared to be a somewhat orderly overtaking of the space.

"So what exactly do you want to talk about, Timothy?" Rollie said.

"You've met my friend?" Timothy said.

"Sure," Rollie said. "Have you taken that banner down like I told you?"

"That's kind of one of the areas we wanted to talk about," Timothy said.

"O.K. Talk," Rollie said. He looked at his watch. "You have five minutes."

Malachi looked at the three chairs across from Rollie's desk. Over to the right, past Rollie, behind his back.

Malachi and Timothy eyed each other again.

And then Malachi said, "War is over. If you want it."

Rollie's eyes flashed at Malachi. "Don't disgrace the name of John Lennon. You hear me."

"We've come to bring a peace offering," Malachi said. "We want to offer you twenty thousand dollars. We want to help you with your financial struggles—get you back from the edge. And we're asking in exchange that you'll allow us to bless the downtown by permitting us to gather as a stable, positive, caring, community of people, who will economically benefit downtown and support the endeavors of our neighbors. We're asking for your endorsement of our church—The Table."

Malachi smiled at Rollie.

As they looked directly at each other, Malachi could visualize Rollie tipping back shot glasses filled with the clear god of lying hope. His eyes. His nose. Skin texture. Rollie appeared to be a regular worshipper. Possibly ardent.

"You're a weasel," Rollie said. "Get out of here. Now!"

Timothy turned and started to walk away.

Every muscle in Malachi's face tensed. His shoulders squared.

By now, Timothy was halfway down the steps.

Still at attention, squarely facing Rollie, Malachi reached under his coat with his left hand. And revealed a white envelope—the common size. It was sealed. He transferred it to his right hand and held it out to Rollie.

Malachi spoke slowly, "Rollie, I'm backing down. But this letter won't—every bit of it will happen. And unfortunately, today we shake the dust off our feet; your life is in your own hands. My heart is broken for you."

Rollie ripped the envelope out of Malachi's hand, spitting out the words, "You're such a weasel. Get out of here!"

Malachi didn't flinch, but pointed to the envelope. "Truer than front page headlines." He shook his head up and down.

And then turned. Unhurried, he began the seventeen-step descent to street level.

Three steps from the bottom, he heard, "Hey wait. What was your name again?"

36. A Yard Barn Yes

"**D**ale, I brought you an apple pie—Dutch apple. For you and Aunt Betty," Malachi said.

"Thanks," Dale said. He opened the bag and peered inside. "Oh yeah. Beth's Bakery. Her baked goods are addictive. Thank you so much."

"I really appreciate the time off to take care of a little church business," Malachi said.

"Well sure," Dale said. "But now, back to Menards' business."

Dale started walking toward the Skytrack with Malachi at his side. "Now, I won't be here tomorrow. Like usual on Saturdays. And we're switching gears a little. Evonda needs a couple of men to assemble yard barns inside. So after you check in with Wilks, go find Evonda and do whatever she needs you to do. You and Martin."

"You got it," Malachi said.

When Dale said "Evonda," Malachi thought to himself, "Maybe I'll get a chance to ask her about the cross she wears."

Malachi had noticed, every time he saw Evonda, she was wearing that same cross.

And there it was on Saturday morning. Around her neck. Malachi had to wait his turn. Command central was hectic at a little after 7:00 in the morning.

Not a place for chitchat. Malachi and Martin were queued up in a chubby line, almost like a moving mob heading toward Evonda.

Cell phones pressed to the ear, blueprints shoved into the armpit, coffee in Styrofoam containers—the tallest available—with lids, and that hollowed-eyes fatigue-look that is the price paid for twelve hour days—or more, seven days a week; this was the badge many of the hardcore commercial construction workers wore. The ones vying for Evonda's attention.

And while everyone was anxious to get to the real task—building a Menards, Malachi observed an unspoken code of respect and camaraderie. No one was maneuvering to one-up a co-worker in the defectively defined waiting line.

"I think you're next, buddy," someone said.

Malachi barely got the words out of his mouth, "We work for Dale Marble Construction," before Evonda had rattled off all the instructions he and Martin needed. North East corner of the building. Next to the paint booth. You're building yard barns. See Chad—he's expecting you.

"You guys know how to build these?" Chad asked after brief introductions.

'Yeah," Malachi said. "I'm sure we can figure it out."

A Yard Barn Yes

"O.K. you two can work on this gambrel model. I'll do the gable one," Chad said.

And then he offered to share his tools. The seasoned traveling construction worker had a sizeable collection of cordless tools housed in a red metal box on casters. More like a mobile workbench with hinged doors on one side.

Dale had even more tools, a lot more. And Malachi had spotted a two-wheeled cart in the job trailer. So he opted to send Martin out to get what they needed while he studied the blueprint Chad had given him.

It wasn't really a blueprint. It was a set of instructions. The same ones anyone who purchased an *E-Z Build G-12X8* would receive as part of the package.

The package, in theory, contained every piece needed to construct a 12' x 8' yard barn with a gambrel style roof—the traditional barn-style. Wood, sheathing, gray vinyl siding, black shingles, hardware for the double hinged door. Everything—but nothing extra. Nothing.

"Hold it. Let's just stop," Malachi said a couple of hours after he and Martin had commenced the actual building process.

"What do you mean stop? We're not getting anything done. I mean seriously…it's almost lunchtime," Martin said. "Let me look at those plans."

"Hey, these Easy Build instructions are messed up," Malachi said.

"Maybe it's not the instructions that are messed up," Martin said.

Malachi glared at Martin. "O.K. you figure them out." He flung them at Martin. "You be the boss. And by the way, we are getting something done. We're just not going Martin-speed. Some things take longer than expected…O.K."

Chad looked over at them. Their voices were well above conversational levels. But then he slipped around the corner of the building he was erecting. Out of sight—without saying a word.

When Malachi turned his back on Martin, he saw Evonda heading toward their work area.

She had a cell phone pressed to her ear. It was like she was marching. Her brown curled hair, which fell over both sides of her shoulders, bobbed in rhythm.

"Incoming," Malachi said at a level only Martin could hear.

Martin looked up and then returned his concentration to deciphering the Easy Build instructions.

Malachi grabbed a cordless screw gun and started borings screws into the floor decking, adding a few more than necessary.

"So how are the green hats doing today?" Evonda said.

None of the other workers wore hardhats. At least none that Malachi had spotted. So the Dale Marble Construction crew had been nicknamed The Green Hats by the other workers.

Malachi stood up, facing Evonda.

He glanced over at Martin and back to Evonda. "Well, you're the boss, so how you're doing is more important. So how are you doing?"

"I'm doing pretty well. Thanks for asking. Do you need anything?" Evonda said.

"I do," Chad said. He had snuck back from around the corner. "These E-Z Build Gable instructions are screwed up. It's impossible to do it the way they're showing."

"Give me a sec," Evonda said as she looked at Malachi. "Do you have any questions?"

"Ah...yeah," Malachi said. "This may sound stupid, but does that cross you're wearing mean anything special to you?"

"Well yes," Evonda said. She smiled, "Yes, it does. It sure

does."

"Evonda," someone yelled from behind her.

It was the painter. He had stepped out of the makeshift paint booth in the adjacent corner of the building.

She turned around. And then the painter continued in a loud voice, "If I don't get a different tip for this sprayer, I'm never going to keep up. Come over here; let me show you the type I need. And I need it right away."

She yelled back to him, "O.K. I'll be right over."

"You need to decide what to do on these screwed up plans," Chad said with an edge of intensity.

"I'll be right back, Chad," Evonda said. "Let me see what the painter needs first."

She spun toward the paint booth and sped off.

"Well, you got your answer," Martin said. "You told me you wanted to ask Evonda that question."

"But now I have another question," Malachi said.

"How screwed up is this plan we're using?" Martin said.

"No. But I am hoping you can figure that out. I already knew that. So that's not the question," Malachi said.

"Oh, I know what it is," Martin said. "Who's buying lunch?"

"No, I know that answer too," Malachi said. "You're buying lunch."

Martin laughed. "Malachi, you're an easy read. The story is always the same. The question you always want to ask people—it's always the same. You just figure out different ways to ask it. Man, I love that about you."

Malachi smiled

And then Malachi yelled, "Hey Chad, you want to go to lunch with us? Martin's buying."

He poked his head around the corner. "Sure. Free food. I'm in."

They all removed their tool belts. Malachi and Martin

took off their hardhats, and then they all headed toward the garden center's main door. Their exit to the outside.

They walked three abreast.

Malachi was in the middle: "So Chad, do you go to church anyplace when you're back home in Iowa?"

37. Jesus at Menards

It was a little over an hour after they had returned from lunch when Malachi heard someone say, "How you guys doing?"

It was Wilks. The tallest of the Green Hats. And with the three-inches of height the hardhat added to his frame, he looked like a giant. Wilks had the swagger and body type of the archetypical rugged carpenter. Tall, square shouldered, that weathered look—accentuated by a well-worn leather pouch around his waist—complete with what appeared to Malachi to be the heftiest Estwing framing hammer on the market.

And he looked especially towering, because Malachi was on his knees nailing the first course of vinyl siding onto the yard barn.

As Malachi stood up, he said, "It's going good. We're in a groove, now that we've figured out the plans. It's going great."

"I just got a call from Dale," Wilks said. "He said we need to work ten today. And a full day tomorrow too. Plus... well...I'll let Dale talk to you about next week."

"What?" Malachi said. "I mean, I'm O.K. with today. But tomorrow?"

"I know," Wilks said. "Dale said Evonda called him and said everybody needs to step it up for the final run to the finish. Not making the deadline—to the day—isn't an option with her. She told him, there are only two options—you're either with me or you're against me."

"Ouch," Malachi said. "Working Sunday?"

He looked over at Martin.

"What do you think, Martin?" Malachi said. "Working on Sunday?"

Before he could answer, Wilks said, "Remember when Dale prayed—our first morning here? He prayed that we could be a blessing to Menards, to Evonda, and to our co-workers here. That's what I remember. I mean...I'm not much at praying. And I'm not much of a Bible guy, but there must be something in the Good Book. I don't know...maybe it says something like, 'Get off your knees. The prayer's been answered—it's you. Now go—be the solution. Go be the blessing.'"

"Hmmn," Malachi said. "You're taking all the fun out of it, Wilks. Pious was going to be easier. Being practical just seems a lot sweatier."

"The cost?" he heard Martin say quietly, while he was still looking at Wilks.

Wilks smiled. "So, you in?"

Malachi glanced over at Martin and then turned to Wilks. "We're in."

Malachi watched Wilks for a couple of seconds as he walked towards the back of the store—heading to the rear exit. He could hear his long hammer jangling in its holder.

And then he turned to face Martin.

"I was thinking as you two were talking; a thought popped into my head," Martin said. "Why don't we do ah… let's see—tomorrow…a Jesus at Menards? Like a noontime chapel service. Half hour, twenty minutes if Evonda would O.K. it. Say—up in the break room mezzanine. Maybe with some food for the workers."

"All of that popped into your head that fast?" Malachi said.

"Yeah."

"Wow," Malachi said. "Let's see. We get home at 7:00. Bone-tired. We need music, a sermon, food, maybe a handout or some way to get the word out. You really think we can pull all that off? It makes me exhausted just thinking about it. I should say more exhausted."

"I agree. There's a cost to being a blessing," Martin said.

"You're right. You're definitely right," Malachi said. "But how are we going to pull it off?"

"I'm not sure," Martin said. "But I was just reading that Bible verse that says, 'But we have this treasure in earthen vessels, so that the surpassing greatness of the power, will be of God and not from ourselves.' The power will have to be from God. He'll show us a way. For now, we need to bust it on this barn. And trust God to pop some more ideas into our heads— right while we're working. His power."

"O.K.," Malachi said. "Here's something that just popped into my head—we need to get Evonda's O.K."

"Yeah," Martin said.

"You go get the rest of the vinyl siding we need," Malachi said. "I'll call Dale. You know where the siding is?"

When Martin returned, he said, "What did Dale say?"

"He said he was sure Evonda would say O.K.," Malachi said. "Ah yeah…he said… especially since she insists we work a minimum of fourteen hours a day next week. And if she doesn't say 'Yes', he'll call me back."

"Fourteen hours a day?" Martin said.

"Or more," Malachi said. "Dale's going to put us up in a motel. Paying for all of our meals too. It's the final week before the deadline. It's crunch time."

"All I can think of right now is the two Bible verses following the earthen-vessel one," Martin said. "'We are afflicted in every way, but not crushed; perplexed, but not despairing; persecuted, but not forsaken; struck down, but not destroyed.' And let us not forget the good news."

"Jesus died for our sins," Malachi said. He smiled.

"Well, good news of minor importance comparatively," Martin said. "Nonetheless, my wallet is smiling. We'll make more money next week than we could make in a month at Walmart."

"We need to praise God we even have a job."

"Amen."

"Hey, let's get this thing sided," Malachi said

"You got the next measurement?" Martin said.

Malachi and Martin efficiently sided one wall after another—with the tan double-four vinyl siding. The workflow was so smooth it looked like they were painting it on.

"Wow, that didn't take long," Martin said. "I'll go round up the shingles if you want to get the roofing tools out of the job trailer."

Soon Martin was chopping shingles to length with The Shingle Shark and flinging them up on the roof, as Malachi fired them down on the felted sheathing with Dale's Senco coil nailer.

They were knocking out the last dozen or so pieces of ridge-cap when Evonda showed up.

"It looks like The Green Hats are on a roll," Evonda said. "You guys are doing an excellent job. I'm going to keep you two working inside on displays all next week."

"Dale called you?" Malachi said from the roof of the yard barn.

"He sure did," Evonda said. "Chapel? I like the idea. Go for it."

"It'll be nice. Real nice," Martin said. "We have experience. We've done something kind of like this at Walmart in the middle of the night. We called it Jesus at Walmart."

Evonda laughed. "So this is going to be Jesus at Menards?"

38. Going to Jerusalem

"**H**ere we go," Malachi said.

Even the groggiest construction worker would have had a hard time missing the notice Malachi posted. Created using three standard size sheets of paper—placed horizontally on a makeshift signpost.

Malachi knew the only entrance to the construction site was through the Garden Center doors. So three steps inside, where every worker had to pass, hopefully as enticing as a low-price guarantee, was the announcement: Sheet one—*Free Food. Pizza...we're talking the good stuff. 12:00 Sharp! This is for you.* Sheet two—*Which Construction Worker Plays the Mandolin...and writes his own songs? Find out. Live on the break room mezzanine. 12:00 sharp. Did We Mention Free Food?* Sheet three: *MANDOLIN.*

MUNCHIES. MESSAGE. The Message: Going to Jerusalem. From the number one selling Book of all time. Featuring the world's best-known Carpenter. Here's the Deal—Join us for a short noontime chapel service. Come be strengthened and refreshed in the Lord.

Timothy and Martin were both carrying three pizzas, while Malachi had three plastic grocery sacks containing five two-liter bottles of pop, napkins, paper plates, and plastic ware.

Timothy had called them when he arrived in the parking lot. Malachi and Martin quickly suspended their construction activity and went outside to give him a hand.

"Right up these steps, Timothy," Malachi said. "Thanks for being our last-minute catering service."

"This is too cool. I wouldn't miss it for anything," Timothy said as they ascended the steps to the mezzanine. "We need to thank my buddy, Adam, too. The guy who runs the Mancino's in Manistee. When I told him what we were doing, he insisted on giving me a sweet deal. And he let me use his thermal blankets to keep the pizzas and bread sticks warm."

Once they arrived in the area, which would be the Menards' store employees' break room, they designated the table nearest the entrance for the food. Timothy would be in charge of keeping it stocked and tidied up.

There were three tables total. Sturdy plastic lawn furniture type. Each had four matching tan high-backed chairs in a distinctively embossed wood pattern.

They left two of the tables set up with their chairs around them. The other four chairs from the food table were placed about the perimeter of the space.

Opposite the entrance door, across the room, a music stand was set up. And off to the right, snugged against the wall, was Malachi's mandolin case and a blue backpack.

Going to Jerusalem

Everyone was moving Martin-speed—an adrenalin induced tempo that seems to make time rush by even faster.

Timothy efficiently made the final preparations for the munchies. Malachi opened his mandolin case, placing a song sheet on the music stand. And Martin removed a Bible and some notes from his backpack.

And then Malachi said, "Fire drill."

They quickly gathered up front.

Malachi prayed, "Not by might nor by power, but by My Spirit, says the LORD of angel armies. We receive Your power—in faith. And put Your words in Martin's mouth as he steps out into a new experience."

"Amen."

"Amen."

"Amen."

Malachi could hear Martin exhaling from his mouth as they rose from their knees.

Malachi looked at Martin. "Wow. Look what the Lord has done." They embraced.

And then they heard sounds coming from the entrance.

It was Dale, with a big smile on his face. He came right over to them, saying, "I'm proud to have you two on my crew."

He looked away, out into the open space beyond the mezzanine's tubular railing system. And then returned his gaze to Martin and Malachi. He shook his head up and down slowly, "I wish I had realized a lot earlier in my life that this is really what it's all about. Martin, Malachi this is a wonderful day for Dale Marble Construction. Thank you guys."

Wilks and Raymond had followed Dale in.

"Came to see what a blessing looks like," Wilks said loud enough so Malachi could hear him.

Malachi smiled.

Raymond appeared to be an easy catch for free food. Two pieces of pizza—double stacked, were moments away from losing their battle for survival.

Malachi tried to stay focused on preparing for the music portion of the service. And he was especially pleased to see Chad show up. A minute or so later, two other workers entered the room.

And then, as they had planned, right at 12:05, Malachi began.

"Hey everybody, we're going to get started. We don't have any amplification, so we would appreciate if you could keep noise to a minimum. If you're so inclined, feel free to enjoy the refreshments during our chapel service."

Most everyone sat down. Wilks and one of the construction workers Malachi didn't know opted to stand near the wall.

As Malachi was adjusting his mandolin strap over his shoulder, he noticed Evonda in the doorway. And then she moved just inside—to the left.

He looked out on those gathered and thought to himself, "This is great. What a nice group. What an awesome place to have a chapel service."

Malachi was facing the doorway located on the opposite end of an elongated space. He estimated the area to be twelve-feet by thirty-two feet in size. The walls were constructed of white-painted plywood. There was no wall to his right. Only a three-foot tall railing dividing the room from the retail space twelve feet below. From where he was standing, he could see the entire main cash register area and a bank of exit doors below. Straight across loomed massive arched windows towering eighteen feet above the store's polished concrete floors. Through them, Malachi had a nice view of the parking lot.

He strummed his mandolin softly and then said, "This

Going to Jerusalem

is a song I have entitled *A Free Store Prayer.* I named it in honor of a store and its owner where I used to live—in St. Amos. The Free Store is a ministry that serves those in need.

He smiled. "And I think this song is also a good prayer for us today as we build a store. As we build this Menards."

Malachi played three chords and then began to sing:

> Jesus, give me a heart to do Your will
> Jesus, give me a heart to do Your will
>
> Hands of mercy. A heart of love
> Hands of mercy. A heart of love
> Hands of mercy. A heart of love
>
> Jesus, give me the strength to do Your will
> Jesus, give me the strength to do Your will
>
> Hands of mercy. A heart of love
> Hands of mercy. A heart of love

As he finished singing, Malachi thought to himself, "If Martin's message is as big a hit as the food, a revival is minutes away."

"Now let's give our attention to Martin as he comes up here to bring us all a message. One he's entitled: *Going to Jerusalem.*"

Only a few minutes into Martin's talk, Malachi thought to himself, "He's gifted." And almost as an extension of his own thought, he heard one of the construction workers he knew say the exact same words, "He's gifted."

Also, Malachi noticed Evonda had now moved all the way into the room and was seated in the furthest reaches.

Martin was preaching on the Biblical account of the ten lepers being healed, while only one returned to thank Jesus.

Martin had everyone's undivided attention. He had the touch. He shared sprinkles of his testimony. He made the story come to life with illustrations, carefully selected wording, facial expressions, and even took some labored steps to portray the leper's struggling with their initial steps of faith. And he repeated the phrase, "Going to Jerusalem," several times. Sure to stir future memory responses of those listening.

He even unpacked the meaning of the Greek word *sozo*, meaning *saved* and *healed*. This ignited some oh-that's-cool expressions on faces around the room.

Martin linked the explanation to a key verse, "And Jesus said to the leper, 'Rise and go your way; your faith has made you well.'" And Martin emphasized, "Your faith has *saved* you and *healed* you."

As Martin drew his message to a conclusion, the room was silent. He had the attentiveness all preachers live for.

Martin's words seemed to flow effortlessly:

"Only one leper returned to Jesus. The other nine actually ended up focusing on themselves, rather than on God. Once they received their healing, Jesus was no longer needed, no longer relevant, as they went back to their former lives.

Going to Jerusalem.

This may sound harsh, after all, they did suffer with leprosy for years. But for them, Jesus was essentially a means to a miracle. Jesus was the way to accomplish their goal—no more leprosy.

They had a measure of faith. They cried eagerly to Jesus when they were in trouble. When trouble passed, however, Jesus was quickly forgotten as they moved on to new opportunities.

Going to Jerusalem.

People still do this. Some are dramatically saved or healed or set free. Jesus intervened at just the right time to help. Their place in heaven seems secure. Yet, in time, they go back to an old way of life—without Jesus.

No praising, worshipping, thanking. Yes, happy to have met Jesus and His miracle or His salvation. But God receives no glory. They have salvation, but where is the Savior in their lives now? They have their healing, but where is the Healer now?

Going to Jerusalem—with no desire to have a loving, joyful, daily relationship with Jesus."

"Let's stand together," Martin said. "In Second Timothy, it says, 'Remember Jesus Christ.'"

Martin's focus was clear. He took a few moments to look around the room.

And then said:

"No, we don't flat-out forget Jesus. But many leave Him behind, even after what He's done in their lives.

Are you going to Jerusalem? When you should be returning to Jesus. Friends, a life of freedom is reason enough to return again and again to Jesus. And worship Him.

I'm going to pray. Thank you everyone for coming. When I finish praying—if today is the day you need to return to Jesus, please come and pray with me. You may need to meet the Savior for the first time. Your body may need healing. Please—this is your day."

When Martin finished praying, with little hesitation, Chad moved to the front. The man beside Malachi, who had commented on Martin's giftedness, kept his head bowed for many seconds and then made his way to the front.

Wilks stared up at the front. Everyone else around him had either retreated to the refreshment table or had made their way to the exit.

Malachi hadn't noticed until after Martin concluded, but two more workers had joined the group sometime during the message.

Dale came up to Malachi, shook his hand, and said, "Martin certainly did an amazing job."

As Malachi stood near the food table, he heard Wilks and two other workers talking about Martin's outstanding sermon.

Wilks said, "He sure got me thinking. I gotta get my family back in church."

Malachi turned to his right and just about bumped into a guy he didn't now.

He extended his hand. "Hey, my name's Ted. You're the guy who played the mandolin, aren't you?"

Malachi smiled. "Yeah, I am. My name's Malachi."

Ted got a big smile on his face. "I've got to tell you something."

Malachi focused intently on Ted. "What's that?"

"Man that was the best, I mean the best. The best pizza I've had in a long time. Thanks for putting this deal on for us workers."

"Well ah...yeah," Malachi said. "Thank you for coming, Ted."

The group dispersed quickly.

Timothy and Malachi cleaned up while Martin finished talking and praying with the two men up front.

Within a few minutes, everyone had left. Malachi, Timothy, and Martin sat at a table.

"Martin, you did an outstanding job," Timothy said.

"I give God all the praise," Martin said.

Malachi sat as Martin and Timothy talked some more.

"You sure are quiet, Malachi," Martin then said.

"Well yeah," Malachi said. "Other outcasts came and joined Jesus and the disciples at the table."

"What are you talking about?" Martin said.

"I was just thinking," Malachi said. "The outcasts are sinners."

"O.K."

"Well, I'm feeling like an outcast," Malachi said. "I mean…jealousy is definitely a sin. And ah…I've never delivered a message as good as your first time out. Not in my entire life. I'm like, what's the deal?"

"I don't know if I should say, 'Thanks,' or 'Can I pray for you?'" Martin said.

"I feel like I just got bumped to second string; well, probably third string," Malachi said. "I don't know, maybe I'm just the water boy now."

"Well, you know it doesn't work that way. God uses all of us in different ways," Martin said. "But what we need to do now is to get back to work. Right?"

"Yeah. You're right," Malachi said. "Though working with you, I feel so unworthy."

"Well, you are," Martin said. "But that has nothing to do with preaching. That's because you can't read a plan."

They both laughed.

And so did Timothy.

39. Water Boy

"It looks like we should be able to finish this last barn today," Malachi said. "And then we can be off to something new on Monday."

"From preaching to pounding nails," Martin said. "Just like that."

"Your preaching was good. Really good," Malachi said. "But you forgot to take up an offering."

"I just figured you and Timothy were going to lavish me with a sizeable honorarium," Martin said. "And then I would bless your finances in return."

"Yeah. Bless me so I can work a hundred hours this week instead of eighty," Malachi said. "No thanks. Don't you dare lay those preacher hands on me to impart your blessing."

Martin laughed.

And then they heard, "I'll take a blessing." The words came from behind them, toward the paint booth area, near the completed Gambrel Roofed E-Z Build Barn.

As they were bantering back and forth, a person had approached unnoticed.

They both spun around.

"I mean another blessing," Evonda said. "Your chapel service blessed us all. This is my ninth Menards' job. And believe me, I've work so many Sundays, and no one has ever done anything like what you guys did today. I mean...nobody's ever done anything church-like. Absolutely zero."

"Thanks," Martin said. "We appreciate you giving us the opportunity."

Malachi was absorbed in thought. Pondering thought. His eyes were fixed on Evonda—on the less than completely answered question hanging from her neck.

"So, Evonda," Malachi said. "The cross you always wear, why is it special to you?"

"Do I have to answer?" she said, as she smiled. "It's special because my son gave it to me. But it's not special in the way it should be."

She was silent for several seconds, shifting her focus downward for a few moments. And then began talking as she raised her head, "I ah...wear it like a good luck charm." She shook her head, "It's sad because the cross and its meaning, its true meaning, used to be special to me. Real special."

She swallowed and slowly drew in a breath through her nose. "But now," she shook her head, "I'm going to Jerusalem. And it's like there's no possible way to get turned around. But I want to."

"But I can't." Evonda stopped. The words seemed to affix themselves to the moment. Like the firm pressing of a rubber stamp on the back of a check. Asserting—For Deposit Only.

"How do I just turn around? Just like that?" she said.

Water Boy

Malachi glanced at Martin. Martin nodded at Malachi.

"You've already taken the first step, Evonda," Malachi said. "A brave step."

She fixed her eyes on Malachi.

"Sure, when Martin talked today, it seemed like there were two ways. And the lines of distinction were clear. Yes, there are two directions, but sometimes an immediate turn-around is just too abrupt. So maybe, you're going to need to curve back to the right direction."

"What do you mean?" Evonda said.

"It's the road of God's grace," Malachi said. "On His road, the but *I can't*, turns into, *I can do all things through Christ who strengthens me.*"

"Just like your song," Evonda said. "Give me the strength to do Your will."

"Yeah, you got it," Malachi said. "So you were listening to the song?"

"It was awesome," Evonda said. "Your song went straight to my heart. I loved it."

Malachi glanced at Martin. And when he did, Martin pointed a finger heavenward at shoulder height.

Malachi nodded his head slightly.

"So Evonda, take God's road of grace back to the place where Jesus is real, where Jesus is special again. I don't know what all you're going through. It's probably all the typical road litter."

Evonda shook her head.

"So get on that road; for you, it might be a long sweeping curve. But just stay on it. Stay on it. Stay on it. And then one day, a lot sooner than you're thinking right now—guaranteed, by the strength of God—you'll look back and realize that the time in your life when, 'Jesus was quickly forgotten as you moved onto new opportunities' will be directly behind you. And Jesus, your Savior, your Healer, your Strength, He will be clearly in focus right in front of you. You will be experiencing a new Evonda. The one gently remolded by God. By his grace. His amazing grace."

By the time Malachi had finished, Evonda's head was bowed. Her eyes were closed.

After several seconds, she said quietly, "That's what I want. God, please give me the strength to do your will."

And then she opened her eyes. "Malachi, you've strengthened and encouraged me. You've given my soul the refreshing drink of water it was craving."

With little hesitation, she said, "Thank you so much, Malachi. Can I give you a hug?"

40. Command Fire to Come Down

"**W**hat did you do, command fire to come down to get Rollie to change his mind?" Timothy said.

"Well, I didn't need that. But I am thankful that God gave me a second plan. Because my faithful-to-the-end brother was already out the door. With the pie," Malachi said.

"Well, I'm not Miss Manners," Timothy said. "But I'm thinking it's proper etiquette to leave, maybe before you've been called a weasel for the third time."

Timothy looked over at Malachi. "Seriously though, I was pretty concerned when I came up the steps and the door was already closed. Believe me, it was fire drill time."

"Prayers were definitely prevailing boldly at The Throne," Malachi said, "even before you started, Timothy."

For a couple of seconds, Malachi looked across the table

toward the riverside of the room. His eyes met with Carl's eyes, and at that moment, his words sounded in Malachi's head as he wondered about his, once again, thinner appearance: "Some people when they have a deep burden from the Lord. One that won't go away. Like something needs to be birthed through travail before God; they're almost driven to seeking the Lord through fasting."

And then Malachi looked around the table. Mandy was to his right. Carl sat across from him—a little to the right. Then Timothy. JC sat next to Martin who was to Malachi's left.

"I wanted to tell everyone at one time what happened with Rollie," Malachi said. "Even though Timothy kept bugging me—in a nice way. Plus I wanted to make sure, with some passing of time, everything was going to work out the way Rollie and I had settled on."

"So this is what happened:"

Three steps from the bottom, Malachi heard Rollie say, "Hey wait. What was your name again?"

Malachi turned around, "My name's Malachi. Malachi Marble."

Rollie brushed the side of his face with his left hand. He shook his head back and forth. And said it so faintly that Malachi's ears almost missed his words, "I don't know what I'm doing. This is crazy."

He stared at Malachi for a couple more seconds and then said, "Can we talk?"

Even after the chairs were arranged and the door was closed, Rollie stared over Malachi's right shoulder for nearly a minute before their conversation began.

Rollie lowered his eyes, but still not looking directly at Malachi. The envelope Malachi had given him was protruding from his left pocket.

"I don't want to hear anything about the Bible and Jesus and God and that gobbledygook," Rollie said. "Now the Bible seems truthful. It's just you Christians. You've screwed it up and confused everything. You've almost made it too weird to talk about or believe. So that whole subject is off limits. Got it?"

"Sure."

"That last group of your type, the ones who tried to start a church down the street, they wanted to talk about the Bible and especially that other book they had—all the time." Rollie said. "God's got a wonderful plan for your life they told me. But their lives didn't seem wonderful. And I know the guy who owns the building they wanted to move into. They were practically asking him to finance their whole project. I mean…is that any way to represent God—always crying about money. And then one of their leaders did some construction work for me once. Only once—what a shyster. Plus, I know a peddler when I see one. It was like when the church leaders were talking to me—they were trying to set me up, like a vacuum cleaner salesman does."

And then Rollie looked directly at Malachi and said, "They weren't like you. They had no backbone. Now you, I'm practically spitting fire in your face and you stand there taking it. Then you hand me an envelope, pointing it at me like you're holding a .44 Magnum."

Rollie reached in his pocket and handed Malachi the envelope.

"Here, you keep this," Rollie said. "I didn't even open it. Didn't have to."

"You didn't even look inside?" Malachi said.

"I got the message," Rollie said. "You know, I always get my way downtown. No matter what it takes. When you handed me the envelope, I fought the thought for a second or two, but I knew it was a good thought, 'These church people are different. They've got that feisty survival instinct that'll breathe some much-needed vitality into downtown Manistee.'"

Malachi smiled.

Rollie began shaking his head back and forth. "Now, did this really happen. Or did I just dream this. Did two church guys actually show up at my door trying to give me money, rather than begging for a donation? Or was I just dreaming?"

Malachi laughed. And then he said, "Praise...Oops...I almost said something about God."

"Well that's O.K. But no more," Rollie said.

Rollie looked up toward the ceiling. "Maybe. Maybe it was God."

And then he peered at Malachi. "But don't start."

Malachi raised both of his hands up to shoulder height with the palms facing Rollie. "It was only one slip."

"Malachi, you called my bluff," Rollie said. "I'm so broke. I've weaved myself into an awful web."

He looked down at the floor.

They were both silent for several seconds.

Rollie's words came out in pieces, "It's scary to think..."

"How close..."

"How close I came..."

"The stupid thoughts that find their way into the head of a desperate man."

And then he looked at Malachi. "But I'm not taking your money."

"You're not taking the money? But we want to help you," Malachi said.

"I'm the weasel," Rollie said. "I need to act like a man. I know how to make money. But I spend it like a foolish child. I'm such a poser. I feel like a weasel."

He shook his head back and forth. "It's weird. It's like, in the last three days, I've seen Timothy either getting in or out of that little black car he drives now. I'm thinking, 'Man, he must have sold his Escalade.' But he always looks so happy."

It was almost a laugh Malachi heard coming from Rollie.

Command Fire to Come Down

"I have so much crap. If I just quit pretending and got rid of the tons and tons of the crap…I mean, I have two Escalades. Maybe my kids would rather have a dad than two thousand dollars in monthly payments. Payments I can't afford."

Rollie stood up and paced back and forth. "And I've got this big castle. And the monthly payment is even bigger. And this is the crazy thing; I just absolutely hate the subdivision I live in. I mean seriously…does the whole lawn really have to look like a putting green? I spend more time and money on that stupid lawn. If I don't, the pious subdivision—self-appointed by the way, lawn police come by with enough glaring self-righteousness to kill crab grass at a hundred feet. And those are the friendly neighbors. I'm serious, Malachi. As soon as you leave, I'm calling my real estate agent, I'm putting that burden on the market today. Today. I mean it. Today."

Rollie then enumerated his financial miseries for several more minutes as he paced the floor.

Like a top eventually losing its momentum, he spun his last woe and sat down. And said, "I don't need your money. I need to quit being so stupid. I can do this. I know I can."

Malachi patted Rollie on the shoulder and then he said, "I'm probably breaking a rule. But I know it's true—God can help you."

"Yeah," Rollie said. "That's O.K., because I'm going to break my own rule too."

Rollie looked off to his left. Away from Malachi. He folded his arms and appeared to be staring at the floor.

He then repositioned himself, looking intensely at Malachi.

He was slowly rubbing his hands together when he said, "This might sound crazy. It doesn't make sense to me. But it was like I couldn't open the envelope. I stared at it—flap side down. After some hesitation, I flipped it over. When I looked down and saw what you had written, my legs almost gave out.

That's a Bible verse? Right?"

"Delight yourself in the Lord and He will give you the desire of your heart," Malachi said. "Psalm 37:4."

Rollie kept talking as if he was going in the wrong direction. "I saw you down there with her once. And if it was that other church-bunch, I would have figured it was a set-up. But I know I can trust you."

"I'm not following you," Malachi said. "I thought you were telling me how that Bible verse made you change your mind."

"Kind of," Rollie said. "I was down at Zeke's less than an hour before you and Timothy came over. I'm a regular. There's a waitress there—is she your girlfriend or something?"

"We're really good friends," Malachi said. "Like family."

"She's not much of a talker," Rollie said, "but a really fine waitress. I was getting ready to leave as she walked over to me. In her hand, folded in half, was one of those square napkins. 'Here's a message for you,' she told me and then went back to her duties. So what do you think she had written on the napkin?"

"Are you serious?" Malachi said.

"Yeah. So when I saw the same words written on the envelope, it was a sealed deal," Rollie said. "Only God could do that. And I'm not even sure I believe in God."

"Maybe not yet," Malachi said.

"Careful, Malachi," Rollie said. "I don't want to put you in the penalty box."

"For an offside," Malachi said.

They both laughed.

"So that's what happened when I talked to Rollie," Malachi said as he looked around the table—this time left to right.

He shook his head up and down when his eyes met Mandy's. He laid his hand on hers. "Look what the Lord has done. His sheep hear His voice. And praise God for when they listen and respond."

41. Grace Night

"Do you want to get some coffee or something?" Mandy said. "It's been a long time since we've had a chance to talk."

Everyone had enough church business for one night. The Rollie-story was the highlight—of course. This became a springboard for making some directional plans for The Table. And everyone agreed, they needed to meet on the next Wednesday also.

Malachi wanted to, and he knew he needed to have a face-to-face meeting with Mandy, especially after the new direction her life had taken. They had talked a few times on the phone—briefly. But with the Menards job—sleep and work had engulfed much of Malachi's life.

He welcomed its conclusion. And had seriously

pondered what Evonda told him, "You should consider getting a job at the Menards store. I can get you in."

He had thought to himself, "Who knows what the future holds—only God knows."

Malachi had zero doubt what his answer to Mandy had to be. And he couldn't help thinking back over the span of their relationship, less than a year, even though it seemed much longer. And so much had taken place over that period of time.

The first time they went out, Mandy was the one who swayed their relationship from restaurant chitchat to first date, though it required nearly nil for effort, besides the asking.

And after that charmed evening together, Malachi was convinced he wanted to marry Mandy.

That first date was near the pinnacle of their relationship. Not long afterwards, it tumbled awkwardly to lowland. One of the benchmarks on this low road—also a long one, was when Mandy accused Malachi of being a stalker.

That was a painful stab to Malachi, which was strangely offset to a degree, because Mandy had allowed Malachi to have basically a mentoring relationship with her only child—Alex. Malachi never saw or talked to Mandy during that period.

"Sure, that sounds great, Mandy," Malachi said. "What did you have in mind?"

"I don't know," Mandy said. "How about Zeke's?"

"The food's good," Malachi said. "And I've heard that the waitresses sometimes hand out Bible verses that will melt your heart and change your life."

Mandy laughed.

It was that same laugh, the one that had initially apprehended Malachi's heart back all those months ago.

As they walked the three blocks to Zeke's, it was

weather and work-talk. And they chatted about what was going on in Alex's life.

Malachi hadn't eaten dinner yet. And it seemed appropriate to suggest getting something to eat. But his insides were jostling around so much that his appetite had nearly vanished.

He had plenty of silent, "God help me prayers," as they walked side by side in the nippy night air.

And Malachi was mentally scripting out how he wanted the conversation to go. Attempting to. Yet no slicing and dicing of film clips running through his head seemed to fade to that perfect, happy ending.

The enemy inside seemed to cheer him on the more he struggled to stomp the pieces together.

And then Mandy said, "I really like that poster Timothy hung up in the church. The one that says, 'Commit to the Lord whatever you do and your plans will succeed.' That's how I want to live my life."

She looked over at Malachi. "That's one thing I love about God. He makes straight the crooked paths. So that means, we don't have to figure everything out ahead of time."

Malachi smiled. He didn't say anything for a bit. They walked along silently. Then he said, "I totally agree with you, Mandy. And you know what, now I'm starting to get hungry. We need to get something to eat."

By the time they sat down in a booth, in the least active part of Zeke's, Malachi and Mandy had small-talked through the basic list.

It was 8:12. Only two other tables were occupied.

They looked at each other without saying anything. They both ordered coffee, and they both ordered omelets.

When Malachi ordered, he commented, "That's exactly what I was hungry for."

Malachi knew, as they looked at each other, they were playing the you-say-something-first game.

Malachi couldn't help it. It just popped into his head uninvited. It was the time-tested used car-purchasing axiom, "Whoever makes the first offer loses."

"So, what are you thinking, Mandy?"

"Well, I wanted you to talk first, and I knew you were thinking the same thing," Mandy said.

She laughed. "This is weird. It was easier for us to talk on our first date."

"Does that seem like it was ten years ago?" Malachi said.

"Just about."

"O.K." Malachi said. "How about this? Let's make this grace night. We both now know about the grace of Jesus and have received His unconditional love."

"Yeah," Mandy said. "That's for sure."

"So, if either one of us says something goofy, unexpected, seemingly hurtful, misunderstood," Malachi said, "we just spread this thick blanket of grace over it. Special grace. It's a no-offense night. We'll cut each other so much slack, we'll both have so much leftover, we'll need doggy bags."

"Doggy bags?" Mandy said with a smile.

"O.K.," Malachi said. "A Styrofoam box with a folding lid. The jumbo size."

By now, a portion of the table was filled with plates, coffee cups, and the like. They had bowed their heads, "And with prayer and petitions with thanksgiving they had let their requests be made known to God."

"So if I say something like...I mean...if I suggested we start dating again and wasn't sure how you would react, but because it's grace night, I should feel at ease to kind of just blurt it out?" Mandy said.

Malachi smiled, "Exactly."

He took a sip of coffee and took a deep breath. "It's kind of like if I thought I was going to say something that sounded stupid…like if I looked into your eyes and told you how easy it would be to fall in love with you, but then no matter how tenderly I say it, I know what I have to tell you will be misunderstood, likely hurtful—I could just go ahead and tell you anyways. Because it's grace night."

Malachi could feel his heart beating. His eyes gazed at Mandy. Once again, Timothy's words from months ago echoed in his head, "Malachi, make sure you know the desire of your heart is the right desire."

"Oh Mandy," Malachi said. "I just love what God's doing in your life. And it would seem almost too perfect that you and I start over again—with God being the center."

Malachi looked down slightly to the left and rubbed both of his hands together.

He looked up. "Mandy, I can't date you."

Mandy's face started to quiver. She lowered her head.

Malachi fought every urge to console her with a hug.

After nearly a minute, Mandy raised her head. "It's grace night."

Now, Malachi was the one with tears in his eyes. He so wanted to hug her.

The desire hadn't fully passed when he said, "You're so amazing, Mandy. And I love you so much. But it's in a different way."

"I love you too, Malachi," Mandy said. "But I'm not sure which way it is. But for some reason, I can't explain it, but I know which way you love me."

Malachi sipped his coffee again and then set the cup down on the table.

"Well now, I'm going to tell you why," Malachi said. "You need to promise me that you won't tell anyone. O.K.

No one."

"I like secrets," Mandy said. "You have my word. It's our secret."

"I'm getting married," Malachi said.

"No you're not." Mandy laughed.

"Yes, I am."

"Elysia?" Mandy said. "Are you moving to China? That's it."

And then Malachi laughed.

"I'm getting re-married," Malachi said. "By God's special grace, I'm marrying Annie."

Tears were already rolling down her cheeks when she looked heavenward. "That's so awesome. God is so awesome."

"That's so awesome, Malachi," she said as she stood up.

They embraced. Malachi sensed Mandy's love—the other kind—grace night love.

42. Special Grace

They had been talking frequently on the phone since Malachi's visit to St. Amos. Two, three, four, five times a week.

The first phone conversation will likely remain at the top of the charts for years to come, in the peculiar-phone-conversations category.

Malachi now smiles as he recalls Annie's words from that day: "Will you marry me, Malachi?"

If Annie's tears on the other end hadn't tenderized his heart, he might have responded with, "Why would I do that?" The warm-fuzzy rendition of that theme.

Instead, Malachi agreed to consider her idea—her proposal.

Eight seconds after he hung up, Malachi had finished the consideration process. Fueled solely on bad vibes, emanating from those daggers-in-the-heart episodes of their marriage.

Then a little more pondering, and after a few dagger retractions, Malachi softened. He knew they had experienced some wonderful times during their marriage. Still, his answer was, No. For what he considered the right reasons.

When Malachi had visited Carl to seek some guidance, an unequivocal: "I see your point, Malachi. Let's pray," would have spun real nice on the turntable of advice that day. No, not Carl. Who would ask this kind of question, but Carl: "What would make you want to marry Annie again?"

As Malachi left Carl's cottage and prepared to trudge up the first snowy grade, he assumed his weighing deliberations would be a trudge as well.

He walked slowly, like he was bound by heavy ropes. And then like backlit flashcards, three pieces of Scripture burst into his brain. A brilliant white background. Piercing black lettering.

"It is no longer I who live, but Christ lives in me."

"Husbands, love your wives, just as Christ also loved the church and gave Himself up for her."

"God hates divorce."

The last one was the exact words Annie and Carl had both already spoken.

And then Malachi's own words breached his thoughts. Now, not just words, but a gutsy revelation, "I do love Annie."

So absolutely true.

I do.

I do.

Slash, slash, slash—the binding was loosed.

And now, through the many phone conversations, Malachi and Annie had rebuilt the part of their relationship, where sharing what was going on in their lives seemed vital. These multi-weekly times together on the phone was their equivalent of sitting across from each other at the kitchen table, sharing their experiences of the day.

Plus of course, dealing with the transitional matters related to their renewed life together. A lot of decisions.

It wasn't a new issue. More like a recurring thread. One Malachi thought was already settled.

And it was. So, when Annie said it, her words were more like a musing, a longing to ease the stress: "Sometimes, I just wish you could move back to St. Amos."

"I know, Annie," Malachi said. "In some ways, that would seem so much easier. But it's obvious that God's hand is upon what's going on in Manistee—at The Table. And work and all."

They were both silent for several seconds.

And then Malachi said, "Annie, I love you so much. I wish I could hold you in my arms right now."

"Malachi, I love you so much too," Annie said. "God will help. Look what all He's done. I'm just tired. You know that."

"You need a dose of God's special grace," Malachi said.

"Yeah, I do. But we've already experienced so much of His special grace," Annie said.

"We sure have," Malachi said. "Hey, I've got a story for you. An amazing God-story. One that'll revive your soul."

Annie laughed. "Sounds like you're about ready to say, 'Coming soon to a theatre near you.'"

Malachi laughed.

"Just about," Malachi said. "Remember this guy Rollie who was giving The Table so much grief?"

"Yeah," Annie said. "The downtown czar."

"O.K. my beautiful wife-to-be, listen to what our amazing God did," Malachi said.

Malachi then told Annie the entire story in detail.

He finished with, "So what do you think about that?"

"That's incredible, a miracle," Annie said. "You're so right, Malachi. God's hand is upon you and The Table there in Manistee. After hearing that, I'm excited about moving to Manistee."

"Praise God," Malachi said.

Jesus at Walmart...fire on the Earth

"Back to the story for a second," Annie said. "So Malachi, what was inside the envelope?"

"I don't know."

43. Growl

"Let me go over this list of points we've made decisions on tonight," Timothy said. "I'll print each one of you a copy, so you have it in front of you. And you'll have something to take with you."

Everyone was sitting in the same seats as last week. Timothy was taking notes on his black, Microsoft Surface RT Tablet. He would cyberspace it up to his Cloud office on the internet, and from there, he could signal his printer in his office, adjacent to the kitchen, to reel off seven copies. One for everyone, including himself.

Within four minutes Timothy returned from the back and passed out a single sheet of paper to Carl, Mandy, Malachi, Martin, and JC.

Everyone studied their copies:

1. The new, The Table banner with phone # (DT's number) and the catchphrase: The church for you, is approved.
2. Church grand opening will be on Easter.
3. Will hold services the Sundays leading up to Easter. This will be our soft opening.
4. Mandy and JC will select the interior color scheme.
5. Timothy will coordinate the painting, minimal construction, and possible additional banners. Will also work on any flyers, invitations etc. to inform the public.
6. Martin will be in charge of the sound system. He will use his equipment.
7. Malachi and Martin will coordinate worship music for The Table.
8. Carl requested that Friday 12:00 p.m. to 5:00 a.m. be set aside as a time for him to come to the church to pray. This is approved.

After four minutes, Timothy said, "Anything need changing or revising?"

"It looks good," Malachi said. "And if you want to, make a note on your copy that we're meeting next Wednesday."

"Everybody's good then?" Timothy said.

He glanced at his watch and then said, "Our timing looks good. We've got a few minutes. Like I told you when we started tonight, the pastor of the church that tried to start down the street called me. He wants to meet us. His group had wanted to have a church at what is now A Place in Thyme. This is the group Rollie said he ran off."

"So what does he want?" Carl said.

"He was like, 'I would like to meet your group and see what you're doing'" Timothy said. "That's pretty much all he said."

Growl

"It's good and Godly to fellowship with other churches," Malachi said. "It will be nice to meet him. That's the way I see it."

"I was just wondering," Carl said.

"I think that's him," Timothy said as he heard a knock on the door.

After a few moments at the front door, Timothy escorted the two men over to the table.

"Have a seat," Timothy said. "I'll grab some more chairs."

"No," the taller man said. "We won't take up much of your time."

"O.K. everyone, this is Elder Tuli Brule and Elder Benny Utis," Timothy said. "And this is our leadership team: Malachi, Mandy, Carl, Martin, and JC."

"Now, Pastor Tuli…" Timothy said.

"Elder Tuli," he said. "That's what my people call me."

"Oh, O.K. Elder Tuli, you're the head elder and…" Timothy said.

"Presiding Elder," Elder Tuli said.

And then he looked around at those gathered. He was in no hurry. "Everyone here helps lead your church, guide your church?" Elder Tuli said.

"Yeah, that's how we do it here at The Table," Malachi said.

Elder Tuli was looking at JC when he said, "Everyone."

"It's really exciting to be a…" JC said. She stopped talking when Elder Tuli turned his back on her.

And then Elder Tuli looked at Carl before staring up at the yellow and green banner hanging on the wall.

His eyes then returned to Carl. And he said, "Is that the NIV Version of the Bible?"

Carl glanced upward.

Timothy spoke first, "Yeah it is."

"We have a saying at our church," Elder Tuli said. "The NIV Version compared to the Authorized King James Version of the Bible is like bring a spoon to a sword fight."

"You have sword fights at your church?" Mandy said.

Without responding, Elder Tuli looked over at Elder Benny and said, in a much quieter tone, "See what I mean?"

Elder Tuli then looked around the room and spoke into the air almost as if no one was there, "Oh the defilement, sacrilege, the lewdness, the blasphemy, profanity upon profanity that ruled and reined in this den of wicked iniquity. The curse doeth still inhabit…"

"Get out of here," Carl said as he stood up. "You heard me. Now!"

"Do you own this place?" Elder Tuli said.

"I do," Timothy said. He pulled both of his long sleeves up to his elbow. "And I'm the bouncer. You heard my friend."

He then walked them to the door.

Elder Tuli turned just before he exited and said loudly, "There's only one remnant left and be it not, yea to…"

Timothy used the door to shove him to the outside, muffling his final words.

When Malachi heard the word remnant, he said, in a whisper, "Dotty."

"Wow, Carl, the old thin-guy still has some growl," Martin said.

"I should have said something sooner," Carl said. "I know this bunch…I mean, I was pretty sure the minute they walked in."

"Are they the we're-the-only-true-remnant group?" Malachi said.

"That's them," Carl said. "And they are so far away from the accepted teachings of the Christian Faith and of Jesus Christ that I should have done what it says in 2 John 1:10-11 without hesitation, 'If anyone comes to you and does not bring the teaching of Christ, do not receive him into your house. And do not give him a greeting. For the one who gives

Growl

him a greeting participates in his evil deeds.' I should have acted sooner."

44. The Kool-Aid

The meeting should have been over. Yet the conversation kept circling back to one basic theme: "They sure were strange."

Malachi was just listening by now. And with what was being said, he was wondering why it took so long for someone to speak-up. It was like a flaming blaze had ignited, but instead of running for the extinguishers, they started roasting hot dogs and were about ready to break out the ingredients for s'mores.

Malachi turned around and stared intently out toward the street. He stood up and started rubbing above his right eye with his right hand. His face became warm on his right side. Between his ear and eye—above his cheekbone.

He was only vaguely aware of the continuing conversation

going on behind him.

Malachi continued rubbing as the warmth washed over him, as nearly a minute passed.

And then he turned back around to the group. "Hey everyone, Elder Tuli is going to rile up Rollie. Stir things up. Meet with him."

"Well that's obvious," Timothy said. "I could have predicted that."

"You have Rollie's number?" Malachi said.

"Well yeah," Timothy said.

"Call him right now," Malachi said.

"It's after 9:00," Timothy said. "I'll call him in the morning."

"Call Rollie right now," Malachi said. "And insist he comes down here. Right now. Don't take no for an answer. Right now."

"I agree," Mandy said. "When the enemy comes in like a flood, the Spirit of the Lord shall lift up a standard against him."

Malachi looked at Mandy and grinned.

"O.K. I'll call him," Timothy said. "My cell phone is in the back."

In just a couple of minutes, Timothy came charging back into the room. His phone was pressed against his ear. His left hand was flailing in the air.

He stopped inches from Malachi. Shoved his cell phone into Malachi's hand. "Here, you talk to him."

All that Malachi said into the phone was:

"No."

"No!"

"No!!"

Then he was silent for over a minute.

Then Malachi held his hand over the mouthpiece and said quietly to those gathered in the room, "Fire drill."

The Kool-Aid

Then Malachi started talking into the mouthpiece again, but all he said was:

"Stop."

"Just stop for minute."

"Stop. Can I say something?"

And then Malachi heard Carl's voice rising as the rest of the members of The Table prayed silently on their knees.

Just loud enough for Malachi to hear: "Lord, you say in your Word, 'Every morning I will put to silence all the wicked in the land. I will cut off every evildoer from the city,' by your strong right hand let morning break in the spiritual realm over Manistee. Now. Now. Let it be now, Lord."

"Are you there?" Malachi said. "Are you there? He hung up on me. Rollie hung up on me."

The room was silent, except for the noise of people getting up from their knees. Carl sat down as everyone else stood around the table.

"Oh man," Malachi said. It was almost an exhale. "The Tuli twosome went right over to see Rollie when they left here."

He shook his head back and forth and looked at everyone. "What a mess. Those guys—I don't know what they said or how they persuaded him to even listen, but they've pretty much convinced Rollie."

Malachi exhaled through his mouth in a sigh. "Well, they told Rollie never to drink the Kool-Aid down here."

"Kool-Aid?" JC said. "Do we have Kool-Aid?"

"No, but Jim Jones did," Timothy said. "It was before your time. This Jim Jones guy led a cult group and by his edict, most of them committed suicide by drinking poisoned Kool-Aid."

"That's awful," Mandy said.

"So now we're the cult," Carl said, "at least in Rollie's eyes. It's like the Bible says, 'For such men are false apostles, deceitful workers, disguising themselves as apostles of Christ. No wonder, for even Satan disguises himself as an angel of light.'

So tonight, Tuli and Utis appeared to Rollie as angels of light."

"So that's how it happens," Mandy said.

The ensuing discussion, though serious, because of weariness and the lack of a feasible game plan, turned into more of a head-nodder than a fourteen-inning 1-0 Tiger's game.

But then a beefy pounding on the door sounded throughout the entire room.

Malachi, who was closest, scurried to the door and opened it promptly.

It was Rollie. He was shouting at Malachi, "Listen weasel! No one hangs up on me. When I talk, you listen. You hear me!"

Rollie's right finger was jabbing at Malachi. "Marble, you need to learn respect. Do you hear me!"

"I didn't hang up on you," Malachi said. "It must have been a dropped call."

Malachi stepped back slightly. The smell of alcohol on Rollie's breath was practically sliceable.

"We have the best tower in this part of the state," Rollie said. "I've never had a dropped call downtown."

"I didn't hang up," Malachi said. "I thought you did. Maybe there's something wrong with one of our phones."

Malachi pointed at Timothy's phone. "Try calling his phone."

By now, both Rollie and Malachi had shuffled inside. Malachi closed the door as Rollie retrieved his phone from his pocket and punched in Timothy's number.

"Hello, this is The Table. The church for you. How can I serve you?" Timothy said when he answered.

"What the...is going on?" Rollie said.

And then Rollie heard Timothy's voice over his phone, "Why don't you join us for some coffee. I make great coffee."

Rollie turned off his phone and looked at Timothy, "I don't know."

The Kool-Aid

"I said coffee, not Kool-Aid," Timothy said. "And you can leave anytime. Any time you're ready. O.K.?"

45. The Letter

While Timothy was getting the coffee around, Malachi made introductions. It wasn't the warmish how-are-you-doing, nice-to-meet-you variety of glad-handing. On Rollie's side of the handshakes that is.

Rollie was acting like they might be radioactive. But then JC decided to contaminate him when she gave him a brief hug and said, "How you doing tonight, sweetie?"

Malachi was sure she had just pulled a major social faux pas. He tensed inside.

But Rollie seemed to drop his lead shield—just a bit. And while it wasn't really a smile on his face, it was livelier than a straight-line grimace.

Malachi glanced over at JC. He question-marked his face. She winked. And then Malachi tried not to laugh.

The introductions soon turned into goodbyes. Mandy was heading home. She worked the early shift at Zeke's. She was going to drop Carl off. Martin and JC were heading out.

Before Carl left, he motioned for Malachi to come up to the corner off to the right of the door. They talked quietly for a couple of minutes. No one else could hear what they were discussing.

And then Malachi said, "Hey Timothy, I need to go get something that's out in my Suburban."

In less than three minutes, Malachi had returned and joined Timothy and Rollie at the table for some coffee.

"So what's the deal, Rollie?" Malachi said. "Give it to us straight."

"Well, I've changed my mind about your church here," Rollie said. "Elder Tuli showed me some things in the Bible and his other book—it was like a light came on. And now I have a much clearer picture about what's going on. He's really into the Bible—believes every word of it. Front to back."

"So you believe in the Bible?" Malachi said.

"Well yeah. I'm O.K. with the Bible," Rollie said. "I don't have any problem with the Bible. I've just never really seen the connection between what it says and what most churchgoers do. I always sort of figured that there had to be more. Like maybe the next level."

"The next level?" Timothy said.

"Well yeah," Rollie said. "And tonight, I finally received the revelation. It was from Elder Tuli and their book—it's that next level. And it's all in their book, *The Ancient Scriptures of the Elder Guides.* When he read from it, the words grabbed me."

"*The Ancient Scriptures of the Elder Guides*?" Malachi said slowly.

"Yeah," Rollie said. "And Elder Tuli started showing me

things in it. When he explained it to me, it was like click, click, click. I was seeing things about life like never before."

And then Rollie stopped, looking intently at Timothy and then Malachi. "I'm not going to let this so-called church you're trying to start lead people astray. You said you wanted it straight. Right?"

"That's what I said. That's what I meant," Malachi said.

"I almost made a big mistake," Rollie said. "But thank God for Elder Tule, because now I see that this place is a cult."

Malachi lifted his left hand from under the table and placed the letter flap side up on the table, so Rollie could see the words, "Delight yourself in the Lord and He will give you the desires of your heart."

Rollie fixed his eyes on it for several seconds.

"So what's inside, Malachi?" Rollie said. "Another trick."

"I don't know," Malachi said. "It's been lying on my dashboard since the last time we talked."

"So you wrote it and you don't know what it says?" Rollie said.

Rollie reached for it. Malachi placed his hand over it. "Carl wrote it. But he asked me not to tell anyone about his involvement. Except you."

"I want to see what's inside," Rollie said.

"Not yet," Malachi said.

"Is this what cults do?" Rollie said.

"I wouldn't know," Malachi said. "But here's a question for you. So how do you know this book, The Ancient Scriptures of the Elder Guides, is true, reliable enough to trust your life with?"

Rollie chuckled. "I asked Elder Tuli basically the same thing. He knew the answer without hesitation. He told me to read it. And as a sign that it was true, my heart would burn within me."

"So you follow your heart? That's what Elder Tuli told

you? That's what you believe?" Malachi said.

"Exactly."

"Here, you can open the letter, Rollie," Malachi said.

He carefully tore the envelope open and pulled out the single sheet of paper. After unfolding it, he studied it for several seconds. And then his eyes retraced the words on the page a second time.

Rollie then drew in a deep breath. He leaned back in his chair.

He stared upward toward the top of the roadside wall for nearly two minutes.

He looked over at Malachi and said, "Crap."

He shook his head back and forth and then said, "So that's in the Bible? The one Elder Tuli insists he believes in. The one I told you I believe is true."

His eyes darted toward Timothy, "Do you have an Authorized King James Version of the Bible?"

"Right here on my Tablet," Timothy said. "Let me get it up for you."

"Look up Jeremiah 17:9," Rollie said. "And let me see it."

"Here you go, Rollie."

Rollie then methodically read the words from the Bible verse out loud, "The heart is more deceitful than all else. And is desperately sick; who can understand it?"

Rollie stared at the screen as if that would make the words dissolve.

He shook his head and then looked at Malachi, "Now, I'm the weasel. Tuli's a weasel. Follow my heart? That's absurd. My deceitful heart? Your heart will burn—that's ridiculous."

Rollie took a drink of coffee and then said, "Malachi, I'm so sorry for the way I treated you. There's no way to justify it."

He didn't say anything for a few moments. And then said, "I ah…" He shook his head. "I need to quit drinking so much. I ah…that's not an excuse. I ah…I do apologize for my behavior."

"Apology accepted," Malachi said. He extended his hand and they shook.

And then he turned to Timothy, who said, "All is forgiven."

"How could I get so mixed up so fast?" Rollie said. "And even if I didn't agree with you, did I need to act like a total raging idiot? And you two have treated me so kindly. You try to give me a pie and cash to keep me from…from…"

Rollie turned his head to the left, looking away from Malachi and Timothy. His focus was downward. He was talking to them. But it was almost as if he was talking to himself, "I'm so arrogant. It's pathetic."

They were silent for several seconds.

"Me too. I've got a long way to go, myself," Timothy said. "More coffee?"

Rollie looked back over at Timothy and Malachi. "Yeah. Sounds good."

From there, the conversation turned a hue confessional, predominately the type that's easier to laugh about. And then it followed a trail of its own. One of those types of conversations that you mentally stop for the briefest of seconds, wondering: "How did we arrive at favorite eighth-grade baseball team memories?"

But then when Rollie laughed for the third time, Malachi was delighted that he knew Rollie played shortstop. And once triggered a game winning double play. An eighth grade rarity.

And then somehow, the talk curved back to what the evening was really about.

"I'm really thankful you guys are starting this church," Rollie said. "I'm one-hundred percent behind what you're doing."

And then his face turned stern. "And I'm telling you one more thing, before I head on out, I'm going to silence Tuli and his bunch. Like right now."

And then he looked over at Timothy. "So what time is it?"

Timothy glanced down at his Microsoft Tablet. "Yeah it is late. It's past midnight—12:03."

"Well, actually, it's early." Rollie smiled. "Morning has broken over Manistee."

46. Spring Surprise Party

"**H**ey Martin, before we go back to work, I've got to tell you something," Malachi said.

"So what's up?" Martin said.

"I'm having a party down at the church on the first day of Spring from 7:00 to 9:00 or so," Malachi said. "That's on a Wednesday evening."

"What kind of party?" Martin said.

"It's a surprise party," Malachi said.

"Oh cool. I love surprise parties," Martin said. "Whose birthday is it?"

"It's not a birthday surprise party," Malachi said.

"So what kind of surprise party is it?" Martin said.

"That's part of the surprise," Malachi said. "I'm not telling you what the surprise of the surprise party is."

Martin looked at Malachi for several seconds.

He smiled. "You're weird, Malachi."

Malachi grinned. "That sounds like a yes. So here's the deal. Don't bring anything. I've got the food covered."

And then Malachi paused for several seconds before saying, "O.K. This is my only request: bring a favorite recipe, a jar of peanut butter—the good stuff, and a photograph of you as a baby—if you have one. And be ready to tell everybody your three favorite colors."

"Sure, sounds ah…" Martin said. "A Spring Surprise Party that's a surprise. Bring—a recipe, peanut butter, baby picture, three favorite colors. Sounds great. Who all's invited?"

"Just a small group," Malachi said. "You, JC, Uncle Dale, Aunt Betty, Mandy, Alex, Timothy, and Carl."

When Malachi opened the door to The Table several days later, he said to himself, "Wow, this looks amazing."

And then he saw Timothy.

"Timothy, it looks remarkable in here," Malachi said. "You did it so fast. The painting and the carpet in one week."

"You would be surprised how many of my regular ex-bar customers are painters," Timothy said. "Wierick and a couple of the regulars sprayed it out in two days and three six packs. The carpet I picked up at Menards—they had that 11% rebate deal going on. A couple more bar buddies installed it. Four hours and two safety breaks. One was before they started."

"Safety break?" Malachi said.

"It's really sad," Timothy said. "But I know what they're doing out in the van. They think they gotta have their weed."

"You're right; it is sad," Malachi said.

"The good news is they did a nice job. The Table is ready for service," Timothy said. "And the better news is, all the construction workers heard my testimony, and I invited each one of them to church. I think that makes about five

Spring Surprise Party

times for Wierick."

Malachi stood admiring the space. The ceiling was painted a sunshine yellow. The walls were seafoam green-ish—slightly toned down with a dash of gray pigment. The commercial grade carpeting was multi-hued. Coffee colored with contrasting splashes of off-white, beige, teak, and burnt yellow. All the trim and doors were black—in a semi-gloss.

"I love the colors," Malachi said. "And those mini white Christmas lights on the riverside wall make it look festive in here."

"It did turn out nice," Timothy said. "Praise God."

"And thanks for helping serve the refreshments tonight," Malachi said.

"I'm happy to help out on the Spring Surprise Party Surprise," Timothy said. "The first annual?"

"Who knows?" Malachi said.

Then Malachi made his way to the front of the church carrying his mandolin. Timothy had left a space between the seats, so he could walk directly to the front.

He turned around and said to Timothy, "I think this walkway in-between the chairs is going to make it a lot nicer for Sunday service."

"Oh I agree. Definitely," Timothy said.

Everyone started arriving. Most were carrying Walmart-style shopping bags to bring in their party items.

When Mandy and Alex arrived, Malachi greeted them and said, "I need to talk to you two in the back."

In a few minutes, they re-emerged from the kitchen area. Mandy walked toward the entry door.

Alex had an especially big grin on his face as he accompanied Malachi to the front.

"Hey everyone," Malachi said. "Thank you so much for coming. Please take a seat. I have a song I would like to sing to get us started."

He then stopped and looked back at Mandy and said, "Mandy, could you wait back there in case anybody else shows up."

"Sure, Malachi," she said.

Malachi picked up his mandolin from its stand as Alex stood beside him.

Malachi worked the strap around his suit coat. He took a deep breath and said, "It's the first day of Spring."

He then started softly playing his mandolin as he talked, "Winter seems to kill things off. And it's easy to think maybe it's dead forever. But in the Spring, what looks dead can come back to life. The great God we serve is in the business of restoration. Can I get an amen?"

"Amen."

"Amen."

"Amen."

Malachi looked upward. And then to the right. And then straight ahead. After another deep breath, he said, "I hope I can do this."

He swallowed; he strummed his mandolin. "I was sure a part of my life was dead, but God surprised me. And here's your surprise. Surprise—you're all at a wedding."

Malachi started singing. Mandy opened the door, and Annie emerged. Together, they walked toward those gathered—as Malachi sang:

> Deep in the heart of God
> Deep, deep, deep
> Is his love for us
>
> His love for us
>
> Deep in the heart of God
> Deep, deep, deep

Spring Surprise Party

Is his love for us

His love for us

When Annie arrived, she faced Malachi as he sang one more chorus:

Deep in the heart of God
Deep, deep, deep
Is his love for you

His love for you

Tears were running down both of Annie's cheeks. She wiped them away with a handkerchief. Malachi's stomach muscles tensed to hold back his emotions. JC wasn't able to. Neither was Aunt Betty. And Mandy was brushing away tears during the entire ceremony.

Malachi tried not to look around.

Annie moved to Malachi's side. And Mandy stood beside her. Alex, the best man, stood beside Malachi.

Carl stepped forward with an open Bible. His eyes were moist.

Carl stood there. It was a long time. He didn't have a choice.

It took almost two minutes, though it seemed longer, before Carl was ready to say, "Should we proceed?"

Malachi glanced at Annie and then looked at Carl before shaking his head.

And then Carl said, "Annie, what would make you want to marry Malachi again?"

Annie said, "'I have been crucified with Christ; and it is no longer I who live, but Christ lives in me; and the life which I now live in the flesh, I live by faith in the Son of God, who loved me and gave Himself up for me.' So in response to God's great love for me, I choose to live a new life that reflects the Christ that lives in me. It is also my desire to undo an act in my life that dishonored the Great God of love. And I desire to marry Malachi, because I love him."

Next, Carl faced Malachi and said, "Malachi, what would make you want to marry Annie again?"

Malachi said, "The Bible says, 'Husbands, love your wives, just as Christ also loved the church and gave Himself up for her.' In response to the love of Jesus Christ and in honor of His amazing sacrifice, I choose to follow the command of this verse. I failed the first time. But I choose to live a new life, reflecting the Christ that lives in me. By His special grace. And I desire to marry Annie, because I love her."

Malachi and Annie then exchanged the traditional wedding vows.

And then Carl said, "By the power vested in me by the state of Michigan and Almighty God, I now pronounce you husband and wife. Malachi, you may kiss your bride."

It was a long kiss. Real long.

When they released their embrace, Annie had tears on her cheeks again. Mandy was crying even more. And Alex had a flashbulb bright smile on his face as he clapped his hands, appearing to be coiled for some joyous body gyrations.

And then Carl said, "Ladies and gentleman, I would like to present to you Mr. and Mrs. Malachi Marble."

47. The Helper

"**S**o why did you have us bring peanut butter and all that other stuff to the wedding?" Martin said. "With all the crying and laughing and good food, everybody forgot about those things."

Malachi laughed. "That was a diversion."

"It worked," Martin said. "Boy that sure was gutsy that you never even told Mandy and Alex until they got there. Wow, that was daring."

"I wavered on that decision," Malachi said. "Like I told everyone, Mandy already knew we were getting married. But not when. I wanted the wedding to be something special for her too."

"When you said, 'Surprise. You're at a wedding,' for a second or two, I thought you and Mandy were getting married. I mean…none of us—except Dale and Betty, knew Annie. But then I saw the bouquet and Annie's dress—then I knew."

Malachi laughed again.

"That was the coolest, most Godly wedding of all time," Martin said. "But hey, we need to get to work."

It was day one on the Swallow Valley Orchards' construction job. The first Monday following the wedding. And after the honeymoon getaway Malachi and Annie had taken to Onekama—the beach town just north of Manistee.

Swallow Valley Orchards—a third generation farm whose main focus was fruit trees. Located just outside the northern boundary of the Manistee National Forest. The sprawling operation encompassed a handful of sights, with their main presence being on Johnson Rd. directly across from Chief Lake.

That's where Martin and Malachi were working. On a chilly day—the second day of spring.

"I'll fire up the Skytrack and bring it around to the south side of the building," Martin said. "Can you grab a couple of gorilla bars out of the job trailer? And look around and see if you can find some pallets. Four would be good."

"You got it," Malachi said.

Martin maneuvered the Skytrack around the backside of the building. He had attached the work platform to the forks. This four-foot by eight-foot box constructed of welded steel, with tubular safety railing on three sides, was the ideal piece of equipment for productive high-above-the-ground construction work.

"I've found some skids, and the bars are right over there," Malachi said. "What else do you need help with?"

"I think I'm all set," Martin said. "Here's the plan. I'll

shoot you up on the platform about two-thirds of the way up. You work the top, and I'll do the bottom. We can probably rip off twelve feet, and then I'll move the Skytrack over."

The building was an aged pole barn. A typical thirty-two foot by sixty-foot with twelve-foot sidewalls rendition. The outside skin was a faded chalky blue. The roof—a rusty, discolored, dirty white.

Soon they were peeling the three-foot wide, full height sheets of metal off the building's frame. When they popped the last fastener loose on a piece, Martin would manhandle the awkward steel sheet and stack it on a skid.

At three minutes after ten, Martin hollered up to Malachi, "What do you think about skipping break? We did talk a long time this morning. And it would be nice to bust this long side out before lunch."

Malachi gave Martin a thumbs-up. "I'm good."

Teamwork and efficient rhythm conquered the big wall a handful of minutes before the noon whistle blew.

Soon they were sitting in the Suburban with the motor running, anticipating the warmth from the vehicle's renowned heater.

"God bless this food. Give us strength to honor You. Help us to be a blessing. Amen," Martin said.

"Dale had to leave so fast to get Wilks and Raymond going on that other job, I didn't even have time to ask him what this place was going to be," Martin said. "So I grabbed the blueprint out of the job trailer."

He unrolled the blueprint as he munched on his peanut butter sandwich.

And then Malachi heard Martin chuckle. "So guess what this place is going to be."

"I don't know," Malachi said. "How would I know?"

"Two guesses," Martin said.

"Ah...ah church?" Malachi said.

"To some people...kind of," Martin said.

"Oh. I know what it's going to be. I've heard about these places," Malachi said. "What a coincidence. I mean... a God-thing. It's like a present."

"A God-thing?" Martin said.

"Yeah...this is going to be one of those wedding chapels," Malachi said. "Isn't it?"

Martin laughed. "I think wedding bliss has infected your brain. No. This place is going to be a distillery for schnapps with an adjoining tasting room and retail space."

"No its not," Malachi said.

"Yes it is," Martin said as he handed Malachi the print.

"Ouch," Malachi said. "Elder Tuli is probably going to drive up in like two minutes. I can hear him now, 'Oh the defilement, the sacrilege.'"

Martin chuckled. "Or Rollie, so he can get a jump on signing up for his frequent-tasters card."

"Schnapps?" Malachi said.

"Yep, Schnapps," Martin said.

Malachi folded his arms and looked out the front windshield.

Martin was looking at Malachi.

"Schnapps?" Malachi said.

"Yeah, schnapps, Malachi," Martin said. "Like mind altering al-key-haul."

He stared outside for just over a minute and then said, "Well praise God. Praise God for work to feed our families."

"What? Aren't you supposed to get indignant? Say, 'Let's go on strike,'" Martin said.

"How many shopaholics do you think frequent Menards?" Malachi said. "Buying stuff because they're out of control."

'Yeah," Martin said.

The Helper

"Did we get our religious shorts in a knot and do a pious pullout over there?" Malachi said.

"I'm hearing you," Martin said.

"So if a person drinks a jug of this schnapps stuff every day, is that their real problem? Or the person who ship-wrecks their finances because they can't quit shopping, is that their main problem? Should that be our number one concern?"

"You're right," Martin said. "They need Jesus. Let them come to The Table with Jesus and the disciples. With their Schnapps bottles, their flaming credit cards."

He stopped and looked at Malachi, "And with their unrepairable, utterly destroyed marriage."

Malachi shook his head as they knuckled bumped.

"Bring it all," Martin said.

"I'll drink to that," Malachi said as he tipped his coffee cup to his lips.

And then Martin said, "Back to work."

When the workday had concluded and they were putting the last of the tools away, Malachi said to Martin, "Do you have time to talk for a few minutes?"

"Well sure," Martin said.

The day had warmed up nicely. The jobsite was on an elevated area of the orchard. A gentle slope rose up to the building from the long rows of fruit trees to the south. Winter browns and blacks were transitioning to minty green.

Still wearing their carpenter's tool belts, they were both standing at the lower edge of the job-trailer's swing-up door. Now open, it formed the ramp into the trailer's interior.

The sun was lowering in the sky. The big barn was casting an ever-increasing shadow to the east, dispelling the brilliance of the day as it stretched toward the ramp.

"Have you noticed that...ah," Malachi said. "Have you noticed how, without even talking about it or planning it, out here on the jobsite, you've become the leader and I've become the helper? It just sort of happened."

Martin looked down. His facial muscles tensed.

And then he looked at Malachi. "I'm sorry, Malachi. But like you said, I didn't do it intentionally or at least I don't think so. I'm so sorry."

Malachi shook his head back and forth. "No. No that's not what I'm talking about at all. You don't owe me an apology. Not at all."

Martin stared at Malachi for several seconds.

"God's been showing me something. Thoughts and feelings I've never had before," Malachi said. "So what's going on is good. It's God's way. But hardly anybody ever sees this. And nobody talks about it. At least I haven't heard it mentioned."

"O.K.," Martin said. "I'm just about as clear on this as a guy who just spent all day in the schnapps' barn product testing."

"Sounds like you need to come to The Table," Malachi said. "The church for you."

They both laughed.

"Here's the deal," Malachi said. "Maybe you've seen this Bible verse that says, 'And God has appointed in the church, first apostles, second prophets, third teachers, then miracles, then gifts of healings, helps, administrations, various kinds of tongues.'"

"Maybe," Martin said. "But I'm not familiar with it."

"I've discovered that I have the sixth spiritual gift on the list," Malachi said. "God has appointed me to be a helper. Working with you, helping at the chapel service at Menards, helping down at The Table—some construction work, cleaning up, whatever. I can tell, that's what God has made me to be. He's gifted me to be a helper. And yes, God has used me to lead things—like Jesus at Walmart, but really, I didn't seem to fit what I was doing. Because I didn't."

Malachi stopped and focused more intently on Martin. "Am I making any sense?"

"Yeah," Martin said. "Definitely."

"I'm just so sure that's my gift," Malachi said. "Now, you're absolutely, positively gifted as a teacher plus a lot of strength in leadership. I'm positive."

"Thank you," Martin said. "And now I am seeing things in a new way too."

"Now, I've already talked to Carl about this, and we'll need to run it by everyone else, but he agrees fully with my observation," Malachi said. "So I'm not going to be up front preaching and teaching on Sundays. Yes, I may do it on rare occasions to help out. However, I'm going to fulfill my calling as a helper."

"So who's going to do most of the teaching/preaching on Sundays?" Martin said.

"You are," Malachi said.

"The new guy?" Martin said.

"The guy who is a very gifted teacher, who whole-heartedly follows the Lord Jesus Christ. The guy who intensely studies the Word of God," Malachi said. "That's the guy."

"So you're going to vacuum floors, and I'll take your job, just like that," Martin said.

"I will definitely vacuum some floors," Malachi said. "But the gift of helps is a lot more than that."

"Like what?" Martin said.

"The Menards chapel service and what happened there is a perfect example," Malachi said. "You used your gift of teaching. Then Evonda comes by later, because she was moved by what you taught. I had helped some with a song. And then I basically took your anointed message and helped connect it to Evonda's life situation. Everything I did fell under the shadow of the most important part—your proclaiming of the Word of God. It's like, you brought the meat and taters, and I was the salt and pepper for the main feast. I helped make it more palatable for Evonda. But she certainly would not have eaten just raw salt and pepper."

"Wow," Martin said. "I've never seen it like that."

"Neither did I until God revealed it to me," Malachi said.

"That's so cool," Martin said. "Nobody ever teaches on that. Maybe you should."

"I could do a conference on the gift of helps," Malachi said.

"Well yeah...maybe," Martin said. "I'm not sure about a conference."

"I could charge like three-hundred bucks to impart the gift of helps," Malachi said.

"I don't know about that. Three hundred bucks?" Martin said. "I just don't see that."

"People easily get four-hundred for a gift of healing impartation and the apostle gift—that must be going for five, six hundred bucks. So three hundred's a bargain. So at the impartation ceremony, I would have everybody come up front with their vacuum cleaners. I would lay my hands on everybody's heads, and they would fall over backwards. With a little help from me—using my helps gift you know. And then I would lay hands on their vacuums and shove them over too. Forty-five people and forty-five vacuums all slain in the spirit—sprawled out on the floor."

Malachi grinned and looked at Martin. "What do you think?"

"I think you've been testing too much schnapps."

48. Jesus at The Table

"**A**re you ready, Martin?" Malachi said.

"Preach the word; be ready in season and out of season," Martin said.

He rubbed his hands together and exhaled as he spoke, "'Not by might nor by power, but by My Spirit, says the Lord of hosts.' I think so. I've never talked in front of a big group like this before. Remember, the chapel at Menards was like only, maybe a dozen people."

"Well, just act like there are only a dozen people," Malachi said. "I mean, it's not like one of those massively popular gift of helps conferences where it's standing room only."

Martin laughed. "Of course, half the seats are taken up by vacuum cleaners."

Timothy scrunched his face. "What are you two talking

about?"

"Sorry, just a joke between us," Malachi said. "So how many chairs do we have?"

"It's like sixty," Timothy said. "Several of my buddies, old bar buddies are coming. Wierick of course."

"Sal told me she'll be here. She'll probably bring her husband," Malachi said. "Gary's almost a definite. From Walmart. You know him?"

"Oh yeah," Martin said.

"And I've got flyers all over town," Timothy said. "Who knows what God's going to do today?"

"Hey, there's Mandy—nice and early," Malachi said.

Malachi looked at Timothy. "With our first guest. I think I know that guy. Well, Martin you head to the kitchen—you need to stay focused. After I greet Mandy and her friend, I'll come back there."

And then Malachi said to Timothy, "Thanks for being the hospitality team of one. When Carl arrives, can you send him back to the kitchen?"

Then Malachi walked toward the street side of the church. Off to the right, Annie was already chatting with Mandy by the time he arrived.

Malachi greeted Mandy and Alex. And then turned toward the man who was with her.

Malachi extended his hand. "You look familiar. I'm Malachi Marble."

"Malachi Marble. Eminem," the man said with a grin. "I'm Jamie Christler."

"So good to see you," Malachi said as they shook hands. "You're looking good. How've you been doing?"

"Ever since we hung out together in jail, I've been on a good path," Jamie said. "God is real to me. Yeah, I've hit a few bumps, but Jesus is my Lord. Just like I told you in jail."

"Praise God, Jamie," Malachi said. "It's so good to have

you visit The Table. I've got to head to the back to prepare for the service. We'll talk more later. O.K."

Malachi glanced at his watch—10:09. Twenty-one minutes until—*let's do church.*

Martin's sermon notes were spread out on a stainless steel countertop. Though he wasn't speaking out loud, Malachi could tell he was practicing his sermon.

He stopped when he saw Malachi.

"Just keep going," Malachi said.

"I'm ready. I'm prepared," Martin said. "But I need to get a couple of these under my belt so I won't feel so jittery."

"You're going to do great," Malachi said. "That guy with Mandy, Jamie Christler, I met him when I was in jail. He attended a little impromptu chapel I had, he and two other guys. Snyder the spider—a bald guy with a tattoo of a spider web covering the top of his head; I don't remember the other guy's name. Maybe they'll show up too. That would be so cool."

Soon Carl arrived.

"Are there many people out there?" Martin said.

"You know how everybody always shows up at the last minute for church," Carl said.

Next, Martin called a fire drill.

And when they stood up, Carl said, "Let's surrender this time to the Lord. This day. This church service."

Soon all three of them had their hands raised in the air and each one affirmed:

"I surrender all."

"I surrender all."

"I surrender all."

And then Malachi softly began to sing:

> Solid is the Rock upon which I stand
> Solid is the Rock upon which I stand
>
> Standing, standing, I'm standing on the promises

of Christ my Savior
Standing, standing, I'm standing on the promises
of Christ my Savior

Savior, Lord, Your My King
Savior, Lord, Your My King

I surrender all
I surrender all
I surrender all

And then Martin and Carl joined in:
I surrender all
I surrender all
I surrender all

When Martin opened his eyes, he said, "Wow, God is surely in this place."

He looked at Malachi and Carl. "Praise God. Now I'm ready."

"Yeah," Malachi said. "It's almost time. We need to get our instruments ready."

They both made their way to the front of the church and took the two steps up unto the small platform.

The one Dale had paid Martin and Malachi to build, plus he paid for the materials—his contribution to the church. And then Timothy painted the platform black.

Martin's Casio RX-350 keyboard was set stage right at a slight angle, allowing Martin to see the congregation, as well as Malachi.

Malachi was thinking how marvelous the sanctuary looked. He loved the color scheme. And Timothy's passion for Vistaprint banners was artistically displayed on every wall—each highlighting a Bible verse. The newest one was now hanging over the entry door. It was Timothy's/Vistaprint's

Jesus at The Table

standard two-foot by three-foot rendition. A black background with white wording. It had a three-inch wide inset border—in the same sunshine yellow as the ceiling. And the stout, contemporary lettering proclaimed, "Other outcasts came and joined Jesus and the disciples at The Table."

"I want to welcome everyone to The Table this Easter morning. Thank you for worshipping with us," Malachi said. "Today, we proclaim—Jesus is alive."

Malachi looked over at Martin. He could tell they were both thinking the same thought.

As Malachi scanned out over the room, one visual was by far the most striking. All the empty seats.

He looked at the door one more time. Besides the regulars, there was Jamie, and someone sitting geographically near dead center of the seating arrangement. Malachi didn't know the man, but assumed he was Wierick. He looked like a Wierick. And then there was an older couple in the far reaches. They appeared skittish. But still brave enough to venture into a new church. Malachi was already envisioning them scooting out as the final *amen* hung in the air.

The most eager looking guest was a lady three rows in back of might-be-Wierick. But on the other side of the aisle. She had that attentive, I'm-ready demeanor.

"Can we stand and worship the Risen Lord with our songs to Him?" Malachi said.

He was right. She popped right up.

This was the first time Malachi and Martin had led worship as a team. Malachi was hesitant. He never played with other musicians. And Martin was so accomplished and confident.

He pressed Malachi by saying, "The Bible says, 'Sing to Him a new song.' Let's go further and have a new sound here at The Table—some God inspired innovation, instead of mundane imitation. Still it was a hefty stretch musically for Malachi. And he attempted to convince Martin to lead worship by himself.

Martin then put forth one of the axioms at The Table, which settled the issue for Malachi. "If we try something at The Table and it doesn't work, we'll change. It's not about being perfect."

Still the first song was nearly perfect. One of Malachi's standards: *Awesome is the God.* It had never sounded better.

And then halfway through the second song, Malachi's lower e-string snapped. He had never experienced that before. It seemed impossible, because Malachi strummed the mandolin strings with his thumb.

Martin the consummate pro, saw what happened and filled in the gaps musically as Malachi extracted the string.

All was well within a couple of minutes, but they never fully got back into sync. It wasn't a bad worship set; however, the music quality took a noticeable dip after song one.

When the music concluded, Malachi sat on the front row with Annie.

Right from the start, it seemed like the amazing Martin from Menards had left the building. The unbiblical word *clunky* would best describe his presentation. He had the Bible verses. His theme was solid. He had three virtuous points.

But it was like he was playing dot to dot in the dark. The connections were repeatedly askew.

The fella, who-might-be-Wierick, seemed to agree with Malachi. And now he was almost positive he was Wierick. Because after Timothy finished his hosting duties, he sat down beside him.

Malachi heard a snore. When he turned around, Wierick had one of those sleepy where-am-I-looks on his face. In addition, it appeared that Timothy's face was a rosier hue than normal.

Malachi was praying for Martin generously during the entire sermon.

And Martin did rally at the end. It was for merely three

minutes and a handful of seconds.

"Let me read these verses," Martin said, "Afterward Jesus appeared to the eleven themselves as they were reclining at the table. And He rebuked them for their unbelief and hardness of heart, because they had not believed those who had seen Him after He had risen."

And then Martin said, "Please stand with me as I close. Today, we celebrate the risen Lord Jesus Christ. We have enough evidence with the Bible, seeing changed lives through the power of the blood of Jesus, through seeing miracles, and so many other ways; essentially we have seen the Risen Christ. Let's rebuke in our lives, by the power of the Holy Spirit, unbelief and hardness of heart."

He stepped out to the side of the podium with his Bible in his hand, "Fully believe in what Jesus Christ can do—past, present, and future. Keep your heart soft to the wooing of Christ in you—the Holy Spirit. And then be empowered to do what Jesus commanded in the next verse."

Martin looked down at his Bible and read, "Go into all the world and preach the gospel to every creature."

"Friends, go and tell every creature about Jesus Christ—our risen Lord."

"Let's pray."

When he concluded his prayer, Martin said, "If anyone needs prayer—for any reason, please come forward."

The attentive lady walked straight to the front.

Malachi glanced back. He was right. The daring, yet hesitant couple had already left. While Wierick seemed fairly awake, with a smile on his face. Though Malachi suspected it was due to an obligation fulfilled.

And then he heard Jamie behind him.

"It sure was good to see you, Malachi," Jamie said. "Do more people usually show up?"

"I hope so," Malachi said. "I'll see you next Sunday."

"Maybe."

And then he heard Martin calling softly, "Malachi."

He turned toward the platform. Martin was signaling for him to come over.

"Malachi, this is Sara," Martin said.

"Nice to meet you," Malachi said. "I'm Malachi."

"Sara, tell Malachi why you decided to come to The Table today," Martin said.

"I was over at Glen's Market looking at the bulletin board after I finished shopping. Some guy came up beside me and pointed at the poster advertising this church and said to me, 'Don't go there. That's a cult.'"

"Really?" Malachi said.

And then she continued, "I hadn't even noticed your poster. I wasn't planning on going to church today. So when he left, I read the poster. The words: *The church for you,* grabbed a hold of me—stirred a sensation in my heart. And wouldn't leave. So I went from no church plans to...I would call it a...a joyful yearning. So here I am."

"Wow, praise God," Malachi said.

"Sara, tell Malachi what you asked me when you came up here," Martin said.

"I told Pastor Martin, his words truly awakened something inside of me. In a good way. And I had this awareness—I knew I couldn't tell anyone about Jesus, because I really didn't know Jesus. So I asked Pastor Martin if he could help me to know Jesus."

She looked at Malachi. "And now I know Jesus. He's in my heart. I can tell."

She hugged Malachi and said, "This is the best church."

And at the same time, he heard Martin say, "God is surely in this place."

49. A Way in Manger

"**H**ow about some breakfast. Are you awake in there?" Annie said as she lightly rapped on the door.

"What? Hun?" Malachi said. "Yeah…ah yeah."

"Are you awake?" Annie said again.

"Oh… ah yeah," Malachi said. "Come on in, Annie."

Malachi stood up and hugged Annie. "Happy New Year my beautiful wife. May God bless your new year."

"Happy New Year to you too," Annie said. "Did I wake you up?"

"No. I wasn't sleeping," Malachi said. "I was just deep in thought. Really deep. It was like a long train passing by slow enough to read every bit of the graffiti. These pictures of the past started to roll by in my mind. Wow, it was wonderful. I was reliving some memories. Some good memories—with some challenges. But God is so good."

"So, do I need to welcome you back to 2014?" Annie said.

Malachi laughed. "Yeah. Pretty much."

"How about some breakfast?" Annie said. "I guess I should say, a New Year's Day brunch. A late brunch."

"That sounds great," Malachi said.

"Maybe you should change out of your pajama pants first," Annie said. "We have a guest."

"Really?" Malachi said.

"Alex wanted to invite his friend Rollie over," Annie said. "He was also hoping he would go to church with us tonight."

"Speaking of church," Malachi said. "Stephen Johnson and his family are definitely coming tonight. You remember I told you we had been e-mailing back and forth."

"Yeah," Annie said. "That's wonderful. It will be so good to see them."

"And he said they have a surprise for us," Malachi said. "Of course, he wouldn't say what. I just hope they didn't buy us a Christmas present."

"Well, you know Stephen," Annie said. "Whatever it is, it will be a blessing. But now, I need to finish getting the food ready."

When Malachi walked into the kitchen, he instantly smiled. He knew the smell. It was Camp Eggs Malachi. Originally, something he cooked over the campfire, back in their camping days. It was simple—scrambled eggs, a healthy dose of cheese, and some salsa.

"Hey everyone," Malachi said.

"This is my friend Rollie," Alex said.

Malachi immediately saw the family resemblance in his facial features. Plus, he had the same girth as his dad.

"Welcome to our family, Rollie," Malachi said.

And then he turned to Annie and said, "Do you need any help?"

"No I'm good," Annie said. "The food's almost ready. You can sit down."

Malachi sat down in his usual seat, the head of the table slot. Their dining room and kitchen flowed together as one space. If Malachi had stretched out his hand to its full extent, his fingertips would have been less than a yardstick from the stove where Annie had just clicked the burner knob to off.

"So good to have you join us, Rollie," Malachi said. "We always say a prayer together as a family before we eat."

Malachi looked to his left at Rollie when he said it.

"What?" Rollie said. "I have to help or something?"

"No, I wanted to make sure you weren't going to run out the door screaming that I had ruined your life forever, because I prayed out loud."

"People do that?" Rollie said.

"Just about. But it's usually adults. They shriek the loudest if someone whispers the name *Jesus*," Malachi said. "Not at our house. We ask our guests who we're not sure of."

"I've never heard anybody pray," Rollie said. "I mean like...live...in person. Is it like they do it on *Duck Dynasty*?"

"Yeah. Theirs is the real deal—pretty much," Malachi said. "You want to go for it. Live in person. I'll do the praying."

"Sure." Rollie said. "Why not?"

"First, God, I ask you to bless those Duck Dynasty guys for showing people a slice of who You are. Thank you for the family you've gathered around our table today. Help each one of us to draw closer to You this new year. With this food, give us strength to honor and glorify Your name. In the name of Jesus. Amen."

"Amen."

"Amen."

"Yeah ah...amen."

"Thank you Annie for making everything," Malachi said.

"This is really good," Rollie said.

"So how's your dad doing?" Malachi said.

"He's really sick this morning," Rollie said. "He gets sick a lot. And this morning, he's really bad."

"That's so unfortunate," Malachi said.

"So I'm trying to figure this out," Rollie said. "Alex and you have different last names. I knew Alex went to The Table, and I've heard my dad mention your name, but until today, I didn't know he was your son."

Malachi looked over at Alex. He smiled. And then looked back at Rollie. "It's a long story. Something only God could do. It's pretty amazing. I'll let Alex tell you what God did. You two can have that talk another time."

When everyone finished eating, Malachi said, "Annie, let me help you clean up. I'm sure Alex and Rollie have something they would rather do than hang out with us."

"I wanted to show Rollie your mandolin," Alex said. "He got a ukulele for Christmas, but he's never seen a mandolin. I was telling him how cool it is."

"Malachi, I'll clean up," Annie said. "You go show Rollie your *cool* mandolin."

Alex and Rollie followed Malachi down the hallway of their moderately sized ranch house. To the last bedroom on the right, Malachi's office.

Malachi turned around just before he walked into the room and said, "It might be slightly messy in here, Rollie."

And then Malachi heard Alex say, "It's a national holiday. I don't think you're supposed to clean your room. Isn't that right, Malachi?"

"I'm not positive," Malachi said. "But why take a chance? Right."

"Your office is cool," Rollie said the moment he stepped in.

Alex pointed to the wall. "There's his mandolin."

Rollie stared at it and then said, "It's like a little guitar."

Malachi reached for it and removed it from its wall bracket. He held it out toward Rollie. "Do you want to hold it?"

"No. I want to hear you play it," Rollie said.

"Well O.K.," Malachi said. "Grab a seat."

Rollie sat down on the chair facing the computer, the one Alex had been sitting on earlier in the day.

The Bible verse scrolling across the screen drew Rollie's attention for a couple of seconds. *"Jesus said, I came to send fire on the earth and how I wish it were already kindled."*

And then he repositioned the chair. He faced Malachi, who was sitting on the edge of the green recliner.

He was cradling his mandolin and had already worked the strap around his back.

Alex pulled the swiveling chair over from the other side of the room. And now he was facing Malachi also.

Malachi strummed a few chords and then said, "This is a little riff God gave me yesterday."

He played the A minor-Chord three times. In a vibrato. A Malachi-vibrato. Two firm strums on the D-chord, two on the C, one strum on the D, the briefest of pauses, two more firm strums on the D-chord, followed by a melodic brushing of the G-chord.

The instant Malachi stopped, Rollie said, "That sounds kind of like a ringtone. Those ones without singing."

Malachi chuckled. "My first ringtone from God. I'll

call it *Fire Drill*."

"How do you know God gave it to you?" Rollie said.

"Wow. That's sort of complex to explain. Kind of...," Malachi said. "O.K. here's one way. That ringtone thing isn't a good example. But God has given me quite a few songs, and if they're from Him, they usually come to me very quickly. And I'm not that talented. Really."

"Does that make any sense?" Malachi said.

"I don't know," Rollie said. "I guess. Maybe?"

"Can you play that Christmas song?" Alex said.

"But Christmas is over," Malachi said.

"Our tree's still up," Alex said.

"So is ours," Rollie said.

"O.K.," Malachi said. "By popular demand—*A Way in a Manger*."

"I've heard of that song," Rollie said. "You didn't write that one."

"You've never heard this version," Malachi said. "And this is an example of what I was saying. This entire song came to me in less than an hour. Chords and all. God gave it to me," Malachi said. "And part of it is an old Christmas carol, which blends together with some new words and music. You'll see."

"Make sure you do the talking part like you did in church," Alex said.

Malachi smiled.

He strummed his mandolin and began to sing:

> Away in a manger
> No crib for His bed
>
> Jesus abide in me
> Jesus abide in me

A Way in Manger

Away in a manger
No crib for His bed
The little Lord Jesus
Lay down His sweet head

Jesus You laid down Your life for me
Your blood has set me free

Jesus abide in me
Jesus abide in me

Malachi stopped singing and spoke as he strummed his mandolin: "This is kind of what I said in church. Maybe Jesus is only half abiding in you. Maybe less. And maybe not at all. Maybe you don't know Jesus. So listen to these words. May they touch your heart in a special way."

And then Malachi continued the song:

So open your heart to Jesus today
His gift is salvation
He's the only way

The Way was born in a manger on, that first Christmas Day
And the little Lord Jesus, He'll return some day

Jesus abide in me
Jesus abide in me

The Way was born in a manger on, that first Christmas Day

Rollie had been watching Malachi closely as he played and sang, except when he glanced above Malachi's head.

Jesus at Walmart...fire on the Earth

At that point, Malachi presumed he was looking at the black baseball cap hanging on the wall above the chair, with the word, *JESUS* embroidered in yellow, surrounded by what looked like dancing white musical notes.

And he definitely shifted his attention to the rough-plaster cross Malachi had created on the wall to the right. Malachi was sure he was reading the blue-lettered Bible verse beneath it: "Come to Jesus—the Living Stone, rejected by people. But chosen by God as valuable. And precious."

But by the time Malachi finished playing the song, Rollie was absorbed in the music.

"Wow. That was so awesome," Rollie said.

He then shifted his eyes down to the floor for a second or two before refocusing on Malachi. "I've got something to ask you. It's something I really need to know."

Rollie seemed animated, like a child getting ready to open a Christmas present.

"What do you want to know, Rollie?" Malachi said.

"Well ah..." Rollie said.

"Go ahead," Malachi said.

"I mean...I don't know if it's okay to ask this," Rollie said.

"There are no dumb questions," Malachi said. "So just ask."

"O.K. then," Rollie said. "How much did your mandolin cost? I have some Christmas money. I want to buy one."

"I got this one for free," Malachi said. "Kind of from God." And then he told Rollie the story about Martin giving him the mandolin. Also, he briefly discussed with Rollie the price range he could expect to pay for a mandolin.

Then Rollie leaned back in the chair and looked around the room and said, "My dad has a man cave. I think your office is a Jesus cave."

Malachi grinned. "I hope so."

"I really like your song, Mr. Marble," Rollie said. "It sounded so nice. But it was like it was in a foreign language—Spanish or something. Because the words didn't really mean anything to me. But it sounded cool. I've never been to church in my life. Not even once."

"Why don't you come with us tonight?" Malachi said.

"I ah...I don't..." Rollie said. "I'm not sure."

"Don't worry. There's no Kool-Aid," Malachi said.

"Kool-Aid?" Alex said. "What?"

"I meant, just come with us, Rollie," Malachi said. "And if at any time you decide you want to leave, I'll make sure I have someone who will take you right home. What do you think?"

Malachi played his ringtoneish-riff and said, "I'll be playing my mandolin tonight."

"Sure I'll try it," Rollie said. "What song are you going to play tonight?"

"The first one will be a new one," Malachi said. "It's entitled, *His Amazing Grace*."

Rollie laughed.

"What's so funny, Rollie?" Alex said.

"Grace," Rollie said. "That's the name of our Doberman."

50. His Amazing Grace

"**T**imothy, it's so good to see you tonight," Malachi said. "I want you to meet Alex's friend, Rollie."

"Hey Rollie," Timothy said as he extended his hand. "Good to meet you. Welcome to The Table."

"Timothy, if Rollie needs to go home early, could you give him a ride?" Malachi said.

"Sure. Absolutely," Timothy said. "No problem."

And then Malachi looked at Alex. "Why don't you show Rollie around?"

They darted off. Annie excused herself as well.

"Rollie?" Timothy said.

"Rollie Jr." Malachi said. "Rollie Kirtner Jr."

"I see the family resemblance." Timothy smiled. "Look what the Lord has done. Does he know we bought this place from his dad?"

"I didn't tell him outright," Malachi said. "But I'm sure after being over at our house today and everything, he's made the connection."

"So how did you get him to come to church?" Timothy said.

"I gave him a Dutch apple pie and twenty thousand dollars," Malachi said.

They both laughed.

And then Malachi told him what had happened.

"Wow, only God could do that," Timothy said.

"And only God could do this," Malachi said. "Just look at this amazing new facility. And we bought it from Rollie Kirtner. Remember when he was our enemy?"

"Yeah," Timothy said. "It's almost like what it says in the Twenty-third Psalm: 'You prepare a table before me in the presence of my enemies.'"

"A lot of people would think starting a church in downtown Manistee would be a gamble," Malachi said. "And then to expand into a space that's three times larger."

"But it's not gambling when you, 'Commit to the Lord whatever you do,'" Timothy said. "Then it's a business. God's business and He says, 'And your plans will prosper.'"

"You bet," Malachi said. He smiled.

They were facing each other. Malachi embraced Timothy.

And then he stepped back, placing one of his hands on each of Timothy's shoulders.

And he said, "Seriously. I want to thank you for bringing a lot of cows home. We wouldn't own this building if it wasn't for you. And I know you're practically camping down at your place."

"I'm just trying to do what the Bible says, 'Suffer

hardship with Me, as a good soldier of Christ Jesus. No soldier in active service entangles himself in the affairs of everyday life, so that he may please the One who enlisted him as a soldier.'"

"Thank you, soldier," Malachi said.

Timothy smiled. "I'm not suffering. Sure, I don't live like most fifty-eight year olds do. It seems like suffering. But...you ever heard of Lester Sumrall."

"Oh yeah," Malachi said. "A mighty man of God. The real deal to the core."

"Well, you know he's gone on to his reward," Timothy said. "This is what he once said, 'The happiest people in this world are those who are vitally involved in the kingdom of God.' So I praise God, I'm not suffering—I'm vitally involved."

Then Malachi made his way to the backroom to meet with Carl and Martin.

Martin was already there. In the prayer room.

Soon Carl arrived.

"Are there many people out there?" Martin said.

"You know how everybody always shows up at the last minute for church," Carl said.

Soon they were on their knees praying. It was a fire drill.

And when they stood up, Carl said, "Let's surrender this time to the Lord. This evening. This church service."

Soon all three of them had their hands raised in the air and each one affirmed:

"I surrender all."

"I surrender all."

"I surrender all."

When Martin opened his eyes, he said, "This is the day the Lord has made. I will rejoice and be glad in it."

He looked at Malachi and Carl. "Praise God. Now I'm

ready."

"Yeah. Praise God," Malachi said. "It's time."

They both made their way to the front of the church and took the four steps up to the platform.

Martin went to his keyboard, sitting slightly left of the center. Malachi was standing to his right, angling toward the middle of the sanctuary.

Malachi glanced to the other side of Martin. For a fleeting second, he looked over at JC, Annie, and Mandy, standing there with mikes and music stands in front of them.

Malachi was thinking how marvelous the sanctuary looked. He was pleased that they had kept the same color theme as their previous facility—it made it feel like home, even though this was only their third service at the new church.

Timothy's banners had been replaced by gracefully hand lettered Bible verses—adding life all around the expansive space. One of the newer members of The Table had discovered a talent he didn't know he had. Malachi felt an inner tingle when he recalled watching Wierick high up on the scaffold, with a steady hand, as he painted the six-inch tall carrot-colored letters on the far-wall. Proclaiming: "Other outcasts came and joined Jesus and the disciples at The Table."

"I want to welcome everyone to The Table this evening. Thank you for worshipping with us," Martin said. "This is our fourth annual evening that we call a Holy Convocation."

Martin glanced over at Malachi.

Malachi looked over at Martin. He could tell they were both thinking the same thought.

As Malachi scanned out over the room, one visual was by far the most striking. There were very few empty seats.

His Amazing Grace

A scattering here and there. The most sizeable block was behind Alex and Rollie, who were sitting directly in front of Malachi—on the front row. However, one thing Malachi didn't see, as his eyes searched the audience one more time, was the Johnson family—Stephen, Gracie, and Sarah.

And then Martin looked down at his Bible and read, "It shall be a holy convocation for you and you shall humble your souls and present an offering by fire to the Lord."

And then he looked up, "So let us humble our souls before the Lord and present our first offering to the Lord tonight—the music we lift up to the Throne of God."

Martin eyed Malachi and then nodded his head.

"Please stand with us," Malachi said. "Let's worship the Lord. Our great Redeemer."

Malachi strummed the G-chord. Martin hit a G-chord on the keyboard. All the voices on stage met together as they began to sing:

> Turn your eyes upon Jesus
> Look full into His marvelous face
>
> Turn your eyes upon Jesus
> Look full into His marvelous face

Malachi's eyes were focused toward the center part of the sanctuary. And then he moved his eyes over to the side, where Alex and Rollie were standing. But then a man moving slowly toward the front drew Malachi's attention. And right behind him was Stephen Johnson and his family.

The man approached a seat a few rows in back of the two boys and then looked up as he stood there.

Malachi's heart thumped. Their eyes met. His heart raced.

> At His feet you'll find
> His amazing grace

Malachi stepped forward enough to catch Martin's attention. And ever so slightly pointed with his head toward the person he had noticed. Martin looked confused, but when he saw Malachi remove his mandolin, Martin knew what to do musically.

Malachi rushed off the stage as the man moved toward him. They grabbed each other in a hug. And the man began to sob.

He wept on Malachi's shoulder.

> Hallelujah
> Praise the King
> Our Great Redeemer
> Merciful to the end

Malachi spoke into his ear, "It's so good to see you… it's so good to see you."

Malachi heard his voice, "Forgive me, Malachi. Please forgive me for everything."

"I forgive you," Malachi said. "I forgive you for all that happened at St. Amos. I forgive you, Pastor Neil."

He held Malachi even tighter. His tears dampened Malachi's shirt.

> Turn your eyes upon Jesus
> Look full into His marvelous face
>
> At His feet you'll find
> His amazing grace

His Amazing Grace

Hallelujah
Praise the King
Our Great Redeemer
Merciful to the end

After a few moments, Malachi turned to go back up on the stage. He looked over at JC and Annie. Annie had tears trickling down her face.

They smiled at each other.

But Mandy wasn't there with them.

Malachi knew it was only his imagination. Mandy had never been up there on the stage.

Malachi had believed up to the end that God would do a miracle. His ardent, faith-filled prayer for Mandy had been out of Psalm 118:17, "Mandy will not die, but live. And tell of the works of the Lord." With eyes of faith he could see her up on the stage someday—singing praises to God.

Malachi's faith had remained firm. To the degree that it was difficult to absorb the words from Mandy's mom— "She's gone."

Malachi was still grieving seven months later.

Mandy had been emotionally stronger through the illness than he had been. And Malachi will never forget what she told him two days before she died, "I only have two desires of my heart left." She touched Malachi's hand. "The one is that you'll take care of Alex—like he's your own son."

Malachi kissed Mandy on the forehead. "I will. I will. You know I will."

"Now, I'm ready for the last desire of my heart," her eyes filled with tears. "I'm ready to see Jesus face to face."

Malachi's mandolin was once again in his hand. As he

joined in the singing of the final chorus:

> Turn your eyes upon Jesus
> Look full into His marvelous face
>
> At His feet you'll find
> His amazing grace
>
> Hallelujah
> Praise the King
> Our Great Redeemer
> Merciful to the end

The music faded.

Malachi spoke—like an amplified whisper; there were tears in his voice as he delicately strummed his mandolin. "You'll find it. You will. You'll find His amazing grace. I have. You'll find it."

And then he said as his fingers played the final chord. "And now, with just our voices."

> At His feet you'll find
> His amazing grace

Author's Endnote

Dear Reader,

Several years ago—some months after I published my first book, Living the God Imprinted Life, I was pondering, more like mentally wrestling with some uncertainties in my life.

Again.

I was walking the streets of Portage, Michigan—the sister city of Kalamazoo. God's still small voice entered into me as I prepared to cross the street: "You're at a fork in the road of your life."

Moments later, as I walked across the intersection, I looked down. There in the street was a flattened silverware fork.

Of course, I smiled. May have shouted a hallelujah or a praise God. I don't remember for sure. However, I do remember; a strange thought, a foreign thought entered into me at that instant: "Get a job at Walmart."

I could have said, "No thank you," for many valid reasons. I didn't. And less than two weeks later, I was a Walmart employee.

So that's the story behind the story. The short version. And now you dear reader, are also part of the story. Many of you have been along with me the entire three-book journey. And others of you have joined us somewhere along the way.

I can't thank all of you enough. I would not be a writer without you. A special thanks to the ones of you who have sent me an encouraging note. So many of you have blessed and amazed me by your kind words. I praise God for you all.

Before signing off, I need to thank my wife Nancy. Without you, I would not be a writer. And I need to thank God for allowing me to even be a writer.

Two more notes. I've included the lyrics and chords for the songs I've written which are in **Jesus at Walmart...fire on the Earth**. For anyone desiring additional information on the songs please contact me. And check out **rickleland.com** . I may post a video clip of a song or two.

To all, thanks again for stopping by. It's always a pleasure to hear from you. You can email me at **rickeland1@outlook.com**. And if you've enjoyed the book, please share a review on **Amazon**. It really helps other discover my works. Thank you so much!

Magnify the Lord with me,

Rick Leland

The Songs

Here are the lyrics and chords for the songs appearing in the book. I wrote them as mandolin songs. Thumb strumming style.

The chords play nicely on the guitar as well. If you have any questions please contact me at rickleland1@outlook.com or go to rickleland.com.

1. Hallelujah
2. Awesome is the God
3. Oh What You've Done for Me
4. Oh God Please Change My Heart
5. Rise Up
6. Standing on the Rock
7. Jesus in the Waves
8. A Free Store Prayer (Your Will)
9. Deep in the Heart of God
10. A Way in a Manager
11. His Amazing Grace

Hallelujah

```
C                    D         G~      D              C
Salvation and glory and power belong to our God
C                    D         G~      D              C
Salvation and glory and power belong to our God


    G           D       C     D
Hallelujah,  Hallelujah, Hallelujah
     G           D       C     D     DDC
Hallelujah,  Hallelujah, Hallelujah


   C            D          G~     D              C
Salvation and glory and power belong to our God
   C            D       G~      D           C
Salvation and glory and power belong to our God


GG           DD       C-CC        D     DDC
Praise God,  Praise God, Praise God.
GG           DD       C-CC        D     DDC
Praise God,  Praise God, Praise God


   C           D         G~     D              C
Salvation and glory and power belong to our God
   C           D         G~     D              C
Salvation and glory and power belong to our God
```

The Songs

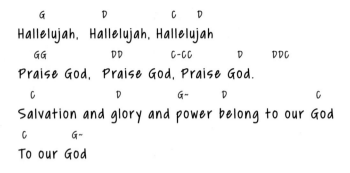

```
   G          D          C    D
Hallelujah,  Hallelujah,  Hallelujah
   GG          DD          C-CC          D     DDC
Praise God,  Praise God,  Praise God.
   C          D          G~    D              C
Salvation and glory and power belong to our God
   C      G~
To our God
```

Words and Music: Rick Leland/ Free Truth Music 2013

Awesome is the God

```
   G            D
Awesome is the God
   G            D
Awesome is the God
   G            D    C
Awesome is the God, Most High

   G
Worthy
   C
Worthy
   G
Worthy

   G            D
Worthy is the Lord
   G            D
Worthy is the Lord
   G            D                    C
Worthy is the Lord, who died upon a cross

   G       D   C      G
Here's my life, have your way
```

The Songs

```
 G       D
For You Lord
 G       D
For You Lord
 G   D           G
No cost is too great
```

Words and Music: Rick Leland/ Free Truth Music 2011

Oh What You've Done for Me

```
 G~                      D        C
Jesus, Oh what You've done for me
 G~                      D        C
Jesus, Oh what You've done for me
 G~                      D        C
Jesus, Oh what You've done for me


 G          D      pause    C
Loved me. Saved me. Set me free
 G          D      pause    C
Loved me. Saved me. Set me free
 G          D      pause    C
Loved me. Saved me. Set me free


 G           D         C
And who  the Son sets free
 G           D         C
And who  the Son sets free
 G           D         C
And who  the Son sets free
CC  D      CC   G
Is free. Free indeed.


 G~                      D        C
Jesus, Oh what You've done for me
 G          D      pause    C
Loved me. Saved me. Set me free
 G          D      pause    C
Loved me. Saved me. Set me free
CC   G
Free indeed.
```

Words and Music: Rick Leland/ Free Truth Music 2013

Oh God Please Change My Heart

```
   G          D                   C
Oh God please  change my heart
   G          D                   C
Oh God please  change my heart
    G          D                  C
Oh God please  change my heart


G          D                         C
Holy Spirit let Your wind blow in this place
G          D                         C
Holy Spirit let Your wind blow in this place


G            D        C
Jesus I will seek Your face
G            D         C
Jesus I will seek Your face


G          D                  C
Oh God please  change my heart
G          D                         C
Holy Spirit let Your wind blow in this place
G            D        C
Jesus I will seek Your face
G          D            pause  C~
Oh God please  change my heart
```

Words and Music: Rick Leland/ Free Truth Music 2013

Rise Up

```
G              D                    C
Silver and gold have I none
 G             D                    C
Silver and gold have I none


G        D        C~
In the Name of Jesus
G        D        C~
In the Name of Jesus


C    G    C    D    D           C~
Rise up.  Rise up. Rise..Rise  up.
C    G    C    D    D           C~
Rise up.  Rise up. Rise..Rise  up.


G        D            C~
In the Name of Jesus
C    G    C    D    D           C~
Rise up.  Rise up. Rise..Rise  up.
```

The Songs

```
G        D        C~
In the Name of Jesus
G           D                    C C
Walk and leap and praise the Lord
G           D                    C C
Walk and leap and praise the Lord


G           D              C
Silver and gold have I none
G        D       C~
In the Name of Jesus
C    G   C   D   D        C~
Rise up.  Rise up. Rise..Rise  up.
G           D                    C C
Walk and leap and praise the Lord
```

Words and Music: Rick Leland/ Free Truth Music 2013

Standing on the Rock

G   D   C
Solid is the Rock upon which I stand
G   D   C
Solid is the Rock upon which I stand

G   D   C
Savior, Lord, Your My King

G   D   C
Solid is the Rock upon which I stand
G   D
Standing, standing,
   C   G
I'm standing on the promises of Christ my Savior

G   D   C
Savior, Lord, Your My King
G   D   C
Solid is the Rock upon which I stand

   G   D
Standing, standing,
   C   G
I'm standing on the promises of Christ my Savior

The Songs

```
G          D              C
Savior, Lord, Your My King
```

```
G      D      C
I surrender all
G      D      C
I surrender all
```

Words and Music: Rick Leland/ Free Truth Music 2013

Jesus in the Waves

G   D
Jesus in the waves
C   G
I'm in the boat

G   D
The boats going down
C   G
But I won't get out

G   D
Come to Jesus
C   G
He'll hold your hand

G   D
Come to Jesus
C   G
He'll hold your hand

Words and Music: Rick Leland/ Free Truth Music 2013

A Free Store Prayer (Your Will)

G   pause   D   C
Jesus, give me a heart to do Your will
G   pause   D   C
Jesus, give me a heart to do Your will

G   D   C   G
Hands of mercy. (pause) A heart of love
G   D   C   G
Hands of mercy. (pause) A heart of love

G   pause   D   C
Jesus, give me the strength to do Your will
G   pause   D   C
Jesus, give me the strength to do Your will

G   D   C   G
Hands of mercy. (pause) A heart of love
G   D   C   G
Hands of mercy. (pause) A heart of love
G   D   C   G
Hands of mercy. (pause) A heart of love

Words and Music: Rick Leland/ Free Truth Music 2013

Deep in the Heart of God

```
G     C                  D
Deep in the heart of God

C            G
Deep, deep, deep

G      D       C
Is His love for us

Am   C     G
His love for us

G     C                  D
Deep in the heart of God

C            G
Deep, deep, deep

G      D       C
Is His love for you

Am   C     G
His love for you
```

Words and Music: Rick Leland/ Free Truth Music 2012

His Amazing Grace

```
G           D           C~
Turn your eyes upon Jesus
G           D                   C
Look full into His marvelous face


 G      D          C~
At His feet you'll find  (pause)
 D ---        G
His  amazing grace


G      D
Hallelujah  (pause)
 D          C
Praise  the King
G               D
Our Great Redeemer
C               D~
Merciful to the end
```

Words and Music: Rick Leland/ Free Truth Music 2013

A Way in a Manger

G   D
Away in a manger
C   G
No crib for His bed

G   D~   C
Jesus abide in me
G   D~   C
Jesus abide in me

G   D
Away in a manger
C   G
No crib for His bed

G   D
The little Lord Jesus
C   G
Lay down His sweet head

G   D   C   G
Jesus You laid down Your life for me
G   D ----   C
Your blood has set me free

G   D~   C
Jesus abide in me

The Songs

```
    G     D~      C
Jesus abide in me


G          D          C          G
So open your heart to Jesus today
 G            D~
His gift is salvation
C             G
He's the only way


 G              D      C         ------
The Way was born in  manger on  that first
 G
Christmas Day
G     (Pause)  D  (Pause)     C            G
And the little Lord Jesus, He'll return some day


 G     D~      C
Jesus abide in me
  G    D~      C
Jesus abide in me


 G              D      C         ------
The Way was born in  manger on  that first
 G
Christmas Day
```

Words and Music: Rick Leland/ Free Truth Music 2013

Made in United States
Cleveland, OH
27 December 2024

12705136R00194